WE ALL HEAR VOICES

WE ALL HEAR VOICES

a novel

SAM TAGGART

iUniverse, Inc.
New York Lincoln Shanghai

WE ALL HEAR VOICES

iUniverse books may be ordered through booksellers or by contacting:

iUniverse
2021 Pine Lake Road, Suite 100
Lincoln, NE 68512
www.iuniverse.com
1-800-Authors (1-800-288-4677)

Because of the dynamic nature of the Internet, any Web addresses or links contained in this book may have changed since publication and may no longer be valid.

This is a work of fiction. All of the characters, names, incidents, organizations, and dialogue in this novel are either the products of the author's imagination or are used fictitiously.

ISBN: 978-0-595-44184-6 (pbk)
ISBN: 978-0-595-68541-7 (cloth)
ISBN: 978-0-595-88517-6 (ebk)

Printed in the United States of America

Thanks to my wife, Annette, for all of her encouragement,
and to Tucker Steinmetz, my friend and mentor.

PROLOGUE

butterscotch

Saratoga Springs, 1938

Eight-year-old Pauly loved the feel of his baseball glove as it molded to his left hand. The soft glove, with its well-formed sweet spot, made him feel ten feet tall. It was his father's glove on loan—a valued possession. Before the Great War, his father had played second base for the Albany Tigers, and Pauly was intent on taking up where his father left off. For now, he was the backup shortstop for the Union Hotel Indians.

"Batter up!" the home-plate umpire shouted.

"Be alert, guys!" the coach called out from the bench. "Move back, Pauly! This guy's a good hitter!"

Pauly did as he was told, moving several feet back toward the outfield.

The young pitcher for the Indians wound up and threw the ball as hard as he could. It was a perfect pitch, right in the middle of the strike zone. The hitter swung, and the bat met the ball over the plate. It was a solid hit, a line drive, straight to Pauly's glove. Like a shot, it was there, landing perfectly in the sweet spot. When the force of the speeding ball was transferred to his hand and arm, the spiral taste of butterscotch flooded his consciousness. For an instant, Pauly was overwhelmed by the sweet, rich, burnt-brown flavor. Standing there with the ball, he was mesmerized by this overpowering sensation, lost in a world of distant dreams. While Pauly drifted into a world of warm, spiral shapes, the runner on third tagged the base and made for home. All of Pauly's teammates, coaches, and friendly spectators loudly urged him to throw the ball home, but Pauly just stood there staring at the ball, oblivious to the world around him.

Slowly, the sweet taste subsided. Pauly reached into the glove, pulled the ball out, and stared at it.

The third baseman, Billy Pitts, ran over to where he was standing. "Pauly, are you okay?" Billy asked.

His friend's voice drew him back into the here and now. "Yeah, I'm okay," Pauly replied.

"Well, throw the ball back to the pitcher," Billy said.

Pauly nodded, looked at the ball for a moment, and then threw it to the mound.

When the inning was over and the team back on the bench, the coach came down to where Pauly and Billy were sitting. "I'm taking you out of the game, Pauly," he said. With no further comment, the coach turned and walked away.

Pauly silently acknowledged the inevitable.

Billy removed his hat and prepared for his turn at bat. "If we get far enough ahead," he said to Pauly, "I bet the coach will put you back in. Maybe I'll ask him to take me out and put you in my place."

"That's okay. You know me—I'd just do something stupid," Pauly said.

He sat quietly for a minute, and then turned to his friend. "Tell me something, Billy … have you ever noticed how it tastes to catch a good hit?" He pointed to his glove. "I mean … that spiral butterscotch taste. Well … not exactly butterscotch, but kinda like that."

Billy turned to him with a funny look on his face. "What are you talking about? That's stupid! It don't taste like *anything* when you catch a ball—it just feels good."

"No, this is different. The taste doesn't come from the glove. It comes from inside," he said, pointing to his head.

"That's goofy," Billy said.

"Who are you calling goofy?"

"You, stupid! Nobody tastes things when they catch a ball. That's stupid."

"Who are you calling stupid?" Pauly said, his voice getting louder.

"I'm calling you stupid, stupid. What are you gonna do about it?"

The coach walked down the dugout to the boys. "Pay attention to the game, men. Billy, you're up. Pauly, leave Billy alone—he's got to concentrate on the game."

After the coach turned and began walking back to the other end of the bench, Billy got in one more jab. "Yeah, Pauly, you're stupid and goofy, just like your crazy old mama."

That was enough for Pauly. Almost before the words had left Billy's mouth, Pauly pounced on his friend's back, kicking and hitting. As is often the case, the second insult was the first to be seen by everyone else. All the coach saw was a benchwarmer attacking his star third baseman. After he pulled the two boys apart, the coach stared intently at Pauly. "Listen, son," he said, "I don't know what this is all about, but put a cork in it. We've got a game to play. On second thought, why don't you go on home?"

With that, young Paul J. Currier was banished from the baseball diamond for the day. It was the last time he played baseball, but not the last time an odd smell or taste would invade his consciousness.

CHAPTER 1

dancing crisp greens

Gum Ridge, Arkansas, 1995

Leonard Johnson was hurrying to finish cultivating the last few rows of cotton before the storm hit. Any amount of rain would gum up his plows and make plowing impossible for the next few days. Early that morning, his wife, Linda, had tried to entice him into staying in bed, but Leonard had been determined. The last patch of cotton was right by the highway, near the house, and everyone who drove by could see that it was full of weeds. "I won't have these people thinking that I'm a drugstore farmer," he had told Linda, and out the door he had gone. When his tractor came to the end of the row, he raised the plow and stepped on the left rear brake. With the plow disengaged from the soft dirt, the tractor spun around on a pivot. He then headed back down the next set of rows. As if on cue, a bolt of lightning split the air, and thunder followed in its wake. In an instant, Leonard—the little man who loved his children and lusted after his wife, who paid his bills when he had money, who had failed to live up to his father's expectations—was gone. The lightning, in its search for ground, stopped the clock that was Leonard's life. All that was left was his body, a burn on his scalp and a dark spot on his heel where the force found its way home.

The tractor died at the same time, but the fixed wiring of the machine was more forgiving, and it would live to roar again.

The thunder faded into the bottomland and was replaced by the sound of rain pelting the tractor's hot muffler.

At the southern edge of the field, across the bar-ditch on Highway 80, the bus from Memphis sped up as it approached the last bridge out of the Le Petite River bottomland. Oblivious to Leonard's fate, the passengers turned toward the flash of light in the dark, cloudy sky. A talkative old man in the front row leaned forward toward the driver and began to talk about the time he had been almost hit by lightning.

"I lived in Tucson at the time," he said, "and, anyway, I was cooking these big-ass steaks. Out of the blue came this bolt of lightning—no clouds, no nothing! It threw me fifteen feet in the air. Wife wanted to take me to the hospital, but I said, 'Hell, no, I ain't going to no hospital!'" The bus driver nodded and smiled.

In the back row of the bus, a young couple engaged in a marathon make-out session had been startled by the lightning flash, but in an instant had melted back into their passion.

Jack sat in the sixth row, by the window. He was lost in a world of warm, yellow-brown triangles that formed and reformed in a kaleidoscope of the lightning's white light. Intermingled with the light was the rich taste of butterscotch, and mixed with this round flavor was a remote memory of springtime and baseball and friends. In the last year, these memories had become more vivid, more real—like a dream just after you've awakened and before it's had time to fade. Most of the time, Jack allowed himself the luxury of retreating into this world of colors and smells and distant voices, but today he didn't have the time.

The bus had already begun to slow as it neared the eastern edge of Gum Ridge. Off to the north of the highway was a large stock car track. Gum Ridge was Jack's final destination, and the track was his reason for being here. He loved the world of stock cars—the bright red and yellow cars racing around the oval; the big, powerful engines that were felt as much as they were heard; the smells of little kids and old people, of dirt, popcorn, hot dogs, and beer—all of this fused into a warm comforting cloud. Track hands were good folks, a family who shared a love of cars and the excitement of speed. Jack knew that as long as he was near a track, he had a home.

At a blinking red light, the bus driver pulled off the highway into the gravel parking lot of the Jay Bird gas station and came to a stop. "This is Gum Ridge and the transfer point for Sandy Banks," he said. "The next bus south will be through in an hour. We'll be here about five minutes, if anyone wants to get out and stretch."

Of the people on the bus, only six got off: a tired-looking woman with two crying babies, the young couple from the back of the bus, and Jack. As usual, Jack waited for the others to get off before he left his seat. He did his best not to draw attention to himself.

The rainstorm had passed quickly, and the sun broke through the clouds as Jack stepped down from the bus. Steam and heat rose from the hot pavement. An ambulance, sirens blaring and lights flashing, rounded the corner at the stoplight and headed back out the Highway 80.

Jack waited patiently for the bus driver to open the cargo hold. Jack was a short, heavyset man who appeared to be melting into his center as he aged. His old plaid shirt had a slept-in look, and his loose-fitting pants seemed on the verge of falling down. The skin on the back of his hands was thin with dark patches of age coloration. His hair was thinning and gray. Patience was an easy virtue for Jack; in fact, it was second nature. While other people complained, he relished the time spent lining up for movies or for the races; it gave him a purpose, a reason for being.

Just before the bus pulled into the parking lot, Jack had noticed a small grocery store and it reminded him that he was hungry. The driver threw Jack's duffel out on the ground. Jack picked it up, threw it over his shoulder, and headed for the store.

Painted on the front window of Mr. Kim's Grocery were two large blue and green dragons preparing to clash over a bloodred sun. The day the sign was completed, Mr. Kim had taken a picture of it and sent it to his grandfather in Wonju, South Korea. On the back of the picture, he had written, "Grandfather, you were wrong. I *did* amount to something. This is my grocery store. It is twice as big as anything in our village. Love and respect, Kim Lee."

Jack opened the warped screen door and walked in. Mr. Kim was standing behind the counter to his right. He smiled at Jack. "Welcome to my store! May I help you?"

Without speaking, Jack walked down the first aisle and picked up a can of potted meat, a package of crackers, and a small jar of tomato juice. He carried them back and set them on the counter in front of Mr. Kim.

"That will be one dollar and seventy-five cents, with tax," the grocer said. While Jack fumbled for exact change, Mr. Kim continued, "Never seen you before. Are you new around here? My name is Kim. People call me the Chinaman. I'm not Chinese, I'm Korean. Most of these people can't tell the difference. I don't correct them anymore. What's your name?"

When Jack was done counting out the change, he looked up at Mr. Kim. "Jack," he said.

"You gonna stay, or are you just visiting?" Kim asked.

"Looking for work."

"Go down to the track," Kim suggested. "They're always looking for help."

"I'm not a track hand. I'm a cook," Jack replied.

"You're in luck! Moon, from the bar across the street, was in here just a little while ago. He bought a marker pen and butcher paper to make a Help Wanted sign. He's looking for somebody to cook. He needs a cook real bad. Be careful, though—he's one slick fella. Tries to cheat me all the time."

With no farewell, Jack picked up his food and walked out of the store.

Mr. Kim stared out at Jack. He was used to being ignored by white people.

Jack crossed the highway and walked east. He passed Sandy's Curl Up and Dye beauty shop and the old abandoned ice plant where Mule Johnson and his friends held their farmers' market on Wednesdays and Saturdays. The last building on that side of the road was Moon's Bar and Grill. Parked out front was an old red pickup with the tailgate pulled down. Jack sat down on the tailgate, opened his can of potted meat, tore open the package of saltines, and unscrewed the top from the tomato juice. While he was eating, he examined Moon's place.

The bar was an old redbrick building with the look of permanence. Above the front façade was a large neon quarter-moon sitting on top of the word "Moon's." The front door was to the far left—it was a heavy, solid-core affair with an oval of cut glass at its center. In the middle of the glass was a caduceus with the words "St. Vincent's Infirmary" inscribed above it. To the right of the door was a large, darkened plate-glass window. On the far right side of the window was a second, smaller neon sign in the shape of a rooster announcing the arrival of Cock's Crow Beer. Below the bird was the phrase "Wake up to the rooster, it'll get your attention." In the center of the window was a poster with a dark figure dressed like a gangster. In an arch above the figure were the words "Home of Powhatan J. Ives," and below it was printed "Learn the true facts inside." Just to the left of the wooden door was the newly made Help Wanted sign: "Experienced cook wanted. Good pay and benefits. Must have references."

Jack removed the sign from the window and opened the door to the bar. It took a minute for his eyes to adjust to the dimly lit room. On his right was a long bar that led to a small office in the front corner. Behind the bar were the grill, a refrigerator, and an old, red cold-drink cooler. The area in front of the bar was filled with small round tables. All of the chairs were turned toward a big-screen TV placed opposite the front door. In the back, near the restrooms, were two pool tables with lighted hoods. Against the wall opposite the bar was an old floor-safe; a wooden sign above it read "The Powhatan J. Ives Memorial Safe."

Business was slow at Moon's Bar and Grill. Mary Ann Phillips, the waitress, was busy cleaning up the bar, Joe Peeler and Art Griffin were nursing a couple of beers, and Albert Lawrence Moon, a rakish man in his midthirties with coal black hair and touches of gray around his temples, was holding forth from behind the bar.

"Leonard knows this old man in Batesville," Moon said, "who knows a guy who swears that he knows where P. J. Ives is buried." He tapped the bar with the side of his hand to emphasize his point.

"Give me a break," Joe said. "You know as well as I do that Leonard's been chasing that ghost since he was old enough to wear long britches."

"Yeah, Moon," Art added, "that's nothing but an empty rathole."

"You two hicks don't know what you're talking about," Moon said.

"Hold on, Moon!" Art said. "Where do you get off, calling us hicks? You ain't no better than us."

"Yeah, this ain't exactly the Peabody," Joe chimed in.

"I swear, I can't believe you people haven't figured this out yet," said Moon. "Being a hick has nothing to do with where you're from. Listen to me one more time—it's not where you're from that counts, it's your worldview. It's how you see yourself in the greater scheme of life." This was sermon number four that he trotted out once a week, and Moon had a full head of steam.

Art and Joe looked at each other and began to chuckle.

"Laugh if you want," Moon continued, "but that's why I own my own business, and you two jerks drive fifty miles a day to work for those Japs at that steel mill."

Mary Ann, an attractive woman with a ready smile, deep blue eyes, and dark brown hair pulled back in a knot and decorated with a large red barrette, finished cleaning the bar and then looked up at Moon.

"Come on, Moon," she said, "you own your own business—if you can call this a business—'cause you conned your mama out of the money."

"Watch your mouth, woman," Moon countered, "or you'll be out of here on your butt!"

Mary Ann smiled. "You can't fire me, Moon," she said. "Who's gonna keep the doors open while you're out chasing women? Besides, you still owe me back pay. That's the main reason I don't quit—if I did, I'd never see a cent of that money."

"Bitch, bitch, bitch," said Moon. "That's all you people ever do. I'll get you paid up one of these days. I'm just going through a tight time right now."

"Listen here, Moon," she said. "'One of these days' means *none* of these days, and you know that as well as I do!"

As they spoke, Jack walked up with the Help Wanted sign. He stood quietly for a minute, waiting for them to finish. When Mary Ann turned back to her salt-shakers, she saw him standing in the shadows.

"Can I help you?" Mary Ann asked hesitantly.

Jack looked down at the floor and mumbled, "I'm interested in the job."

Mary Ann walked toward him. "I'm sorry, I didn't hear what you said," she said.

From his perch behind the bar, Moon sized Jack up quickly. "We don't give handouts," he said. "You get on out of here."

Looking at Mary Ann, Jack spoke in a slightly louder tone. "I'm a cook. I need a job." He pointed to the sign he carried.

"What did he say?" asked Moon.

"He says he's a cook," she replied. "He wants the job."

"You're kidding me. He's a bum."

"I know it's a stretch for you, but try to be civil, Moon," she said. "At least talk to the man. You couldn't be any worse off than you are."

Moon poured a glass of tea and then looked across the room toward Jack. "Are you still there?" he asked.

"Yes, sir," Jack said. "I'm a good cook, and I need a job."

"All right, all right. Come over here."

Jack slowly walked over to the bar. His stooped shoulders made him appear shorter than he really was. He didn't shift his weight from one leg to the other when he walked—it was more of a shuffle.

"Well, Mr. Cook, first things first. What's your name?" Moon asked.

"Jack."

"Jack what?"

"Just Jack."

"Just Jack, huh? Well, Just Jack, why should I hire you to cook for me here in my fine establishment?" Moon spoke in a mocking tone.

"Like I said before, I'm a good cook."

"I can't just take your word for it. You got any references?"

An awkward moment passed as Jack looked at him, rather puzzled. In all of his days of cooking in greasy-spoon cafes and bars, he had never been asked for references, and he didn't quite know how to respond.

Mary Ann walked over to him and put her hand on his shoulder. "You know, honey, from people you've cooked for."

Jack took a second and then said, "Well, let me see … one time, in Virginia, I cooked a foot-long dog for the Queen of England. And then, back in the seventies, I lived in Tuscaloosa, and Bear Bryant used to ask for my cheeseburgers, special. He gave me one of his checked hats. I like hats and caps. I lost the one he gave me, but it was pretty well worn out anyway. One time, a long time ago, I think I cooked a chicken-fried steak for Mr. Harry S Truman. I don't really remember where that was."

Smiling, Moon looked at Art and Joe. "What have I always told you? If you're gonna lie, lie big!" Moon turned back to Jack and said, "Now, friend, are you gonna stand there, flat-footed, and tell me that you cooked for all them famous folks?"

"Yes, sir, I guess I am," Jack replied.

"Well, I'll tell you what … I'm a gambling man." Moon reached into his pocket, pulled out a roll of money, and stripped a couple of twenty-dollar bills from it. "It's almost lunch, and I'm hungry. Go over to the Chinaman's, and buy what you need. Watch out for him—he'll cheat you every time. Come back in here and give it your best shot." He turned back to his friends and said, "I think that's pretty fair, don't you guys?"

Joe and Art readily agreed.

Jack looked at the money, then back at Moon. "I don't need this much," he said.

"Take it anyway, and hurry up," Moon said. "I ain't got all day."

Jack walked out the front door. Moon laughed as he slicked his hair back. "The Queen of England, my ass."

Joe looked toward the door to make sure Jack was gone. "Well, Moon, that's the last you'll see of those two twenties."

Mary Ann watched out the front window as Jack headed across the street. "I don't know … I got a feeling about this guy," she said.

Moon grinned at Art. "Yeah, kinda like the feeling you had about your first two husbands."

"Watch your mouth, asshole," she said.

A few minutes later, Jack returned with a sack of groceries. He walked around behind the bar and put the sack on the counter. He reached into his duffel bag and pulled out a worn-out apron and a blue-green baseball cap with "Jesus Saves" printed in large, yellow letters across the front. "Where's the utensils?" he asked Moon.

"You mean like knives and stuff to clean the vegetables?"

"No, sir, I mean like soap and water and cleanser and rags, so I can clean the grill."

"Can't you cook on it like it is?" Moon asked.

"No, sir. You try to cook on a stove that dirty, it'll make the food taste horrible," Jack said.

"Sure, I knew that. I was just testing you."

Mary Ann disappeared into a room at the south end of the bar. It had once been the kitchen but now served as a storeroom. They could hear her rummaging around, and she came out a couple of minutes later with a bucket full of cleaning supplies. "Some of this stuff hasn't been used in a while," she said. "If you need something else, I'll be glad to go and get it for you."

Jack smiled at Mary Ann. He unloaded the bucket and began cleaning the dirty stove. He disassembled the grill, scraped the grease traps, and scrubbed the stovetop. Behind him, the boys were kidding Moon—even if he didn't get a cook out of the deal, at least his grill would be clean.

Jack finished cleaning the stove and sharpening the knives. When that was complete, he emptied the contents of the brown paper sack onto the prep table: a large piece of round steak, a few potatoes, a bag of fresh purple hull peas, a handful of yellow crookneck squash, some fresh tomatoes, a bunch of green onions, and a head of lettuce. It was nothing fancy—just basic fare. The same was true of the spices: a little oil and some flour, sugar, salt, pepper, garlic, and fresh basil. Freshness was something that the bar hadn't experienced in a while. After the departure of Mamie—Moon's mother and the only real cook the place had had—food at Moon's had been reduced to popcorn, beer nuts, packaged sandwiches, and pickled eggs.

While the potatoes boiled in preparation for mashing, Jack salted and peppered the steak, gently coated it with a light dusting of flour, and slowly browned it in a black cast-iron skillet. He diced the squash into tiny triangles, coated them with garlic powder and pepper, and then cooked them quickly in a small amount of oil. When Jack threw the diced squash into the hot oil, steam and smoke rose up into the vent hood.

An old familiar voice spoke to him from above the stove: *"Yeah, stupid, you really think you're smart, don't you? They're not going to like this pile of crap you're cooking. They'll figure you out soon enough. You think you're some kind of great cook, don't you? Well, let me tell you something ... you ain't nothing! You'll probably burn this place down, like you did that place in Little Rock."*

Jack stood motionless, staring at the hood. "No! I didn't burn it down!" he said.

Mary Ann was close enough to hear "burn down."

"Yeah," she said. "I'm surprised this place ain't burned down, with all the grease and dirt. It's a real firetrap."

Moon and his buddies had returned to their table to watch a video of the Delta 500 stock car race. Moon caught the tail end of Mary Ann's comment. "Phillips, leave the man alone—let him work," he said, "and get the boys another round of beer."

Mary Ann walked behind Jack to get to the cooler. As she passed, Jack got a whiff of her perfume—a hint of fresh towels just out of the clothes dryer. The soft, round aroma lingered like the vapor trail of a jet. He watched her as she walked down the wooden grate that raised them off the floor.

I like her, Jack thought. *She smells good and seems real nice. I like this place.*

His thoughts were interrupted by the voice from the vent hood: *"Right, just 'cause she smiles at you and smells good, you think she's a nice person. Look here, fool, she's smarter than the rest of this bunch. She'll figure out your secret soon enough. She wants something—they always do."*

From across the room, Art shouted, "Hey, Jack, when's that food gonna be ready? I'm starving!"

"Five minutes. Can't hurry it."

By the time the meal was complete, the stale smell of beer and cigarettes had been replaced by the rich aroma of home cooking. For those who benefited from Jack's magic, his passion for flavors and smells evoked memories of childhood, of early mornings before school, of cold winter evenings around the kitchen table. Without having tasted the food—without even having seen it—they experienced a lifetime of rich images.

Mary Ann served the meal, and Jack cleaned up. Moon and the boys said very little; they simply cleaned their plates and looked around for more.

"Damn!" said Art. "That's good! Hell, Jack, you cook better than my mama. Where did you learn to cook like that?"

"Here and there," Jack said. He scraped the potato pan clean.

Joe leaned back in his chair. "Hey, Mary Ann, bring me a toothpick! Say, Jack, where you from?"

"Oh, I travel around a lot."

"Well, how did you end up in our little one-horse town?" Art asked.

"I follow the race circuit. Never been here before. One of the race crews over in North Carolina was talking about this being a nice track, so I decided to come take a look."

"Sounds like you get around a lot."

"Yeah, I guess I do," Jack said.

Moon knew an evasive answer when he heard one—he was a past master at the art. He got up and walked over to the bar. "You in some kinda trouble?" he asked.

Jack turned back to the stove. "No, no trouble. I just like to see the country."

"Well, I'll admit that the food was good," Moon said. "But it wasn't *that* good."

The others looked at Moon as if he were crazy.

He looked around. "Well, it *wasn't* that good," he insisted, then returned his attention to Jack. "I tell you what though ... I'll give you a break. You come to work for me, I'll give you some pointers, and, pretty soon, you'll be a really good cook."

With that, everyone but Moon and Jack started laughing.

"Well, do you want the job or not?" Moon asked.

"Yes, sir, I do. I sure do."

"When can you start?"

"Now, I guess. I don't have anything else to do."

Mary Ann walked around the bar with a pan of dirty dishes. "By the way," she said, "any benefits the cook gets, *I* get."

"What in the hell are you talking about, woman?" Moon asked.

She held up the sign. "Like the sign says: 'Good Pay and Good Benefits.' I assume you mean like health insurance and retirement. You know ... benefits?"

"Leave me alone, Phillips. I've got more important things to think about."

While Moon and Mary Ann discussed the phantom benefit package, Jack turned back to the stove. The vent hood began speaking again: *"You didn't tell them about me and the medicine, did you, Jack? You didn't tell them that you take the medicine to keep me from telling the truth. But I got you there, 'cause when you shut me up, you can't smell. When you can't smell, you can't taste; and when you can't taste, you can't cook. Serves you right for trying to shut me up. All you think about is cooking and eating. I ought to kill you right now and get you out of your misery. Right now, before you burn this dump to the ground."*

Most of the time, these voices were no more than a nuisance to Jack—scary, but just a nuisance. With the voices came the capacity to smell, taste, and cook; beyond that was a complicated flood of synesthesia that rose up in a panorama of violent-loud reds, dark-rumbling blues, and crisp-dancing greens. As the colors mounted, the voices grew louder and more adamant. Ultimately, they would stop him; life would come to a standstill. The only modulator that quieted the voices, pushed them into the background, was his medicine. And therein lay the problem: the medicine that brought Jack out of his immobility changed his cooking. It dulled his senses and muted his creativity, at least for a while.

The pay phone on the east wall rang. Joe got up, walked over, and picked up the receiver. "Hello," he said, "this is the turkey roost. Who in the flock do you want?"

Joe looked toward his friends for a sign of approval after this attempt at humor. He was in the middle of mugging when a stricken look spread across his face. "Yeah, I'll tell everybody," he said. He absentmindedly cradled the receiver. "Leonard's dead," he said. "He got struck by lightning."

CHAPTER 2

we all have a history

Albert Lawrence Moon spent most of his life convincing himself that bad ideas were good ones. The Bar and Grill was the closest he had ever come to a good idea, even though it had mostly been the result of luck.

He was the only son of John David Moon and Mamie Parker. To be more accurate, John David Moon had been married to Mamie when Albert Lawrence was born. No one in town had been under any illusions as to who Moon's real father was. Albert Lawrence had been conceived in the backseat of a 1957 Chevy parked under the Highway 80 bridge north of town. The car in question belonged to Glen Marshall III, the youngest son of the Marshall family. There was one small problem: Glen was married. For months, he had been promising to leave his wife and run away with Mamie, but when she told him of the pregnancy, Glen's pursuit came to a halt. Soon after, he was called away to California on urgent family business. Mamie was a realist. She understood that she could cause a stink and get some money out of the Marshall family—others had done so before her—but, in the end, she knew that this would only poison the well for everyone else. The Marshall family controlled almost everything in Gum Ridge, and they could be quite vindictive. The other reason Mamie let the matter drop was that she was a romantic; she was convinced that, someday, Glen would see the error of his ways and come back to her. Even if he didn't, this would be a little chit in the bank that might come in handy in the future. So, she got busy and married the first good-looking man that came through the door. John David Moon was a guitar player at Curly's in Truman. When the baby was three months old, she came home from work one evening to an empty house. John David was gone for good. Mamie saw this as a sign from God; she gave up on men and concentrated her efforts on raising her son.

Mamie became a fixture in Gum Ridge. She waited tables at Peeler's Cafe and saved every penny she got, hoping that her son would go to school and make something of himself. From the time he was a small child, she would tell him, "This money I'm saving is so you can get a skill—something you can carry with you. Then you won't be stuck in no dead-end job in no dead-end town."

But Moon had too much of his father in him. He tried every scheme he could think of to get the money out of his mother. To her credit, she didn't budge. Moon finally joined the navy and moved away. No one knew exactly what then happened between Moon and the navy, but the rumor was that they didn't part on the best of terms. Within a year, he was back in town and up to his old ways. For a couple of years, he floated from one job to another, and then he came up with the idea for the bar and grill. Mamie figured that this was as close to an honest occupation as he would ever come, so she agreed to bankroll the cafe. She would wait tables as well.

Moon wanted the old building at the corner of Highway 80 and Border Street for his cafe, and the reason was a man named Powhatan Jay Ives. Ives was a mysterious man who had showed up in town, stayed for a few months, and disappeared, abandoning a large sum of money.

On a warm spring day back in the late fifties, Mr. Ives had walked into Marshall Realty looking for a place to rent. He explained that he was a lawyer and needed something out of the way and private. The building on the corner fit his needs and was cheap. Mr. Ives set up a makeshift office in the front of the building and lived in the back half. No one saw much of him. Despite urging from Glen Marshall, he didn't even put his name on the front door. His car sat in front of the store and was seldom moved. He would occasionally go down the street and buy groceries at Wilson's store, but, for the most part, he stayed in his storefront office.

It had been Glen's habit to collect the rent in person. That way, he got to look over the property, but, more importantly, it gave him a chance to get out of his office. He and his father didn't get along very well.

One cold Monday morning in early November, Glen pulled up in front of the building. It took him a minute to realize that something was wrong. The driver's side door of Ives's Nash Rambler was open, and the keys were in the ignition. The front door of the office was wide open, and no one answered when he called. Inside, there was no sign of life—just an old, broken-down desk covered with stacks and stacks of money. Behind the desk, on the floor, was a safe full of money arranged in neat bundles. On the desk with the money was a ledger full of entries written in code. The entries for each day were exactly the same. When the police added up the money, they found there to be exactly fifty thousand dollars.

The State Police never found Mr. Ives, and no one ever came forward with a credible claim for the money. Ives and his story became the subject of an episode of *Stranger Than Fiction*. The *National Star* printed a story saying that aliens had kidnapped Ives. Another story had it that he had been a communist with ties to the NAACP. The Marshall family sued the Ives estate claiming all of the money, but the judge laughed them out of court. Eventually, the State claimed the money, and everyone forgot about P. J. Ives—that is, everybody but Moon.

Moon had grown up listening to the old men sitting around Peeler's, drinking coffee and talking about P. J. Ives and all his money. Moon's idea was to parlay that old story into a way of making his own money—that was why he had to have that particular building.

When Moon first tried to rent the building from Marshall Realty, Glen Marshall laughed at him. Glen's dislike of Moon was a poem with several verses— Moon's parentage was only the first stanza. The second was Glen's daughter, Sybil—she had fallen in love with the young Moon, and when Glen found out about the budding love affair, he forbade her to see him. One Sunday morning, he caught Moon climbing out of his daughter's bedroom window and almost killed the boy. Soon after that, Marshall's daughter left for a private school in Missouri.

"I'll burn the building down and doze the lot clean before I rent it to you," Marshall said as he pointed Moon out the door of his office. The following Monday morning, Mamie, dressed in her Sunday best, showed up at Marshall's office without an appointment. She presented her IOU from years before, and, in fifteen minutes, walked out with a deed to the property and an option to buy the two lots next door. Moon had himself a cafe.

With Mamie cooking and Moon tending bar, things went pretty well, except for one problem: Moon couldn't keep his hand out of the till. After a couple of years, he had exhausted Mamie's reserves, so she bailed out and went back to waiting tables at Peeler's. This is where Mary Ann came in—she was between husbands and didn't have anything else to do, so she agreed to wait tables for Moon until something better came along.

Mary Ann had first married at sixteen to a man named Sam, who hauled soybeans for White's granary. They'd had great plans for big cars and fancy homes, but no money. Soon, Sam started drinking beer instead of going to work, and

Mary Ann joined him. One day, her mother came by, looked at the two of them sitting at the kitchen table, shook her head, and walked out the back door. As she left, she shouted back over her shoulder, "If you two are trying to drown your sorrows, remember—they know how to swim!" That really made Sam mad, and he started cussing her out for being a busybody. He could have cussed at Mary Ann, or even hit her, but she wasn't going to sit there and let him talk about her mama like that. She walked out and never looked back. When she finally got the nerve to go home, her mother never said a word. Mary Ann never drank beer in front of her again.

Eventually, she hooked up with a fellow named Hershel, who drove an eighteen-wheeler coast to coast. He was a good man, and he didn't drink heavily. At first, she liked riding cross-country with him. Long after the relationship was over, she would talk about seeing the Rocky Mountains through the windshield at daybreak. By the time they broke up, she had seen all but three states. After a while, she got tired of being on the road and set up an apartment on Maple Street. Hershel helped with the rent and the food; he would come home every two or three weeks. In time, his visits got farther and farther apart—and then he just didn't come back at all. She cried over him for a long time.

One morning, she was having coffee with her mother and moaning about how he had betrayed her. Her mother put her hand on Mary Ann's arm, looked her straight in the eye, and said, "When you take up with a man, you got to take him for what he is, not what you want him to be. You done tied yourself to a traveling man. Honey, most of this is your fault. The only way you're ever gonna hold a man is in your arms, and that's hard to do when he's halfway across the country."

Soon, she had moved back in with her mother and gone to work for Moon. Mary Ann made it clear to Moon: "Not only do I not know how to cook, I ain't even curious. I'm just here passing time and waiting for some tall-cotton cowboy to come in here and sweep me off my feet. The minute that happens, I'm out of here."

Soon after Mary Ann had come to work for Moon, the folks from Empire Stock Car and Drag Strips, the biggest dirt-track racing company in the South, decided to build a track across the street from the bar. The land had been owned by one of the heirs of the Bozeman family—the other family that had dominated the western half of Cooper County for the last century. When word got out about the sale of the land and the track, a loud groan was heard from the back office at Marshall Realty.

Even though the track brought in a lot of new people to Moon's place, the season was short enough that nobody else opened up another cafe or bar. Moon had no competition and a captive audience, but he still couldn't cook. Soon, he was down to his beer-drinking buddies and the occasional stranger who didn't know what he was getting into.

Then came Jack. His flair with food transformed Moon's. Within months, the struggling bar had been turned into a bustling little cafe. They reopened the kitchen that had become a storeroom after Mamie left. Jack could cook anything: hamburgers, fried chicken, catfish, roast beef, meat loaf, enchiladas, spaghetti … Every day, there was something special, and the regulars didn't bother with a menu. The most common order was "Whatever Jack's cooking."

CHAPTER 3

wild game

Kate Ellis was on a mission when she came into the grill—a mission that had nothing to do with food. She sat down at the bar just as Jack walked out of the kitchen carrying a large plastic bag in each hand.

"You must be Jack," she said, smiling. "What's for supper?"

Jack looked at the sacks, and then back at Kate. "This isn't supper, this is trash," he said. Without further comment, he walked out the side door.

Mary Ann came out of the kitchen just behind Jack, drying her hands with a dishrag. "Sorry, hon, didn't hear you come in," she said. "What can I get you?"

"Draft beer would be good," Kate said.

Mary Ann didn't recognize her. At first, she thought that Kate might be someone from the track—somebody's girlfriend—but there was something familiar about her voice. "Do I know you?" Mary Ann asked.

"Well, I would hope so—I've lived here all my life," Kate said as she lit a cigarette.

"You look familiar, but I just can't seem to ..."

"I'm Kate Ellis. You knew me as Mary Catherine Ellis."

"The preacher's daughter?"

"One and the same."

"The one who always sang so good?" Mary Ann asked.

"Sings, not sang. I still sing," Kate said.

"Well, haven't you changed!"

"Yeah, I guess ... a little." Kate smiled, acknowledging the compliment.

"Are you here visiting?" Mary Ann asked. "Your mom and dad moved away, didn't they?"

"Yes and no. Yes, they moved, but no, I'm not visiting. I'm teaching English at the high school now."

As they talked, Kate looked around the room as though she were looking for someone. Finally, she asked, "Is Moon around?"

"No, he's over at the track. He'll be back around five. He has his daily routine—little spots he hits each day. I can reach him, if you want."

"No, just tell him I stopped by." Kate downed her beer and left.

Mary Ann watched Kate jump into her little yellow Volkswagen Beetle and take off.

The early supper crowd was beginning to gather when Moon came in the side door. The first to catch sight of him was Mary Ann. He was dressed in a white linen suit, white leather shoes, and a red bow tie.

Mary Ann bit her lip to keep from laughing. "What's with the Colonel getup?" she asked.

"I'll have you know that I've decided to enter into a joint venture with the Harris Brothers over at the track that will be mutually beneficial to my corporation and theirs," he said. The Harris brothers, John and Jerry, were fraternal twins who had been imported from Newark, New Jersey to run the racetrack. They were the privileged sons of a union boss, and they had been in trouble since they were born. Shipping them against their will to rural Arkansas had been their father's way of getting them away from temptation. It hadn't worked.

Joe and Art were watching a bowling tournament on the television. Art looked up when Mary Ann commented on Moon's attire. He poked his friend in the side. "Look at the ice-cream man," he said.

"What's this all about, Moon?" Joe asked.

Before Moon could cloud the issue any further, Mary Ann said, "It means that he owes the Harris brothers money, and they want him to dress up like a clown."

"That's just like you people," Moon said defensively. "You never see the broader picture. This isn't about the money. Just think of all of the exposure this will bring to the cafe when the people hear me over the PA system—and especially on the radio!"

"What are you talking about, Moon?" Mary Ann asked.

"Didn't I tell you? I'm the new race announcer for the track!" Moon said proudly. "Think about it—I study the drivers and car more than anybody. When you're making book, you got to know what you're doing." Moon failed to mention that he had lost a thousand dollars to the Harris brothers and that this was his way of working off the debt.

Mary Ann changed the subject. "By the way, Moon, this woman was in here looking for you."

"It's not my baby, and I can prove it!" Moon said.

"Wait a minute, Moon …"

"She was free, white, and twenty-one! At least, that's what she told me."

"Look, this girl was in here this afternoon …"

"I wish these women would learn to take responsibility for their own bodies. It takes two to tango, you know," Moon said. He went behind the counter and poured himself a glass of tea.

"She wasn't pregnant," Mary Ann said.

"Well, at least she finally admits it."

"Will you shut up and listen to me?"

"What?"

"I'm not talking about one of your pregnant girlfriends."

"Well, what in the hell are you talking about?"

"I'm talking about Mary Catherine Ellis."

"And who's Mary Catherine Ellis?" asked Moon. "I don't know anyone by that name, and she's a liar if she says I do."

"You might not remember her, but you *do* know her," Mary Ann said. "At least, you knew her in another life. She's the Methodist minister's daughter. Her hair always looked like wet noodles, remember? Anyway, she don't look that way anymore—she's a knockout. She was in here this afternoon looking for you."

"What's she doing here? Those folks don't even live here anymore."

"She's teaching English at the high school."

"What's some goody-two-shoes schoolteacher want with me? I ain't put the make on any of the high school girls in a couple of years, and anybody that says different is a liar!"

"I have no idea what she wanted with you. She didn't say, and I didn't ask. But I didn't get the idea that it had anything to do with high school girls or church."

Moon walked to the cash register, opened the till, and extracted a handful of money. "Well, I don't have time for an English lesson right now. I've got to get some bets straight before I go over to the track." While Moon was stuffing his pockets, Jack came out of the kitchen.

"Jack," Moon said, "there's a bunch of ducks in the trunk of my car. I want you to fix them for tomorrow's lunch. I got a good deal from a friend. We're gonna have to find a way to cut down on the grocery costs around here. What do you think happens when you cook all this food and nobody eats it? I'll tell you what happens—I get stuck with the bill! You people got me buying watermelons for a dime and selling them for a nickel. We ain't gonna stay in business very long if you guys don't start watching the cost."

Jack stopped and thought for a second. "Mr. Moon," he said, "I haven't been buying any watermelons. In fact, the watermelon season is over."

Mary Ann had seen this coming. "No, Jack, honey, this hasn't got anything to do with watermelons. It was just a figure of speech. Moon's saying that we're spending too much money on food."

"Oh," Jack said. He walked back into the kitchen.

After Moon left for the track, Jack came back out to the front and stopped Mary Ann. "I guess I've been costing Mr. Moon lots of money. I don't want to get us in trouble. What do you think I ought to do? I could start fixing pancakes and canned vegetables every meal. That wouldn't cost very much."

Mary Ann put her hand on his shoulder. "Sweetie, this hasn't got anything to do with the stuff you're cooking. Right now, there's more money going through that cash register in a week than it used to see in a year. Trouble is, Moon empties out the till every night. What money he doesn't spend on his girlfriends he loses at the track or the casinos over in Tunica. The boy can't resist a bet. You just keep on doing what you're doing, and don't worry about it."

The wild smell of fresh-killed ducks and the dark, grainy texture of the meat created a dilemma for Jack. The problem wasn't what to do with the ducks; it was what *not* to do.

When the evening meal was done and everyone had cleared out, he laid out the birds on the prep table. A few of the small, young birds he placed in roasting bags with celery and apples and cooked them slowly. He removed the breasts of most of the others and marinated the meat in red wine, pepper, and thyme. When the lunch crowd began to gather the next day, he would grill and thinly slice the marinated breasts. He chopped and crushed the carcasses, extracting as much blood and juice as possible. To the extract he added a sauce of red wine, flour, butter, pepper, onions, and thyme. He used this gravy on the grilled breasts and the roasted duck. With the older ducks and the ones mangled by shotgun pellets he made a pot of duck soup sweetened with raisins and apples. While the birds were cooking and the soup was stewing, Jack fixed a large pot of rice to soak up the gravy.

Mary Ann arrived at the usual time on Sunday morning. "Morning, Mr. Jack," she said as she came through the back door. "This place smells wonderful. You must have gotten an early start."

When there was no response, she walked to the kitchen door. Jack was standing in front of the stove, looking up at the vent hood.

"Jack?" she said again.

This time, Jack turned toward her.

"Are you okay?" she asked.

Jack said nothing, but nodded.

After an awkward silence, Jack walked toward the side door. "I need a cigarette," he said, and out he went. It wasn't difficult to tell when Jack was bothered—he would sweat profusely and stand staring into the vent hood. Another clue was his smoking. Most of the time, he didn't smoke at all, but when he got nervous, he lit one after another.

Mary Ann watched her friend walk out the door, but she didn't say anything. This wasn't the first time she had dealt with somebody like Jack. When she was a child, Uncle Curtis, her mother's brother, had lived with them. He had stayed in a small apartment off the garage in the backyard, and, for the most part, he had kept to himself. He never hurt anyone, but he had this strange look—a distant stare—that scared her. When Mary Ann asked her mother about Curtis, she responded, "Behind that stare is a lonely soul with no real home. Ordinary things keep him beat down. You just stay out of his way when he starts acting odd." At times like this, Jack had that same look in his eyes, and Mary Ann had decided that it was best to just stay out of his way.

She went about getting the cafe ready for the lunch crowd, and, in a few minutes, Jack came back in and returned to his kitchen.

After Jack returned to his cooking, Mary Ann ventured into the kitchen. "Jack, from the looks of this kitchen, you must have been cooking all night," she said.

Without looking up, Jack said, "I didn't want to waste any of the ducks."

"Where did you get all of the recipes?" she asked.

"What recipes?" he responded.

"You mean, you just made all of this up out of your head?" she asked, truly amazed.

"Yeah, I guess so. But it's different than that."

"What do you mean?"

"I don't know, for sure. It's just kinda like the smell of the raw meat has all these points and edges. Cooking is like smoothing the edges and rounding off the points."

"Oh," Mary Ann said. She didn't have the least idea what Jack was talking about.

It made no difference that Jack couldn't explain where his recipes came from or why his food never tasted the same twice in a row; the ducks were a success. By one o'clock, they had all the customers seated and the orders in. Several weeks earlier, Mary Ann had talked Moon into hiring her friend Joy to help with the Sunday lunch crowd. Mary Ann and Joy waited tables, Moon manned the cash register, and Jack worked as fast as he could to keep up with the orders.

Moon stuck his head into the kitchen. "You got table four's order ready?" he demanded, looking around the kitchen. "That old woman is about to have a hissy fit. She thinks we're doing something to personally humiliate her because table three got their food first."

"Five minutes on number four," Jack said. "Soup's faster than breast. Can't hurry it."

"Well, hurry it up anyway. We got to keep our customers happy. And, by the way, this kitchen is a mess. Get this crap cleaned up!"

When Jack walked back to the oven to check on the grilling duck breast, the vent hood said, *"He's right, you know—this place is a mess. Hell, you're a mess! He'll probably fire you before the day is out. You screwed up three orders today! What are you thinking about?"*

"I'm tired," Jack said to the vent hood.

Mary Ann was standing behind him and heard his comment. "I bet you are," she said. "I'm already tired, and I slept all night. This is the last order. Things are beginning to slack up. I can handle it from here. Why don't you go out and have a smoke?" She patted him on the back.

"I got to finish these orders first," he said. He finished the orders as methodically as usual, took off his apron and cap, and went out the back door.

A few minutes later, Moon came into the kitchen. "Where's Jack? I've got a to-go order," he said.

"Don't know," said Mary Ann. "He went out for a smoke a little while ago."

"You mean, just like that? He walked out in the middle of a meal? Who's gonna clean up this mess? Who's gonna fill this order?"

Mary Ann walked over to where Moon was standing. She reached out and took the order ticket from him. "I'll take care of that and anything else that comes in. As for Jack he didn't just walk out in the middle of a meal, I told him to take a break. He's been working all night, and he was tired. If he doesn't come back, Joy and I will do the clean up."

"Mark my word; anything extra I have to pay Joy in overtime comes out of his paycheck." Moon turned, walked up out of the kitchen, into this office and slammed the door.

CHAPTER 4

hide and go seek

Jack didn't return from his break. The girls plated up the rest of the orders and began cleaning up the mess. After the last customer left, Moon emerged from his office behind the bar, cleaned out the cash register, and left grumbling about "going broke."

"What's this about Moon going broke?" Joy asked as Moon pulled out of the parking lot in his old Corvette. "How could he possibly be going broke? He had a quarter of the people in town in here for lunch today—even a few of the teetotaling Baptists!"

"He's not going broke," Mary Ann replied. "He just needs something to complain about."

"What about Jack?" Joy asked.

"Yeah, it's a little odd that he didn't come back in and say something about leaving," Mary Ann replied. "But hell, he was up all night cooking those ducks, so I don't blame him. I would have been looking for a bed three or four hours ago."

The grill was closed on Mondays. As she did most weeks, Mary Ann got up early, washed a few loads of clothes, and then drove to Batesville to see a movie. Since the track was closed until Thursday, Moon spent the first part of the week in West Memphis at the dog track or Tunica at the craps tables. He and the God of Chance were on a first-name basis. No one ever questioned that he was lucky or that he had a way of making money—his problem was holding on to it. He had a tendency to get greedy, and he could never stop after a good night at the tables.

Mary Ann showed up at the usual time on Tuesday. Ordinarily, Jack was there already, planning the evening menu, so, when she found that he wasn't there, Mary Ann began to worry. Despite her reassurances to Joy on Sunday afternoon, she had been concerned—all of this was different for Jack. For him to leave without cleaning up and then to not show up for work was certainly out of character. In the months since he had walked into the bar, he had not missed a day.

Mary Ann fixed a pot of coffee, poured herself a cup, and began to formulate a plan. There was no use in trying to find Moon—if not for an empty cash register, Moon wouldn't even know if she were to close the place for the day. Instead, she called Joy.

"Hey, Sis," Mary Ann said, "I got a real big favor to ask. Jack didn't come in, and I'm worried that something might be wrong. Could you come down, sling some hash, and serve a few beers for a couple of hours while I try to find out what's going on? I promise there won't be many customers. Tuesday during the day is mostly just sitting around twiddling our thumbs. You can? Great. I'll see you in, what, thirty minutes? Okay, good, I'll see you then."

As a child, Mary Ann had spent more than a few afternoons riding around town with her mother looking for her Uncle Curtis. Whenever he disappeared, her mother would give him a day or two, and then she would go looking for him. One time, Mary Ann asked her how she knew where to look. Her mother had just laughed and said, "Honey, Curtis is like that old mockingbird in the backyard. He ain't never gonna stray too far from his territory."

Sure enough, there were only a few places he would be. Usually, it was down by Don's fish dock on the river or near the railroad bridge at the end of Border Street just beyond Sylvia's cafe. On occasion, he would wander off as far as the Highway 80 bridge north of town. Wherever he was found, he would just be sitting there, real quiet. Whenever Mary Ann's mother found him, she would sit down and start talking. Most of the time, she talked about whatever was on her mind—maybe one of her relatives or one of her long-lost husbands. Soon, Curtis would quit staring off into space and start listening to her. Mary Ann asked her once where she learned how to do that. She said, "Sweetie, all of us get crazy every once in a while. We get to worrying about how bad things are. Sometimes, if it's bad enough, it can just about overwhelm a person. When that happens to me, it helps to just get out and get busy, even if it's listening to somebody else's problems." Usually, if she talked long enough, she could get Curtis laughing. Mary Ann's mother could make anybody laugh.

With Joy holding down the fort, Mary Ann took off on her treasure hunt. The first stop was Jack's apartment. Jack lived in a walk-up garage apartment behind the old Bozeman house. When Old Man Bozeman and his wife died, none of their kids came back to live in Gum Ridge. Over the next several years, the house and the pecan orchard behind fell into disrepair. John Baker, the high school band director, eventually worked out a deal with the Bozeman family—he would keep up the house and tend to the pecan orchard in lieu of rent.

The apartment was perfect for Jack. Originally, it had been created for the children's nanny. At the top of the stairs, the door to Jack's apartment opened into a narrow hall. On the left was a small bathroom, and on the right was a closet. The hall opened into a large room with windows in the front and back walls. At the front of the room was a small kitchen area with a fifties-style dinette table and three old, red vinyl chairs. At the other end of the room was a sitting area with a wooden rocking chair, a small table, and an old radio that Jack had found in the closet. The window, beside which the rocking chair sat, faced onto the pecan orchard. Jack spent hours looking out at the orchard from his chair. Just beyond the large room was a small bedroom with just enough space for an army cot and a thin mattress. The Bozemans had made the bedroom small to discourage the nanny from having visitors.

Mary Ann walked up the steps and opened the screen door. She knocked on the glass-paneled door to the apartment. There was no response. "Jack, are you in there?" she asked, slightly raising her voice. After three or four attempts with no answer, she tried the door. It was unlocked—but, of course, Jack never did lock anything. The one time she had left him to lock up the cafe, he had simply wandered out the back door at the end of the day. When she returned the next morning, everything was standing wide open, and the money was still in the cash register.

Standing at the door of Jack's apartment, she was faced with a dilemma. Jack had not asked her to come looking for him; he was an adult and could do anything he pleased. It was just possible that he had gotten tired of Moon's behavior and had decided to hit the road. From what Jack had said, it sounded like he had been all over the South and the East Coast over the last thirty years. Maybe this was how Jack left one place and ended up in another—one day, he just didn't show up at work; he got on a bus and left.

"Well, if he's gone," she thought out loud, "he won't care whether I go in or not. And if he's sick, he might need my help." This was another of those lessons her mother had taught her. The first time she had heard it, Mary Ann was twelve years old and trying to decide between two dresses. Her mother was getting frustrated. "Mary Ann, honey," she said, "I don't have all day, and it ain't gonna get any easier while you stand there and stew. Make up your mind, and get on with it."

Mary Ann opened the door and, for the first time, was a little scared. Jack was not a young man. What if he was dead? The day Curtis died, they found him sitting in an old lawn chair down by the railroad bridge. What would she do if Jack was dead? As she walked down the dark, quiet hall, she thought she heard a sound from behind the closed bathroom door.

"Jack, are you in there?" she whispered.

Again, there was no response. She scanned the bottom of the door, checking to see if there was any light. There was none. When she reached to grasp the doorknob, she heard the sound again.

"Jack?"

She turned the knob and pushed gently on the door. It didn't budge, and it took her a minute to realize that, unlike normal inside doors, this one didn't open into the small bathroom; it opened out into the hall. She heard what sounded like a moan coming from the bathroom. She slowly opened the door, and, when it was barely cracked, somebody—something—forced itself through the opening rapidly, making a loud crying sound. The scream scared her, and she stumbled backward, falling against the opposite wall of the hall. Instead of attacking, the something in the bathroom streaked toward the kitchen. From her position on the floor, Mary Ann realized that she had just been accosted by Jack's cat, Gracie.

Mary Ann regained her composure, stood up, and brushed herself off. Freed from her prison, Gracie made a beeline for her litter box. When she was through, her second stop was the food bowl. Mary Ann switched on the light in the bathroom and looked behind the door to make sure that Jack wasn't lying on the floor. While the cat took care of its needs, Mary Ann surveyed the rest of the apartment. Other than Gracie, there was no sign of life.

Jack's duffel bag was lying beside the bed. There were three or four back issues of *Stockcar World* and a book of Van Gogh paintings that had been checked out of the Cooper County Library.

Jack was not the kind of person who left his cat locked in the bathroom. The cat and the presence of his duffel bag made it clear that Jack hadn't jumped a bus. But where was he?

"Morning, H. T.," Mary Ann said upon arrival at the police station. "I need your help." H. T. Lincoln was the chief of police. Moon, Mary Ann, and H. T. had known one another since they were children.

"Anything for a pretty lady," he said. "What can I do you for?"

"I think we have a problem."

"What do you mean, 'you think'?" he asked.

"Well, I don't know for sure. Jack didn't show up for work this morning, and that's not like him."

"You mean Jack the cook?"

"Yeah," she said.

"From what I've been told, it ain't unusual for cooks to kinda disappear right along. They aren't the most dependable bunch of folks. How long's this fella been gone?"

"The last time I saw him was Sunday afternoon."

"That's not really very long," H. T. said. "What makes you think he's gone missing?"

"It's just not like him, and his cat was closed up in his bathroom." Mary Ann proceeded to tell H. T. about the cat attack at the apartment.

"Well, to tell you the truth, there isn't a lot I can do unless he's been gone more than a couple of days, but I'll tell the boys to keep a lookout for him. Did you ask around at the track?"

"I didn't think of that," she said. "He could be over there, I guess. Most of the time, there isn't any sign of life over there until the middle of the afternoon."

"Like I said, I'll tell the boys to keep an eye out for him," H. T. said. "Where can I get hold of you?"

"Joy's working the cafe. If you find something, call and tell her, and I'll call in every so often."

"Sure. Sounds like a plan." H. T. smiled at Mary Ann. He liked looking at her—he always had.

Mary Ann checked up on Joy at the cafe and then went to the track. There weren't any races during the week, and the only people at the track were the manager and a couple of the maintenance men. No one had seen Jack.

Mary Ann began the next phase of her search at the Highway 80 bridge north of town, because that was where she went to think. The bridge crossed the river at the old Chickasaw Indian crossing. It was a long, narrow two-lane affair over the

Green River. The river at this point was still a clear mountain stream with narrow rapids and long, deep holes of still water. Just beyond the bridge, the bottomlands began to flatten out, and the river spread out into a slow-moving delta stream. The water flowed under the bridge in a deep channel next to the rock bluff on the west bank. Most of the bridge crossed over a wide sandbar that was dry except in flood season. Here and there on the sandbar were the black-ringed remnants of campfires left by fishermen and canoeists.

This sandbar had been the setting for many of Mary Ann's wonderful memories. As a child, she had fished there with her mother during the spring. In the summer, when the water dropped, the long, deep hole of pale green water was where she would go to swim. In the fall, as the maple, oak, and birch trees changed colors, she would sit there for hours, considering her life. Mary Ann had taken Jack out to see the leaves when they had turned that fall. That particular afternoon, as they walked along the riverbank, Jack had fixated on a bright red maple tree. For an hour, he had sat and stared at the tree and its fiery red leaves.

"Pretty, huh?" Mary Ann had said.

"Yeah, and loud, too," Jack had replied.

"What do you mean, loud?"

"Don't know how to explain it—but it's not just pretty." Jack pointed to a yellow-leafed birch at the water's edge. "See that pretty yellow tree on the bank? It makes a sound as well—kind of a soft hum. But that maple is loud. Sometimes, when the sun hits them just right, the sounds and shapes come together, like in a Van Gogh painting."

"Okay," Mary Ann said. The closest she had come to experiencing anything like Jack described was one time in the Rockies, west of Denver. Hershel, the boyfriend/truck driver, had scored some mescaline and convinced Mary Ann to take a hit. They had been parked in a grove of aspen trees, and, as the sun came up, the yellow aspen leaves seemed to be shouting at her. It had not been a pleasant experience—it had been as though she were two people, one enjoying the ride with the bright colors and the other scared out of her mind of losing control and not being able to find her way back. That day on the riverbank had been the first time that Mary Ann had understood that Jack really saw things a bit differently than other people.

Mary Ann now thought that, since Jack seemed to have enjoyed that afternoon, he might end up here. For an hour or so, she walked up and down the bank, looking in all of the secret places of her youth. But Jack was nowhere to be found.

Her next stop was Don's fish dock back in town. After passing under the bridge, the river made several S-shaped loops before it arrived at the high bank that formed River Street in Gum Ridge. Here, the river was no longer the fast-running mountain stream it had been just a few miles before. The stream, once clear and rocky-bottomed, here took on a deep look and had muddy banks. Don's dock was a sturdy platform that had lasted through repeated floods and dry spells. It was where Mary Ann's mother had been most likely to find Uncle Curtis. Don's stocks-in-trade were catfish, buffalo, and drum. Each morning, a small crew of dedicated fishermen ran their lines and supplied him with a steady stream of bottom-feeding fish. Over the last several years, however, this section of the river had been overfished, and Don was having trouble competing with the fish farms.

Mary Ann walked across the narrow planks that connected the tin-roofed houseboat to the bank. When she was a child, one of Mary Ann's great fears had been that she would fall off of the walkway and be eaten by the great alligator gar that lay in wait under the dock. Never mind that no one had ever seen scale or fin of the monster fish—it had still been her greatest fear.

There was a fish fry every Friday night at Moon's, and the fish came from Don's. This was another of those places that Mary Ann had introduced Jack to when he had first come to town.

"Morning, you old river rat," Mary Ann said as she walked onto the dock.

Don held his hand up. "Morning, Mary Ann. I'll be with you in a second." He was raising the live well from a hole in the center of the boat. The live well was a frame covered with heavy-gauge wire mesh, and, as the box emerged, the water in it began to boil with activity. In the increasingly shallow water of the basket were a half-dozen twenty-pound fish maneuvering for position.

Don secured the rope that had pulled the box from the water, put on a heavy canvas glove, reached in, and grabbed the largest catfish by the gills. In one broad motion, he pulled the fish from the cage and slapped it onto the cutting table. With his other hand, he grabbed a large, flat-headed hammer from his collection of medieval tools and, with one blow to the head, quieted the flopping fish.

"Ruby Cole called a few minutes ago, wanting catfish for tonight," he said. "And you know how she is. If it ain't ready when she gets here, she's just liable to walk off and not buy it. The way things are these days, I can't afford not to cotton to her whims." As he spoke, the old man nailed the catfish to a wooden block at the head of the table and made an incision behind the gills. He then took a large pair of pliers and proceeded to skin the catfish. "What do you need, Mary Ann? I got a little of everything fresh in the hole. You pick it out, and it's yours."

"Don't need any fish today," she said. "I'm looking for Jack. Have you seen him?"

"No, can't say that I have," he said. "Last time I saw him was last Friday, when y'all came down here to get your fish. Why, is something wrong?"

"I don't know—but something's just not right. He didn't show up for work this morning, and that's not like him."

"Well, I ain't seen him, but I'll keep my eye out for him," he promised.

"Thanks, Don."

Sylvia Prince, an ageless woman with long, black, flowing hair, was the gypsy fortune-teller of Gum Ridge. She moved with an elegant grace. Her grandson, the only other living member of her family, often remarked that his grandmother never walked, she floated and danced her way through life. Sylvia and her husband had befriended Curtis later in his life, and it was actually Sylvia who had found him sitting dead under the railroad bridge.

Mary Ann crossed the railroad tracks and stopped at the tall metal gate in front of Sylvia's house. There was a note on the gate: "Have gone fishing, should be back by supper." Mary Ann got back into her truck, turned right onto Border Street, and drove over the levee. Just on the other side of the levee was a parking area where she stopped her truck, got out, and walked the two hundred yards down to the river. As expected, she found Sylvia sitting in a metal folding chair with a single fishing line cast into the stream. Snuffy, Sylvia's dog, was playing with a stick that Sylvia would pick up and throw every few minutes.

"Good morning, Sylvia," said Mary Ann. "Catching anything?"

"Oh, hello, dear. Yeah, I've caught a few." Sylvia got up and stretched. "I didn't hear you come up." She reached down and took the stick from her little dog. "Snuffy and I were playing his favorite game." She threw the stick into the water, and the dog immediately took after it. She turned, walked over to Mary Ann, and hugged her. "It's so nice to see you! It won't take but a few minutes for me to clean these fish, and it would tickle me no end to have you stay for a bite to eat."

"I'd love to, but I really don't have time. I've got a bit of a problem, I think."

"What's going on?" Sylvia asked.

"You've probably heard we've got a new cook at the cafe, and I'm here to tell you, Jack can cook up a storm."

"I've heard. Is he really as good as they say?"

"He's good, all right," Mary Ann said. "In some areas, he might even be able to give *you* a run for your money, and you know how I feel about your cooking."

"Well, now, that almost sounds like a challenge! I've got to come down and see this for myself."

"That's part of the problem," Mary Ann said.

"What do you mean?"

"Jack's a little like Curtis. He's real quiet. He walked out of the grill on Sunday, and then didn't show up for work this morning. I'm hitting all the spots where he just might be."

"Unless he's over across the river—and I doubt that, 'cause the water's kind of high—he's not been down here. I've been up and down the bank all the way to Depot Creek, and there wasn't anybody around but me and Snuffy. Do you think something could have happened to him?"

"I can't get the idea out of my head that he might just sit down somewhere and never wake up—kinda like Curtis did," Mary Ann said.

"I guess we can hope that nothing's happened," Sylvia said. "You know what Melos used to say … 'I'd rather live to be ninety as an optimist and find out the day I died that I was wrong, than live to be ninety as a pessimist and find out I was right.'"

"Well, I got to run," said Mary Ann.

"I really do miss having you around," said Sylvia, smiling. "Keep me posted. If you do find him, I'll come by and meet the competition."

Mary Ann was concerned that Joy might not be able to handle the evening alone. It wasn't that there would be much business, but Joy wasn't the most capable person especially when it came to the cash register. When Mary Ann arrived, there were a couple of cars and trucks in the parking lot. Any concerns that Mary Ann had had about Joy were soon allayed. She found Joy frying burgers, Art and Joe watching a rerun of a television game show called *Take a Chance*, and two of Joy's girlfriends nursing beers at the bar.

"You doing okay?" Mary Ann asked. She hung her coat on the stand near the back door.

"Yeah, we're doing fine. I got plenty of help in case there's a rush," Joy said, looking over at her friends at the bar. "Did you find Jack?"

"No, I didn't, and nobody has seen him. Did H. T. call?"

Joy shook her head. "What are you gonna do now?" she asked.

"Don't know. But I think I'll make one more trip by his house. John wasn't home earlier, and I was thinking maybe he's seen Jack."

"Sounds like a good idea to me. Don't worry about this place—we got everything under control here. By the way, that Ellis girl was in here again, looking for

Moon. We gave her an earful about him." Joy smiled a broad, mischievous smile. "Didn't we, girls?"

The other two nodded. Joy added, "If she's still interested after what we told her, that girl's beyond hope."

For the first time that day, Mary Ann had something to smile about. "You know what Mama used to say when I came home and told her I was in love? She'd smile and say, 'Mary Ann, love and lust are just a misunderstanding between two fools.'" Mary Ann went over to the coat rack put her sweater back on. "I'm going back to Jack's apartment. I should be back in a little while."

"Take your time," Joy said. "We're doing fine." She dished up the hamburgers for Art and Joe.

Mary Ann pulled into the driveway of the Bozeman home. From her car, she could hear the awkward sounds of a trumpet lesson. John Baker tutored some of his young students after school. It took several rings of the doorbell to get his attention.

"What can I do for you, Mary Ann?" John asked after opening the door.

"Have you seen Jack?"

He puzzled for a minute. "Come to think of it, no, I haven't. Is anything wrong?"

"I don't know. He didn't show up for work today, and that's not like him."

"Have you been to his room to look?" he asked.

"Yeah, I came by this morning, and he wasn't here. I was going to take another look."

"Do you need for me to do anything?" John asked.

"No, I don't think so. Thanks."

"Let me know if you don't find him, and I'll keep an eye out."

John closed the door and Mary Ann walked around the side of the house to the garage apartment. When she opened the door at the top of the stairs, Gracie dashed out and ran down the steps. *Damn,* she thought, *now I got to try and catch that stupid cat. I can't let it stay out all night.*

Mary Ann made a quick scan of the apartment and assured herself that there was no sign of Jack. She was beginning to get a bit discouraged. *Jack might just be gone for good,* she thought. *I'll really miss him if he doesn't show up.*

She stood at the window and looked toward the river. The sun hung low in the sky to the west. The long, red rays of evening sun filtered through the pecan orchard, whose evenly spaced trees created a dramatic pattern of alternating light and shadow. Fifty yards from the house was an old tree that had split down the center—half of the tree was dying, and the other half held on to life. Gracie circled the base of the tree. It was obvious that something propped against the base of the tree had caught the cat's interest. *That's curious,* she thought. Then she realized it: Gracie had found Jack.

Mary Ann hurried out the door and down the steps. She walked across the orchard and felt a light, moist, cool breeze come off the river. She pulled her sweater closed over her chest. *It's about to get really cold,* she thought. Leaves and pecans crunched under her feet. *What am I going to do? What if he's dead?*

Her mother's words came to her as she walked: "Don't worry about it, honey. That's what life is all about. Just make it up as you go along."

He was covered in a thin blanket of pecan leaves. If he had been lying by the tree instead of sitting up, he would have looked like nothing more than a mound of leaves. He sat with his knees pulled up to his chest. His eyes were open just a little too wide. Like a child who doesn't want to be noticed and refuses to make eye contact, Jack's stare was focused on the horizon. Gracie had curled up in a ball next to Jack's legs.

"Jack, are you okay?" There was no response. "Jack?" she repeated. Mary Ann sat down on the ground beside him and looked at her strange friend. She really had no idea where to start, but she had watched enough medical shows to know that the first thing to do was take his pulse. She reached out, took his left wrist, and turned it over. His heart was beating regular and slow. He didn't resist the movement, but his arm stayed in whatever position she placed it in. *How odd,* she thought. She straightened out his legs and brushed away the leaves. He didn't seem to be in any pain, and there was certainly nothing wrong with his breathing, but there was still no response—not a blink, not a twitch. It was at this point that she realized how much Jack really did seem like Curtis. When Curtis got like this, her mother would sit down beside him and start talking, and he would eventually respond. So Mary Ann began to talk about first one thing, and then another— her beer-drinking first husband, Hershel and his truck, and her favorite place in the whole world, the Rocky Mountains. After exhausting the trucking stories, she talked about her family and how they had come to live in Gum Ridge—she could talk about that bunch for hours.

As the early December sun set, it got colder, and she started to get discouraged. The talking didn't seem to be working.

Maybe I should call the doctor, she thought.

She was considering her next move when Jack turned his head toward her and a smile of recognition came across his face. "Mary Ann," he said. It was as if she had just sat down beside him. She understood—it was Jack who hadn't been there.

"Jack, are you okay?" she asked.

"Yeah, I guess so."

"Would you like something to eat?"

"I sure would; I'm really hungry," Jack replied. "I feel like I haven't eaten in days."

"Come on, I'll help you up. Let's go and see if we can find something to eat."

He struggled to his feet. "I'm stiff. I guess I'm getting old," he said.

"It happens to all of us, sweetie. By the way, Jack, how old are you?" Mary Ann asked the question more to make conversation than anything else.

A puzzled look came over his face. "I don't know," he said. "I haven't thought much about it."

"You mean … Oh, never mind," she said. "Let's get you in the house and get something warm into you."

Back in his apartment, she helped Jack into his rocking chair and covered him with a blanket. When Jack was comfortable, she began looking through the cabinets for food. The pickings were slim; all she found was a jar of instant coffee, a few cans of clam chowder, and a package of saltines.

"All I could find was some canned soup and crackers. Is that okay? If it isn't, I can go get you something good to eat. It might not be what *you* would fix, but it'd be better than canned soup."

"I like canned soup," he said.

"Okay, clam chowder it is," she said. "You want some coffee?"

"Please. That would be good."

Mary Ann opened the chowder and poured it into a pan. "Jack, a little while ago, out in the orchard, you said that you didn't know how old you were. I don't mean to pry, but what do you remember about being a kid?"

He thought for a minute, then replied, "Just bits and pieces … like dreams of kids playing baseball. Nothing, really."

"What's the first thing you *do* remember?"

"I don't know. I don't think about that much." He considered the proposition for a minute. "Well, I guess the first thing I really remember was Bud Gates at the Bud's Root Beer place in Little Rock."

"How old were you then?"

"I don't know. About the same age I am now, I guess."

"Now, Jack, from what you've told me about traveling around to all those racetracks, that must have been a long time ago."

"Yeah … I guess you're right." Jack got a strained look on his face, and then he looked out the window. He turned back toward Mary Ann and said, "No, that's not right. That's not the first thing I remember." He hesitated. "But you've got to promise you won't tell anybody. Okay?"

"Sure."

"The first thing I remember is Charlotte and the State Hospital in Little Rock. Now, you can't tell anybody, 'cause if Mr. Moon finds out, I'll lose my job."

CHAPTER 5

voices of fate

Little Rock, Arkansas, 1961

It was early evening, and John Allen St. Clair and Jack had just finished their meal at Tom and Jerry's Restaurant. They were walking back to their hotel when John Allen reached out and grabbed Jack's arm. He clutched his chest with his other hand, gasped, and fell over dead at Jack's feet.

"J. A., get up! Wake up!" Jack said. "Stop fooling with me! Get up!"

Jack knelt down and rolled John Allen onto his back. As the last spark of life flowed through his body, J. A. seized and threw up. Through a scrambled fog of disbelief, one thing came through loud and clear to Jack: something was dreadfully wrong with his friend.

The clerk in the army-navy surplus store noticed the two men on the sidewalk, came to the door, and heard Jack's plaintive cry: "Help! Help!"

The clerk ran back inside and called an ambulance, but it was too late. John Allen had been dead before he hit the pavement. The coroner would rule that a massive coronary thrombosis had been the cause of death. His liver was also shot, he had early emphysema, and showed the beginnings of prostate cancer—all of this in a man of fifty-five.

Jack sat there on the sidewalk and didn't move, but he wasn't alone; the voices were back.

From a blue 1960 sedan sitting by the curb, he heard, *"You've done it now, Jack. You've killed him! You killed your friend! You'd better run, you worthless piece of crap, or they'll put your ass in jail. Worse than that … they'll find out your secret!"*

As Jack struggled to understand what was going on, he thought, *I didn't do anything.*

From a piece of newspaper lying on the street came another, less-threatening voice: *"Run, Jack, run. Get out of here. They'll put you away. Run away, Jack, find a place to hide."*

For all his desire to flee—for all the sadness he felt for his lost friend—Jack couldn't move. He simply slumped to the ground. While the voices argued his fate, he sat on the pavement. Alone except for the voices, he shared the responsibility for his friend's death—he and fate.

By the time the ambulance arrived, a group of bystanders had formed a wide, loose circle around John Allen.

"What happened here?" one of the ambulance attendants asked as he leaned over to evaluate John Allen's body.

The store clerk explained what he had seen.

"This guy's dead. What about the other guy?" the attendant asked.

The clerk shrugged and pointed toward Jack. "He's over there, propped up against that car."

The two attendants loaded John Allen's body into the ambulance and then turned their attention to Jack.

One of them leaned over Jack. "Mister, are you okay?"

His question was met with no reply—not a blink or a twitch. Jack just sat there.

"He's either in shock or he's really drunk. Either way, we can't leave him here on the street. We'll let the folks at Central Hospital figure this out."

The emergency-room entrance of Central Hospital was only a few blocks away. It was early in the evening, and the Saturday-night knife-and-gun club had not yet convened, so the emergency room was quiet. When the ambulance arrived, a large, stout, black man dressed in white came out with a wheelchair. He gently molded Jack into the chair and rolled him into the building through the big double doors. Once inside the emergency room, Jack was descended on by a team of medics led by a young intern. They examined him, drew blood, catheterized him, EKG'ed him, and x-rayed him. Everything was normal, and the intern was stumped, so he called in the staff physician.

The young medic described the pertinent positive and negative findings.

"Blood alcohol?" the older doctor asked.

"Negative."

"You've checked an EKG?"

"Yes, sir."

"Any family or friends?" The older doctor thumbed through the chart as they talked.

"Not that we know of, sir—no wallet, no ID. They found him lying in the street downtown. The only other thing unusual about him is that he doesn't respond to anything. Watch." The young doctor picked up a hypodermic needle and jabbed Jack's big toe with it. There was no response of any sort.

"Well, son, this isn't anything we're going to figure out here, and he doesn't seem to have any medical problems. This man needs the help of a psychiatrist. Since he doesn't seem to have any resources, I think it's best that we forward him to the State Hospital. Why don't we send him over there and see what they can do with him?" The older doctor closed Jack's chart.

After a number of telephone calls and an argument about court orders and "John Doe" admissions, Jack was transferred to the State Hospital for Mental Disease.

The only memory Jack would retain of his ride to the second hospital was that of the sound of the cinder driveway as the ambulance turned off Markham Street and weaved its way up the tree-lined drive to the main entrance.

The ambulance crew unloaded Jack and transferred him from the emergency gurney onto a bed in the hospital intake room. The charge nurse signed the transfer sheet, and the emergency crew made a quick exit. Jack was now the responsibility of the State Hospital. The nurse completed the paperwork on this third John Doe of the week and then rang the night physician's room, telling him of the new admission.

Not the least bit pleased that he had been awakened from his sleep, the admitting physician trudged down to the intake room and glanced over at Jack. "He looks dead to me," he said. "Are you sure he's alive?" He never personally touched the patients who came in the middle of the night—you could never tell where they'd been or what they might have been doing.

The big black aide standing next to the cart said, "Yes, sir, he just ain't moving."

The doctor glared at the aide. "I don't remember asking you for your opinion," he said. "When I want your opinion, boy, I'll point to you. I was talking to the nurse."

The nurse, standing two steps behind the physician, spoke up. "Yes, sir, he's alive. At least, he was when he left Central Hospital." She walked up to Jack, picked up his right arm, and took his pulse.

"Well, if he *isn't* alive," the doctor said, "I don't have to admit him, and it would save me a hell of a lot of time and paperwork." It was five AM, and he'd had every intention of being out the door and heading for his favorite fishing hole by six. This case would tie him up for at least two hours.

The nurse resumed her position behind the doctor. "I'm afraid he's alive, at least for the time being."

"Shit, I'll be here all morning," the doctor said.

"Who should we assign him to?" the nurse asked.

"Give him to that know-it-all. What's his name? You know ... Mullins, the kid from California. See if he can figure this one out." The physician turned and left the room. He would never lay eyes on Jack again.

Jack's new home was an open sixteen-bed ward divided into four cubicles, each with four metal cots and small dressing closets. The ceiling was dominated by a large light in a wire cage that came on promptly at five thirty in the morning and went out at nine in the evening. Jack's bed was the first one on the left as you entered the first bay, nearest the lights and noise. By the window and across the cubicle was Jack Lambert—*this* Jack was a paranoid schizophrenic. He and the other paranoids ruled the institution; they parceled out favors and meted out punishment to transgressors. Across the way was Robert the Birdman—Robert babbled incessantly and made loud screeching sounds. Weldon Mopp III was in the bed next to our friend Jack and shared the window with Lambert. Weldon was just mean; he would stand in the hall and cuss at everyone as they came along.

It didn't take long for Dr. Mullins to diagnose Jack as a catatonic. His first note in the chart read, "A conversion reaction or shock is a possibility, but this man looks like someone who has been ill for a long time. He responds to a different set of signals than the rest of us. The best course would be to watch him and see what happens."

Jack lay in his bed, in whatever position he was left, while life went on around him. Despite his calm exterior, a war raged within him.

From the end of Robert's bed, he heard, *"Jack, you rotten son of a bitch, you killed your friend. You're a dirty, low-life scum. Somebody ought to take you out and shoot you. If I had a gun, that's what I'd do. You don't deserve to be alive. God gave you a gift, and you screwed everything up. The police should be here soon to give you what you deserve—a slow, painful, horrible death."*

From the window over Jack Lambert's bed came, *"Don't tell 'em who you are! They'll figure out what happened and arrest you. They'll take you away to prison. You really can't trust any of these people. They won't understand. If you talk, they'll know who you are."*

From inside himself, he heard, *"But I'm hungry and thirsty. I don't like it here. These people scare me. I want to go home."*

From the window: *"Don't trust the colored man with the white shirt and pants. He'll poison you the first chance he gets."*

From Robert's bed: *"You know you deserve all this. What are you whining about? You should have known that this was going to happen. Hell, John Allen probably isn't even dead! He's probably just trying to get you in trouble, so he can get rid of you."*

"No, he was my friend!" Jack said out loud.

The window spoke up: *"Shh! Jack, be quiet, they'll hear you! They'll know who you are!"*

Confirming the doctor's intuition, tincture of time eventually won out. The threatening, fearful voices began to fade, and the cry of hunger and thirst became louder and louder.

"Eat! Drink!" it said.

Three times a day, Parker, the big black aide, came to Jack's bed and left food. After the aide left, Jack Lambert would steal the sweets and crackers. For the first few days, Parker came back and tried to cajole Jack into eating, but the best he could do was entice him to drink small amounts of liquids—food seemed out of the question.

After supper on the fifth day, when Parker came around to get the tray, it had been picked clean. "Looks like you gettin' your appetite back. That's good! You want some more?" he asked Jack.

"Needs more salt," Jack said, his head turned toward the wall.

"What?"

"The stew, it needs more salt," Jack repeated.

"Well, I'll be! The boy can talk, and he's a food critic, too!" Parker laughed as he walked away with the trays.

Parker took the tray back to the kitchen and told the nurse about Jack's comments. She called the doctor and told him of the development. Mullins smiled and lit a cigarette.

Later, on rounds, he approached Jack's bed. "Good evening. I'm Dr. Mullins. Mr. Parker says you have a problem with the stew." He pulled one of the old metal chairs up to Jack's bedside.

"The stew needs more salt," Jack said. "Let it set overnight. Be a lot better."

"I'll talk to the cooks. Was everything else okay?"

"The bread's fine, but the stew needs more salt."

"When you were checked in, you had no identification. We were just wondering what your name was."

Jack sat staring into space and did not respond. Mullins interrogated him for the next few minutes, but, with the exception of those regarding food, all questions were met with a blank stare.

Later, Mullins wrote in Jack's chart, "Made improvement today, catatonic state is lifting. Won't say his name. No obvious visual hallucinations, could be some auditory hallucinations going by report of the nursing staff. Can't really decide if he needs chlorpromazine. Will give him a few more days. Dr. Gerald wants to shock him. Will give him a few more days and think about it."

Several days later, Parker was working with Jack Lambert. "Come on, Jack, it's time to get up," Johnson said, attempting to prod Lambert out of this bed.

The Jack in the opposite bed sat up.

"All right, Jack," Parker said to Lambert, "take off that nasty shirt. You've peed on yourself, and you've been wearing that stinky old shirt for three days."

In the other bed, Jack took off his shirt.

"Now, Jack, stand up and let me get these pants off."

Out of the corner of his eye, Parker noticed that the quiet man in the first bed was moving to his command. He tried a little trick.

"Raise your hand."

Jack didn't move.

Then, he said, "Jack, raise your hand."

Jack dutifully raised his right hand.

"Now, Jack, lower your hand."

Jack did as he was told.

Later, as Dr. Mullins was about to make his rounds, Parker told him of the discovery.

Mullins walked up to Jack's bed and said, "Good morning, Jack."

Jack's eyelids moved just slightly—just enough for acknowledgment.

"Jack, we aren't going to hurt you," the doctor said as he laid his hand on Jack's shoulder.

From the window over Lambert's bed, Jack heard, *"Don't trust him, Jack! He works for the police! He'll find out you killed your friend!"*

"No, I told you I didn't kill my friend," Jack mumbled.

Neither the doctor nor any in his entourage could understand what Jack had said, but it was obvious that all was not well. No amount of prodding could get him to make any further comment.

Mullins's note for the day read: "Patient showing progress. Have determined that name is Jack. Responded to name with paranoia, could not understand con-

tent. Am leaning more toward medicine. Again, nursing staff reports brief out-
burst directed at window, suspect he is having auditory hallucinations."

In the days and weeks that followed—and with constant prodding from
Johnson—Jack began to move around his little area, and then, gradually, the
whole ward. The hospital was always short of staff, and life on the wards was a
cooperative affair. Patients who were willing and able were quickly recruited to
help with the daily chores that kept things moving. With very little prodding,
Jack began to help with the food and with cleaning the dishes.

Each day on rounds, Dr. Mullins asked Jack the same questions, and got little
or no response. On one of these fishing expeditions, the doctor asked, "What
would you like to do?"

To Mullins's surprise, Jack replied, "Cook."

"Can you cook?"

"I can eat," Jack said.

The doctor nodded, smiled, and later made a note: "Patient made an attempt
at humor."

In fact, it hadn't been an attempt at humor. Very simply, Jack equated the
ability to smell and taste with the ability to enjoy and decipher his food. His
understanding was that if you could enjoy food, you could cook.

Just as Jack's catatonic state had been triggered by the stress of John Allen's
death, stability on the ward allowed it to ease up. As Jack improved, the staff let
him range further and further from the ward—first to the common dining area,
then to the large dayroom, where there was a mix of men and women.

The dayroom off Cedar Wing, where Jack lived, was full during the day. For
the most part, the patients there moved around like three-year-olds in a sand
box—playing, but not with each other. Each had his or her rituals that filled the
day, like touching certain places—solid points that didn't move, realities that
didn't change with the light. Jack moved around easily in this soup of real and
unreal. There was something different here, and he knew it. Here, in this place, it
was normal not to be normal. The problem for Jack was that he couldn't find an
anchor.

One day, as he was beginning to feel more in control and the voice from the
bed had begun to fade, Robert the Birdman let loose with a barrage of horrific
sounds. This agitated everyone in the building, patients and staff alike.

A young woman who wandered the wards offering sex with everyone began to
cry. She lay on the floor in the middle of the dayroom and sobbed. "Nobody
cares," she said. "I'm just gonna die. My leg hurts; it must be broken. I hurt it
when I had my heart attack. My chest is killing me."

The voice from the bed said, *"Jack, these people are crazy. This is your punishment for killing your friend."*

"I didn't kill my friend."

"But, Jack, why else would you be here? It's because you're shit. No, you're worse than shit—you're the stink off the shit!"

"Don't!" Jack cried, looking across at Robert's bed.

Weldon looked up from his position across the room. "I didn't do anything to you yet, asshole," he said.

Weldon rose from his bed and began to circle Jack, stalking his prey like a big cat.

Parker appeared and quickly sized up the situation. "Weldon, you little shit," he said, "you touch a hair on Jack's head and I'll have your ass for breakfast! Do you understand me?"

Without making eye contact, Weldon withdrew to a wider orbit.

Parker turned back to Jack. "Hey, buddy, Dr. Mullins wants to see you."

As if nothing had happened, Jack rose from his seat and walked, head down, toward the nurses' station.

As he walked in front of the TV, the fat woman who talked to God shouted at him, "Get out of the way, dickhead!"

A voice spoke from the back of Johnson's head: *"Remember, Jack, Mullins is not your friend, no matter what he says. You don't have any friends."*

From the smooth, sandy surface of the cigarette-butt can, he heard, *"Yeah, you gave that up when you killed your friend."*

When Jack entered the conference room, he knew something was up. Around the table sat a group of very official-looking people. Most were in white coats and had their heads down, scribbling on an assortment of documents. When he entered the room, they looked up. Dr. Mullins was sitting to his right. He motioned for Jack to sit down at the end of the table.

"Jack, this meeting is what we call a 'staffing,'" Mullins said. "All of these people will be involved with your care while you're here with us."

The doctor went around the room, introduced each person by name, and explained a little about what they did. Jack heard little of what was said. His attention was focused on the security guard standing over by the wall.

"… and this is Miss Charlotte Jones, your social worker," Mullins continued.

As Mullins talked, Jack thought, *She seems like a nice lady; she's got a nice smile.*

From under the table: *"Right, stupid—can't you see this is a trick? They're just trying to get you to say something, so they can catch you. They know who you are, they know what a scumbag you are."*

Dr. Mullins concluded his introductions. "And this is Dr. Gerald. He does all the EST."

From the social worker's wrist, he heard, *"Watch out for that guy—you heard Sue Ellen talk about him. She said he damn near electrocuted her."*

"After reviewing your case," Mullins continued, "we feel that we've come to an impasse in your therapy. You've been here for several weeks, and you don't seem to be getting any better. There's some question as to whether you're hearing voices. We've decided to start you on some medicine. We're going to start you on chlorpromazine—let's see if that will help. Mr. Parker here says that you like to cook. Would you like to start helping in the kitchen?"

From Charlotte's wrist: *"Don't let on—don't tell 'em you want to cook. They'll guess who you are. They'll guess your secret."*

As Jack's voices and the conversation among the medical staff flowed around the room, Jack sat mute and motionless.

"Well, Jack, what do you think?" Charlotte asked. "Is there anything you want to say? We're here for you."

Jack didn't respond, but he managed a quick smile at her.

Again, from under the table: *"Sure they are! Who does she think she's kiddin'? They know about you, and, sooner or later, they'll do what you should have done yourself—they're gonna put your ass in a grave. This medicine crap is a trick!"*

Parker helped Jack to his feet. As he left the table, Charlotte reached out, touched his forearm, smiled, and then went back to her papers.

That evening, as usual, the night nurse came around with her pill cart. When she opened the brown glass jar containing Jack's new medicine, he got a whiff of a foreign odor. Unlike the lush smells of food, the rich fragrance of a woman's perfume, or the fresh aroma of a spring day, the medicine had a jarringly bitter metallic scent, full of sharp edges.

"Here you are—take this, it's your new medicine," she said.

He placed the pill on his tongue and, with a gulp of water, swallowed it.

"Now, this second one is to counteract the side effects of the first," she said as she handed him a second tablet.

Jack lay back in his bed, not knowing what to expect. Soon, he began to feel sleepy. The night passed quickly.

The next morning, with the new medicine flowing through his body, Jack knew that something was different. Life seemed blurred—the corners of the room weren't as clear or succinct. At breakfast, the bacon looked the same, but its taste was gone. The coffee steamed and felt hot, but something was missing.

In a brief moment of awareness, he realized they had discovered part of his secret—if he couldn't smell or taste, he was lost.

On the other hand, the voice from Robert's bed—the mean angry one, the one that accused and threatened him—was gone too. Well, it wasn't exactly gone, but it wasn't as loud or insistent.

From the window, he heard, *"Take care, Jack! They're gonna dope you up and take your mind. They'll take your taste and your smell and never give them back."*

The drug haze got worse as the days went on. It was like driving on a foggy morning with the mist coming and going—you expect the sun to break through any minute, but it never does. Eventually, all that was left was a cold, empty world. There were no threatening voices, but it felt quiet, lonely, and sad.

At night, when the lights went out, a new voice came to him through the fog: *"This is the rest of your life—no more smell or taste. It's sad, but it had to be this way, Jack. That's the way life is. When you go to sleep, at least you get a chance to rest. Maybe you won't have to wake up. Maybe you can just sleep from now on."*

Time passed slowly, and the days melted into one another. To those around him, Jack was the quiet little man in Bed Number One who didn't speak unless absolutely necessary. Parker and the nurses regularly commented on how well he looked, but when Jack looked in the mirror, he saw an old man—an emotionless old man who didn't hear threatening voices and wasn't plagued by self-doubt or fear. At the same time, he could no longer be enthralled by the smell of onions cooking on the stove. The feel and smell of fresh, clean towels brought forth no real memories.

Unlike Robert the Birdman and Jack Lambert the paranoid, who were constantly in trouble, the weekly staffings for Jack were quick and easy. Parker would usher him into the room, each member of the team would say a word or two, Jack would be given a chance to respond, and that was it. The one bright spot in Jack's life was Charlotte Jones. She smiled at him in a way no one else did. He was convinced that she cared for him. Parker was his friend, but Charlotte's smile lit a spark. Even though his senses had been dulled with medicine, when he walked near her and drew in a deep breath, her fragrance was disorienting.

Most patients like Jack—the ones with no family—would gradually drift further and further into the depths of the State Hospital system. Any objections they voiced were considered evidence of their need for further hospitalization. There was, however, a movement afoot in the more enlightened circles of mental health to allow those patients who were stable and of no risk to the general population to be deinstitutionalized—that is, to be allowed to move out of the hospital and live on their own.

One morning, Jack was ushered into the staffing room.

"Jack," Charlotte said, "we have some very good news for you! You may get to leave the hospital sometime soon. How do you feel about that?"

"What?" Jack asked. "What do you mean?"

From under the table: *"You know what it means, shithead. While you've been taking that damn medicine, they've figured you out! They don't want a rotten son of a bitch like you around here. They're gonna send your ass to jail where you belong and throw away the key."*

Jack began to sweat and looked quickly from one person to the next. "But I don't want to go to jail. I want to stay here."

From Charlotte's wrist: *"Be careful, Jack—they don't know anything yet, but they'll turn you in if you say anything."*

Across the table, Dr. Mullins grinned and said, "Jack, we aren't going to send you to jail. You don't *have* to leave, and you can come back any time you like. Charlotte will be there to help you along the way. You'll have your own place to live, your own money, and privacy. You'll be able to cook your own food and go where you please."

Through the haze of the medicine, Jack knew that something was wrong about all this. "No!" he said, almost shouting. "What about my friend, Parker?"

"We'll take care of Parker. Don't worry about him; we'll take care of him," Mullins said, attempting to reassure him.

They don't understand—this is home now! Jack thought. *These are my family, my friends, my protectors—I don't* want *to leave!* He turned to Charlotte. "But, Charlotte ..." he pleaded.

"I'll be right here, Jack, and I'll see you every day. We'll find you an apartment. We'll let you stay there for a little while each day for the first few weeks, and you can come back at night. We're not going to just throw you out."

For Jack, this was a lot to absorb in one sitting. As Parker led him from the room, Jack began to sweat. By the time he was back on the ward, all he could think about was getting back to bed.

With coaxing from Charlotte, Jack slowly bought into the idea of living in an apartment and getting a job. She found him an apartment and paid the first month's rent out of her own pocket. As a backup, she contacted some social-work friends in Chicago who were active in the deinstitutionalization movement, and they promised assistance if she needed it.

Jack's apartment was a back-porch room on B Street that belonged to Ruth Bass. Ruth's husband had been a good journeyman carpenter but not much of a planner. What had begun as a small two-bedroom house with a sleeping porch had slowly expanded over the years into a rabbit warren of nooks, crannies, attics, lofts, and halls. After her husband died, Ruth started taking in boarders to make ends meet. Ruth's love was her flower garden. Covering the sidewalk in front of the house was a rose trellis that created a sheltered bower.

The first day, as Jack and Charlotte walked under the blooming vines, Jack stopped and took a deep breath. "Old-world roses," he said. "Those are old roses—from southern Germany, I think."

"How do you know that?" Charlotte asked.

"It's the shape of their scent. The new ones they've bred have no form. What smell they have is incomplete. Like fog—it's blurred. These old ones have a wavy form with no points, no angles."

"Jack, are you telling me that that those smells have a shape to you?"

"Yeah, they do. Can't you feel it?"

"No," she said. "Do you realize that most people don't do that?"

"No, not really," he said, shaking his head.

"How long have you been able to do that?"

Jack thought for a second. "Don't know. Always, I guess."

"Do smells help you remember?"

"Maybe, I guess. I don't know."

"Do you remember any smells from your childhood?" Charlotte was hoping to stimulate his memory.

"No. Well … yes, there is one smell … or taste, really."

"What's that?"

"The spiral taste of butterscotch and baseball."

"What do you remember about butterscotch and baseball?"

"Nothing, except that they go together."

As they stood under the trellis talking about smells, tastes, and shapes, Ruth emerged from the front door dressed for her gardening chores. She was a tiny woman with dark, wrinkled skin. She was dressed in oversized jeans that had once belonged to her husband, a long-sleeved shirt, and a large sunhat. She carried her pruning scissors.

She smiled, laid down her tool, and extended her hand. "You must be Jack. My name is Ruth Bass. You can call me Ruthie. I understand you're thinking about moving in with us. Hope you're not allergic to cats, 'cause we got a houseful. Are you quiet? We can't have anybody noisy. You want to see your room?"

Unsure of which question to answer, Jack just stood there.

Charlotte noticed the impasse and said, "Why don't we go and look at the room?"

"Okay, sure," said Ruthie. "Let's go this way, it's the easiest." She led Jack and Charlotte around the east end of the house and into the backyard.

"You have a nice place, Mrs. Bass," Charlotte said as they followed the brick path around the house.

"It's nothing fancy, but it's comfortable." Rounding the corner, she pointed out the back door at the east end of the porch. "From your room, this is the quickest way into the kitchen. I don't mind you joining the rest of us for meals, as long as you chip in for the groceries. If you use something around here, replace it. We work strictly on the honor system. If you smoke, I'd rather you not do it in the house. We don't allow visitors after ten at night, unless we're having a big get-together. Rent is due by the fifth of the month. Please pay me, not George— that's my son—because he sometimes forgets what the money's for. Here we are."

She explained about the awnings and the storm windows, and how most of the renters sat out in the backyard when the weather was nice, to smoke and listen to Cardinals baseball. "One other thing," she added. "The cats know their place. They won't come into your room unless you invite them. Trouble is, if you invite one, they *all* think they have permission. So, if you don't want these cats in your stuff, don't ask them in." As if on cue, Jasperina, a gray tabby, made a figure eight through Jack's legs three times and then stretched herself out around his feet, using his right foot as a pillow. Jack reached down and picked up the little gray-striped cat, rubbing her chin as he held her.

Ruthie laughed. "I think that when these cats find out somebody new is moving in, they get under the house, have a meeting, and designate one of the group to break in the new human. Looks like Jasperina got the nod this time. Now, like I said, if you don't want them bothering you, you've already made your first mistake."

The first few days, Jack and Charlotte worked on getting his place in order. At lunch, she would take him back to the hospital, where he would spend the rest of the day. On the third day, after spending the morning at the apartment and as they were heading back to the hospital, Charlotte suggested they stop at Bud's Root Beer Place on Markham Street for a cheeseburger and fries.

Entering the glass door to the cafe, Jack noticed a sign in the front window:

SHORT ORDER COOK
NEEDED
APPLY INSIDE

They sat down in the glassed-in dining room that overlooked Markham Street, and Charlotte excused herself to go to the restroom.

Bud, the owner, was cooking hamburgers, answering the phone, making shakes, and working the cash register. Like a street mime spinning dishes on sticks, he gave each activity just enough attention to keep it going.

Jack got up and approached the counter.

"I'll be with you in a minute," Bud said.

"You need a cook?" Jack asked.

"What? I can't hear you for the fan."

"Do you need a cook?" Jack asked again, this time a little louder.

"Does a wild bear shit in the woods?"

With no change of expression, Jack replied, "Sure, I guess so. I don't see why not."

"It's a joke, son," Bud said. "Of course I need a cook. Can you cook?"

"Yeah, I can cook."

"Well, get your ass back here and help me."

Within two minutes of the time the exchange began, Jack had a job. He donned an apron, put on a paper aviator cap, and began frying burgers.

When Charlotte returned, she saw that her charge was gone. Fear built as she went quickly to the front window and surveyed the street, looking for signs of Jack. Just as she began to have visions of Jack wandering, lost, on the streets of Little Rock, she turned toward the register and saw Jack standing in front of the grill. He was smiling, busily flipping meat patties and totally immersed in his new job.

"Jack?" she said.

"Charlotte," he replied.

"What are you doing?"

"I'm cooking." He pointed at Bud. "He said I could have a job."

She looked at Bud, who wasn't completely sure what was going on. Bud nodded.

"I need a job," Jack said. "You told me so. I need to eat—you told me that."

Bud walked over to the register. "What are you lady, his keeper?"

"No, I'm just a good friend," Charlotte said.

"Well, your friend here seems to know his way around a kitchen. What would you like, lady? It's on the house."

Jack had a job.

After the lunchtime rush was over, Charlotte took Jack back to the hospital and returned to Bud's to explain Jack's situation.

Bud quickly interrupted her: "First of all, is he dangerous?"

"No, absolutely not. He's a nice little guy and wouldn't hurt a flea."

"Will he show up for work?"

"I believe he will. He always does what he says he'll do."

"Will he steal from me? I can't afford to have somebody steal."

"I really don't think so. If anything, he's *too* honest."

"Well, what's the problem?" Bud asked.

Charlotte paused. "You see, it's like this … Jack hears voices."

Bud smiled. "Honey, we all hear voices. Some are just louder than others. We all have fears that haunt us and push us to distraction. Sometimes, they make us do things that look real stupid." Bud sipped his coffee. "I don't know, but I guess it's just harder for some people to keep the voices separate. Life isn't easy for any of us. You know what I mean? I can usually tell if I'm going be able to work with somebody, and Jack seems like a regular kind of guy. Now, you tell me: do you think working here is going to hurt him?"

Charlotte reached out and put her hand on Bud's forearm. "No, sir, not at all. I think it will be wonderful for him."

"Well, it's done then," he said.

"What time do you want him here in the morning?"

"What morning? He said he'd be back at five thirty tonight and help me with the evening rush."

"Jack told you that?"

"Yeah."

"Good," Charlotte said.

It took a couple of hours of bickering to get the assistant administrator to allow Jack to leave for the evening.

"Just this once," the administrator said. "The director wouldn't like this at all."

Charlotte finally won out by saying that she would stay at the cafe and bring Jack back when the shift was over.

The real fight took place the next morning at staffing.

"Jack has a right to a normal life," Charlotte said. "Just like all of us! His own place, a job. Who are we to keep him here if he's doing well—and he is—and if he doesn't want to stay?"

"Look here," the administrator said as he pulled himself up to the table, "you don't know how things work around here. When this fellow came through our front door, he became our responsibility. This probate order …" He raised the piece of paper over his head. "… says that I can do anything I want with Jack, and it makes me responsible for all his actions. What's going to happen when Jack goes out there on Markham Street and takes his clothes off? Or when he takes a knife to one of the folks who come into Bud's? We have responsibilities to this community, and if he hurts somebody, whose butt do you think is on the line? Certainly not yours. It's *mine*, and don't you forget it. Dr. Mullins understands the problem. Don't you, Doc? What do you think?"

Dr. Mullins had taken in most of this argument in bemused silence. He slowly pulled out his cigarettes and lighter, lit a smoke, and took a long draw as he relaxed back into his chair. "Well, sir, I tend to agree with Miss Jones. Jack hasn't shown any signs of hurting anybody. He made the move to get the job himself, and, according to Miss Jones, he seems to know what he's doing in a kitchen. Since we started him on the medicine, he's been sleeping better, and his affect has been a bit more appropriate." He turned to Charlotte. "We still have to deal with his having no family—who's going to be responsible for him."

"Where I trained in Chicago," Charlotte said, "we had a group who would act as legal guardians for people like Jack. That's something I've wanted to get started here anyway. I'll go to the court and have myself appointed his legal guardian … if you all will authorize it."

"I don't know about that," the administrator said, "what with you being an employee of the hospital."

"I'll make it clear that I'm doing this as a friend of the court, and not as an employee of the State Hospital," she said.

"I don't know—it seems awfully risky to me."

"Sometimes we have to take risks. I don't think Jack will disappoint us."

"I'll talk it over with the director."

"In the meantime," Charlotte continued, "Jack has a job, and Mr. Gates needs him."

"All right … but only temporarily, until we get a decision from the director."

For the first few days of his temporary privileges, Charlotte accompanied Jack to and from work. Privately, she was a little fearful that he would wander off. The first time she was late getting to the hospital, Charlotte worried that he would be disappointed. To her surprise, he was already gone—he had left for work without her.

When she walked into Bud's, Jack was busy at the prep table slicing tomatoes. "Morning, Jack," she said.

"Morning, Charlotte," Jack replied. "You want a cup of coffee?"

"Yeah, that would be nice. Did you have any trouble getting to work this morning?"

"No," he said. "Just like other days."

From that day on, Jack walked to work alone, and nobody seemed to notice. The hospital director never made a decision one way or the other. Except for Charlotte and his medicines, Jack was lost to the system.

Bud and Jack became fast friends. Jack came to work early, stayed late, and worked harder than any help Bud had ever had—especially his children. One evening, as they were closing the cafe, Bud asked, "Jack, you ever been to the stock car races?"

"No," Jack replied.

"You ought to go with me some Thursday night. I love the races. I love pretty cars anyway, but the races are even better. Some of my buddies drive, and I like to go on the nights that they race. It's like a poor man's horse racing. We can do a little gambling, drink a little beer. You want to go?"

"Sure. I can't drink, though, because of my medicine. Is that okay?"

Bud laughed. "Yeah, Jack, that's just fine."

The instant Jack climbed onto the metal stands surrounding the raised dirt oval, he felt overwhelmed by the sights and sounds of the cars as they sped around the track. Other than cooking and eating, nothing had ever grabbed his fancy like the stock car races. Medicine or no medicine, the noise of the cars blasted the voices away for a while.

Bud and Jack found seats high in the stands and watched the preliminaries. Jack delighted at the roar of the engines when the green flag fell for the first race and the cars sped away with complete abandon. His attention was focused on a canary yellow '55 hot rod with a bright red bolt of lightning streaking down its side.

Bud had pointed out the car to Jack during the warm-up rounds. "That boy's got a great crew—they're all mechanics during the day, and he drives like a bat out of hell."

When the car sped past Jack's position in the stands, he sensed the taste of raw wild onions from a freshly plowed field. The taste was full of sharp angles. All the politeness of social convention was shed as the car jockeyed for position in each turn, slamming fender-to-fender, bumper-to-bumper. The driver of the yellow car pushed his vehicle to its limit and then spun out of control, rotating to a stop in the grassy infield. The car's energy dissipated as steam rose from its ruptured radiator. Jack felt a cloud of warmth, fresh with the smell of sandalwood that left a round taste in his mouth. It was the round taste of yellow—the feel and taste of bright sunshine, a spring daffodil, or a child's golden hair.

As they left the track that night, Jack turned to Bud. "Can we come back next week?" he asked.

"So you liked the races, huh?" Bud said.

"Yeah, I liked them a lot."

"Sure, we can come back. In fact, I'll get my nephew to help at the store, and you and I can make this a regular Thursday-night affair. What do you say?"

"That would be great," Jack said. A bond had formed between Jack and the races. Unlike the human friendships that would come and go in Jack's life, the races would stay close to him for the rest of his days.

For a while, things went well for Jack—the parts to the puzzle seemed to fit together. The first blow to his little world came when Charlotte came for one of her weekly visits.

"Jack, I've got some bad news," she said. "I'm leaving—going back to Chicago. I'm afraid I'm never going to fit in here in Arkansas. The folks over at the hospital and I don't see eye to eye on many things. I really wasn't sure what to do about you. You seem to be doing so well. I don't want to see this get messed up for you. I talked to Dr. Mullins, and he said that, until they get another social worker to take my place, he'll help you get your medicine. Is that okay?"

Jack had begun to sweat. "Yeah. No. I guess so. I don't know," he said. Jack loved Charlotte. He loved her smell, her touch, and the way she smiled at him. She had saved him from a state hospital life, and he knew it—a dark, quiet life in which he would have taken more and more medicine. Over the preceding year or so, Jack had reduced his own dosage, and the voices had grown no worse. He had decided that there were worse things in this world than the occasional threatening voice. He hadn't told Charlotte of his little deceit—he had feared that, if she knew, she would stop coming to see him. Worse than that, she might have sent the security guard to find him and take him back to the hospital.

Jack sat silently and began to cry. Charlotte cried as well.

"I miss you," he said.

"But, Jack, I'm not gone yet."

"I know, but I already miss you."

"I miss you too," she said. "Maybe we can write."

After Charlotte left, Jack quit taking his medicine altogether. For a while, he expected someone to show up at his door and demand that he return to the hospital. Jack even considered running away—to where, he didn't know, but far away from the hospital.

For a year or so, Bud and Jack worked side-by-side six days a week, and, on Thursdays, they went to the races. At times, Jack would remember glimpses of his life with John Allen and the restaurant in Memphis. In some ways, Bud reminded him of John Allen. But, as with everything else in life, Jack's relatively comfortable new existence didn't last for long.

Bud's business had begun to dwindle. Root beer and burger stands were no longer novel, and there were all sorts of hamburger and pizza joints springing up. Bud's place sat on a piece of prime real estate.

"Jack, old buddy, I been thinking," Bud said. "It's about time I retired."

Jack turned away from the grill. "What?"

"I got a friend with a little cafe down at Carlisle—across from the track— who's looking for a cook. You'd be close to the races, and you could meet some new people."

"But, Bud, I don't care about new people. I like it here. Did I do something to make you want to quit?"

"No, of course not. But look, man, I ain't making no money. I'm getting old, and I just can't keep up the pace anymore. The folks from Burger World made me an offer. They want the land, and they've offered me quite a bit of money. I'm thinking real serious about selling. You understand, don't you?"

Jack turned back to the grill, and, from the vent hood, he heard, *"Well, stupid, you did it again. I knew he'd get tired of your sloppy mess sooner or later. Hell, sometimes you slobber into the food! What a piece of crap. You ought to take one of those knives and cut your own throat. This is all your fault."*

"Jack, is something burning?" Bud asked from the other side of the counter.

The voice interrupted again: *"Next thing you know, he'll die, and it'll be your fault, just like with John Allen. You remember—that other friend you killed?"*

"No, I didn't! He was my friend!" Jack shouted at the top of his lungs.

"Jack!" Bud screamed. "The grill's on fire! Get out of the way!" Bud rushed around the counter with the fire extinguisher in his hands and began to spray the grill.

Jack backed up and watched indifferently as Bud put out the fire.

"You did it now. Now you really screwed the pooch."

"Jack, are you okay?" Bud asked as he turned from the fire.

Jack stood helpless, tears streaming down his face.

"This is my home," he said. "I don't *want* a new apartment. I don't *want* to go to a new cafe."

Jack did move on to Carlisle, and then to a place in Georgia. For years, he followed the southeastern circuit, and he finally ended up in Gum Ridge. The glue that held each of these places together was the stock car tracks and the people who worked there. Like carnival people, they moved around a lot, and so did Jack.

CHAPTER 6

the race is on

Winter came and went in Gum Ridge. After the episode under the tree, life at the bar had returned to some semblance of normal. Moon never learned that Jack had disappeared for a day—or, if he did, he never mentioned it. With spring came the new racing season.

It was a quiet evening at Moon's. Joe and Art were watching *Take a Chance* on the TV over the bar. It wasn't the show itself they enjoyed, as much as it was the young woman who escorted the guests on and off the stage.

Joe motioned to Mary Ann. "Bring us a couple of beers."

"Sure," she said. "You guys want something to eat? Jack's got some fried chicken left over from lunch."

"No, I'd just like some popcorn, if it's fresh," Art said.

"It's fresh—I popped it myself this afternoon," Mary Ann said.

When she walked around the bar, Joe turned to Art and said, "You know, I think she gets better looking every day."

Art smiled. "Yeah, you're right. I think it's her smile. When she smiles, it's like she sees right down into your soul."

"No, that's not it at all," Joe said. "It's that nice set of legs leading up to that tight round ass, that's what it is."

"Yeah, I guess you're right. But what I said sounds better."

Joe pointed at the television and said, "Now, you want to talk about a fine-looking woman, get a load of *that*." The game-show hostess was walking across the screen with the first contestant. "Oh, sweet Jesus, you can damn near see through that dress!"

"Wouldn't you like to work with *that* every day?" Art said.

"Who cares about the days? Wouldn't you like to nestle up between those tits at *night*?" Joe replied.

Mary Ann arrived with two beers and a bowl of popcorn, just in time to hear this last comment. "They're not real," she said.

"Right," Joe said. "And where'd you get *that* information?"

"I'll have you know that one of my magazines had a special article devoted just to her," she said. "They interviewed her doctor and everything."

"Phillips, I think you're just jealous," Joe said.

"Did you know," Mary Ann said, "that women who are that big have to do special exercises every day to keep from getting humpbacked? It's not worth the effort. If I was like that, I'd get 'em lopped off. Anyway, it ain't what you got that counts, it's how you use it. If anybody should understand that, you boys should. Now, if you don't need anything else, I'm gonna take a break."

At table three, Joy and one of her friends were discussing the lack of desirable men in Gum Ridge. Joy spread her arms wide in an exaggerated motion. "Look at that, there ain't a keeper among the lot of 'em!"

Mary Ann joined them and laughed. "What do you expect?" she said. "It's like Mama always says, 'If you want a stallion, don't go looking in the donkey corral.' And, sweetie, we are *definitely* in the back lot."

"You can say that again," Joy said. "My husband, Larry, may not be very exciting, but he's a good man. I just wish he didn't have to work all these evening and night shifts."

Mary Ann got up. "Joy, honey," she said, "I got to go back to work. The natives are getting restless."

Actually, everything was pretty well under control, but Mary Ann had noticed that they had a special guest—Glen Marshall III.

Glen was dressed in a dark three-piece suit, and it was obvious that he was out of his element. Moon's was where the hired help went, and his father had taught him not to fraternize with the help—it wasn't good for them.

Jack was flipping burgers at the grill when Glen walked up to the bar. "You must be Jack, the famous cook I've heard so much about. What are you cooking?" he asked.

Jack ignored him.

"Is Albert Lawrence around?" Marshall asked.

"Who?" Jack mumbled.

"Albert Lawrence Moon," Marshall said.

Without further acknowledging Marshall's presence, Jack walked over to Moon's office and knocked on the door. "Mr. Moon, there's a man out here who wants to talk to you."

"Who is it, and what does he want?" Moon shouted.

Jack turned back toward the grill, but before he could repeat the question, Marshall shouted, "Tell him it's Glen Marshall, and I want to talk to him about the bar!"

Jack turned back toward the office door like a mechanical duck in a shooting gallery—the kind that changed directions whenever it was hit. Before Jack could say anything, Moon came out of his office with a glass of ice tea in one hand and a copy of the *National Star* in the other. "Well, if it isn't His Highness! I'm surprised you'd lower yourself so far as to come in here. What drags you down here with us mere mortals?"

Glen, a man for whom anger was a way of life, tried to suppress his irritation. "Strictly business, son. I assure you, strictly business." When Glen was a child, his father had repeated over and over again, "Remember, boy, everything boils down to money and power. Business is how you use money and power. So, everything boils down to business. You know why I give to the church, don't you, son? Makes people think I give a shit."

"Well, pray tell," Moon said. "What business could you possibly have down here?"

"It's like this, Albert Lawrence," Glen said. "Any time you're ready to sell, I'll buy this place back from you, lock, stock, and barrel. I might even throw in a little extra, just for good measure. You know … sweeten the pot." His father's second-favorite saying was, "Make 'em think they're getting something for nothing, and greed will take over from there."

"No, Glen, I don't think so," Moon said. "I'm doing pretty well here. You'd have to set the ante pretty high before I could see my way clear to do any business with you."

"Hold on, son. Everybody in town knows that this bar's nothing but a front for your bookie business. You don't know any more about running a real business than you do about flying to the moon. You ought to at least let someone in here who can mine this place for what it's worth." The longer Glen talked, the more transparent grew the veil over his ever-present anger.

Moon smiled at Marshall, put down his tea, leaned over the bar, and said, "First of all, I'm not your boy. You got that? And second, I got big plans for this place. Pretty soon, I'm gonna get me a big satellite dish, and then I can get sports twenty-four hours a day. The guys around here will love it—I'll pack 'em in! Of course, I *could* use a little loan to get me off the ground—short term, of course. I got another idea that's even better. You see that safe over by the wall—the old P. J. Ives safe? I'm gonna find me a way to make money off that story. I ain't figured out just how, but soon as I do, we're gonna take off like gangbusters!"

"Albert Lawrence," Marshall said, "I don't think the bank will loan you money for this place. But, for a controlling interest, I could personally put up the money you need to make a go of it. As for that P. J. Ives fantasy … That's a rat hole. Nobody cares about that old story—it's ancient history."

"Thank you, Mr. Wise Man, for your sage advice. Actually, I wouldn't take money from you *or* your bank on a bet. I got other sources."

"Well, if you're talking about those hoods over at the track, be careful. They'll take you for a ride in one of those shiny new limousines, and you won't be coming back."

"Thanks for the advice, but I can take care of myself." Moon turned away and walked back toward his office.

Marshall pointed at him and said, "Mark my words, boy, this place will be belly-up in six months!"

"Yeah, yeah, yeah," Moon said. He entered his office and slammed the door.

As he exited the bar, Marshall bumped into Richard Kyle. Richard leased a rice farm east of town and was a bit of a local legend. In high school, he had been an all-state running back for the Gum Ridge Lions; now, he and his Ford Fairlane were perennial favorites at the stock car track across the street.

"Sorry, Mr. Marshall, didn't see you," Richard said.

"Well, watch where you're going next time," Glen said, glaring at Richard.

"Yes, sir, I will."

Richard walked by the table where Joy and her friend were sitting. "Evening, ladies," he said. He pulled up an extra chair to Joe and Art's table, sat down, and raised his hand to get Mary Ann's attention.

"The usual?" she asked.

"Yeah, please."

Richard turned to Art. "Who put a bug up Marshall's ass?"

"He was talking to Moon right before you came in," Art replied.

"Well, that explains part of it. Moon probably owes him money. Speaking of money, I got some real good news! We're about to step uptown with the Fairlane. Mr. Jacobs over at the dealership wants to put some money into the car. He came out to the farm today. Said that, since I've started winning some races, he'd let us use one of his back bays to keep and work on the car. It's a pretty good deal. He'll give us all the spare parts and tires we need, at cost. All we got to do is paint his name on the side of the car."

Art slapped Richard on the shoulder. "Wow, man, that's great! When does all this start?"

"Whenever I like. I was hoping you guys could help me with the move tomorrow night. And, by the way, you boys are gonna be able to crew for me this weekend, aren't you?"

The two men looked at each other and nodded. Over the last six months, they had become his volunteer regular crew.

Mary Ann placed Richard's beer in front of him. "You need anything else?" she asked.

"Sure would! In fact, I'm starving!"

"We got some fried chicken from lunch, or Jack could fix you something fresh—a sandwich or something."

"The chicken, to go, sounds good," Richard said.

"Chicken it is."

Mary Ann walked away, writing down his order.

Joe winked at Art. "You know, Richard, I think Mary Ann's got the hots for you."

"Why do you say that?" Richard asked.

"Oh, it's just the way she talks to you," Joe said. "She treats you different. When she talks to us, it's like she's talking to a buddy. She looks right through us. The minute you walk in, she kinda softens up. Anyway, I was listening in on her and that table of hens over against the wall a couple of nights ago. Joy was saying how she heard a rumor that you worked them rice fields naked. They was laughing about how they was gonna get a good pair of binoculars and see for themselves. Mary Ann was talking about your legs. She said she liked a good pair of legs!"

"Shit, man," Richard said, "I ain't got no business dating. Since Jean left a couple summers ago, I've hardly looked at a woman. Any woman I would have ain't gonna put up with the mosquitoes and mud on a rice farm."

"Nobody said you had to marry her," Art said. "Hell, man, quit being so serious!"

"I'm not interested in one-night stands," Richard said. "I had plenty of that when I went off to school. Didn't care for it then, and the idea still doesn't appeal to me. And the other thing that's holding me back is that I've made more money racing than farming over the last two years, and it looks like this year ain't gonna be no different."

"Wow," Joe said, "you must be doing better at racing than I thought! I know that since me and Art been crewing for you, you've won a few races but I had no idea you were doing *that* well."

"No, Joe, wait a minute," Richard said. "You don't understand. It's not that I'm making a lot racing—it's that I'm not making anything farming."

"Oh, I see," Joe said.

Art leaned over the table. "If you ain't making no money, why do you keep doing it?"

"I ask myself that same question every day," Richard replied.

"If you need money," Joe said, "now that I'm a supervisor, I can get you work at the steel mill anytime. You'll have to start out doing the grunt-work, but, as smart as you are and as good as you are with your hands, they'll run you up the scale in no time."

"Thanks, but that's part of the problem," Richard said. "I don't want to work for somebody else. I don't want to be cooped up all day long. Think about it … I've always been on the farm. The only time I've ever been away was that short stretch at college. And, every day I was away, I missed the farm."

Mary Ann emerged from behind the bar with two plastic sacks full of trash. "Last call, boys!" she said. "We're gonna close up in about fifteen minutes." She carried the bags toward the side door.

Richard watched her nudge the door open with her leg. "I wonder if she and Moon ever had anything going," he said.

Art leaned back in his chair. "Don't know for sure, but if they did, neither one of them will admit to it. Mary Ann's always talking about how she's waiting for some dark, handsome stranger to come rescue her from this dead-end town. Maybe you're him."

"Either one of you guys know if she's dating anybody?" Richard asked.

Both shrugged.

"You ought to ask Jack," Joe said. "If anybody knows, it's him."

Art got up and fished around in his pocket for his keys. "I'm going home," he said. I got to be at work early in the morning. We're putting in some new molds."

"Yeah, I forgot about that," Joe said. "What time you gonna be by?"

"About five thirty," Art answered.

"That's fine," Joe said, and then turned his attention to Richard. "We'll see you tomorrow night at the shop, about seven thirty."

Richard went up to the bar. "Jack, I need to ask you something."

Jack looked up and smiled. He liked Richard; he liked the way he drove.

"Tell me, Jack, do you know if Mary Ann is dating anybody?"

Jack shook his head.

"Does that mean you don't know, or she isn't dating anyone?"

"No," Jack said.

Richard still wasn't sure what Jack meant, but, as he was preparing to rephrase his question, Mary Ann came back inside.

"Mary Ann," Jack said, "are you dating anybody?"

"Why, are you thinking about asking me out?" she said.

"No, but I think Richard is."

Richard and Mary Ann both blushed.

Jack removed his apron and quickly headed toward the door. "I'm going out for a cigarette."

Richard and Mary Ann regained their composure, then began to laugh.

Mary Ann was the first to speak. "The answer to Jack's question is no. I'm not dating anyone. Are you?"

He shook his head. "I really haven't dated anybody since Jean left,"

"Damn, Richard, that's been years!"

"I know. Farming takes a lot of time, and my heart wasn't in it, I guess. The other thing was that there just didn't seem to be anybody I was interested in."

Neither of them said anything for an awkward moment, and then Richard spoke. "Well, sometime when you're off—I assume you get some days off—maybe we can work something out in between racing and farming and your work. I was just wondering."

"Would I go out with you?" Mary Ann asked. "Of course I would."

"Good. I was hoping you would."

"What I'd really like to do is go to that big new movie theater in Jonesboro. We could make a day of it—two or three movies in one afternoon!"

"That sounds like fun," he said. "How does next Sunday sound?"

"Could we maybe do it on a Monday?"

"The farm don't care if or when I take off. Let's make it next Monday, then."

"It's a date. If you don't mind, you can pick me up here at the cafe at about two thirty in the afternoon. That'll give me a chance to get some chores done."

"Two thirty, Monday. Great."

As Richard left, Mary Ann noticed that he didn't put his cap back on until he had gone out the door. She liked that. Her mother had always said that a man who wore his cap indoors was hiding something. It might be nothing but a bald head, but you could never tell.

Jack walked back into the cafe.

"Richard and I are going to the movies next Tuesday," Mary Ann said.

"Good," Jack said. "I like him. He'd be a good man for you to marry and have children with."

"Hold it just a minute. This is one date, and you have me tying the knot and raising a new generation of Kyles?" Mary Ann smiled. "What makes you so sure?"

"He's honest in little things. I've watched him at the track and here—he treats everybody the same, and most of the time he tastes like horses."

"What does that mean?" she asked.

"It's a gray cloud that rolls in like big waves on the water."

CHAPTER 7

a long line of blue-green haze

It was a warm evening, and a full moon rose over the track like a giant floodlight. The roar of the early hobby stock races echoed from the racing oval. The crowds had begun to converge for the night's racing card.

Jack had spent the afternoon preparing a rich Italian sauce. He had begun by sautéing a handful of onions and fresh garlic in oil until the bite of the onion had softened to a warm, smooth shape. For freshness, he had added mushrooms, green bell peppers, and shredded carrots. When the vegetables had begun to fuse with the onion, he sprinkled in—a few pinches at a time—salt, pepper, and oregano. When the vegetables were well seared, he added large chunks of fresh, peeled tomatoes. As the mixture began to cook down, he added several jars of his tomato sauce. Jack had a special way with his sauce; it always had that fresh tomato taste. To the raw sauce he added a measure of Mount Judea's best red table wine. While the sauce cooked, he combined ground beef with eggs, breadcrumbs, garlic, and Parmesan cheese, and formed the mixture into balls. He browned the meatballs in a skillet and then set them aside. Midway through the cooking of the sauce, he added the meatballs to it. Before long, supper was ready.

Jack hadn't taken his medicine in a month. Traveling around over the years, he had learned by trial and error how best to use it. In the early days, when the voices were the worst, he had taken it all the time. Chlorpromazine left a bad taste in his mouth—a bitter, metallic taste. It took care of the voices, but, no matter how little of it he took, he was always aware of its presence. When haloperidol came along, it proved a little better. It was tasteless and odorless, but it still dulled his senses. Each new town had had a mental-health clinic where he could get his medicine. Each time, he had gone through a new evaluation. In most clinics, they would try some new combination or some new technique, but, after a while, they would always come back to the same routine.

"How are you?" a doctor would ask.

"Fine," Jack would say.

"Okay, here's your prescription. See you in three months."

And that was all there was to it. Jack understood that as long as his behavior wasn't too outrageous, no one paid any attention. So he began manipulating his dosage. If he went for more than three or four weeks with no medicine at all, the sounds and threats and fears became intolerable. If he waited too long or had too much excitement, the voices multiplied and became an army. Being among friends helped; having something to do helped; feeling good helped; living in Gum Ridge helped. For Jack, there was something very comforting about Gum Ridge and its people. Most places he had lived, there had been a sense of isola- tion—he would walk down the street, and everyone would look past him as though he didn't really exist. In many ways, he had become a part of the stoves that he had worked at every day. Whenever he took his apron and cap off, he ceased to be. He had just been the cook who talked to the stove, and when he dis- appeared, no one ever came looking. A day or two later, someone else would take his place in front of the grill. But here, in Gum Ridge, when he walked down the street, people honked and waved. When he got sick, Mary Ann came looking without him asking. Jack liked Gum Ridge.

Mary Ann emerged from the kitchen with a two orders of Jack's spaghetti for a couple at table three. "Here you are," she said, setting the plates down on the table. "Can I get you anything else?"

They shook their heads and began to eat.

Kate Ellis walked in the bar. She was one of those girls who turned people's heads—men and women alike. She was pretty, but not ravishing—it was her presence, the way she carried herself that people noticed. When she walked into a room, she became the center of attention, and it didn't bother her at all. Kate had watched her mother change from a thin and attractive young woman into a dumpy matron of the church, and Kate had no intention of letting that happen to her. Kate surveyed the room like a young cat in heat, and her glance momen- tarily settled on Art and Joe, who had spotted her the second she walked in. The look on her face communicated clearly, "No, boys, not interested."

She moved toward the bar, the sway of her hips and breasts obvious beneath her thin cotton dress. "I'd like a beer, Mary Ann," she said softly.

Mary Ann responded without looking up from the bar. "Sure, sweetie, name your poison."

"Draft beer, something like that."

"One draft, coming up." Mary Ann grabbed a cold mug from the freezer and began to fill it.

"Did you tell Moon I was looking for him?" Kate asked.

"Yeah."

"Did he seem interested?"

"Yeah, I guess so. In his own odd sort of way, I guess you can say he was interested."

"What do you mean?"

"How well do you know him?" Mary Ann asked.

Moon emerged from his office chewing on a pencil and studying the *Racing Form*. His hair was slicked back, he was dressed in a Madras shirt, stone-washed jeans, and snakeskin boots. "Phillips, get me a glass of tea," he said. Moon used the same scanning technique as Kate did whenever he entered a room. He slowly surveyed his kingdom. Everything was in order—there were no bill collectors or extra girlfriends, and there was no one angry, aside from the usual troublemakers. And then, his vision focused on a pretty new face—a vaguely familiar new face.

"Can I help you?" Moon asked Kate. "Phillips, get the lady a drink."

"She's already got one," Mary Ann said, pointing at the beer sitting in front of Kate. Mary Ann had seen this play before. She knew the plot and most of the dialogue, and the ending was always the same.

Moon smiled at Kate and unconsciously winked. It was a reflex of familiarity that was automatic when he talked to women, young or old. "My name's Al Moon, but most people just call me Moon," he said. "This is my restaurant. Is there anything I can get for you? The kitchen's still open, and we could get you a plate of wonderful Italian spaghetti. The sauce is magnificent. My man, Jack, is quite a cook. And what's your name?"

Kate always enjoyed being wooed. Kate's feminist friends were quick to point out that this whole process was degrading to the intelligent, integrated, modern woman. According to them, sex was a tool used by the male-dominated world to keep women in their place. In that world, a prick was more important than a brain. The problem for Kate was that the feminist world was cold and empty, and sex was addicting. She liked the way it felt to have men follow her with their eyes. It tickled her when she caught them talking to her breasts. She had honed her skills for years. Her courses in psychology had introduced her to the concept of intermittent reinforcement, and she had discovered that it worked.

"My name's Kate Ellis. I teach English at the high school."

"Wait a minute," Moon said. "*You're* the teacher that Phillips told me about? Damn! Excuse my French, but they didn't have anything like you when *I* was in school. If they had, I would've studied more. We had fat, ugly old Mr. Ferguson."

"Yeah, he was still there when I was in school," Kate said, smiling

"When you went to school? You mean, you went to school here?"

"Yeah, sure," Kate replied. "Graduated just a few years ago."

"I can't believe I didn't notice you. How come we never met?"

"Oh, we met. Several times in fact. But I've changed a little. I'm Reverend Howard Ellis's daughter."

"That couldn't be. She was a skinny little girl! Her hair was always kind of limp."

"College will change you," Kate said.

"I'll say," said Moon.

For Moon, women were a game; in fact, they were his sport of choice. Why waste time dribbling a ball up and down a court when he could be up in the stands with the ladies? There had been a constant stream of women in Moon's life, but it had always seemed to him that they were all just variations on the same woman—she just happened to have many different faces. This little girl, however, seemed different, and he knew it instantly. Later, he would tell his friends that it was love at first sight. With the first smile from Kate, this brash hustler felt something soften in his soul. While they talked, all he could think was, *Please, let this moment go on forever.* She was clearly different from the little country girls who wouldn't look him in the eye. He'd never met anyone like Kate. From that first instant, his assumption was, *We will marry, and I will grow old with this woman.* Never mind that he'd never sustained a relationship for longer than six weeks in his entire life.

Kate, despite her appearance, was less than confident. Moon was a challenge—an emotional dream. As a skinny little kid, she had watched him race his motorcycle up and down the streets of Gum Ridge, thumbing his nose at the adult world. Many nights as a teenager, she had gone to sleep thinking about how romantic it would be to throw caution to the wind and ride off into the night with Moon. And now, the train was finally pulling out, and she had a ticket. In fact, she was the engineer.

"How about taking me for a ride in that pretty little red convertible you've got sitting out in the parking lot?" Kate asked.

Without hesitation, Moon put down his glass of tea, walked over to the cash register, and pulled out a stack of twenties. "Close up, Phillips," he said to Mary Ann. "I won't be back this evening." He walked out from behind the bar and extended his arm to Kate. "Permit me to escort you to the car, Madame," he said. She smiled and accepted his arm, and the pair walked out the door.

Mary Ann watched them leave. "Did you hear those two?" she asked Jack.

Jack nodded.

"I hope that girl knows what she's getting herself into," she said.

"What do you mean?" Jack asked.

"You've seen how he treats women. All he wants to do is get into her pants. As soon as he does, he'll drop her like a hot rock."

"You think Mr. Moon will ever get married?"

Mary Ann laughed. "I pity the poor fool who marries Moon. He'd be faithful for about as long as it takes to close the church door after the wedding. Speaking of weddings, Jack—you ever been married?"

Jack thought for a minute. "No, I don't think so," he said. He took off his apron and hung it in the kitchen. "You remember I asked you if I could leave early tonight to go to the races? I'd like to see Richard run his car."

"Sure. I got everything under control here," she said.

The tall metal grandstand extended all along the home stretch of the oval track. Jack liked the seats on the top row at the head of the stretch. He liked this position because, most of the time, he didn't have to worry about getting a seat. As Jack started his climb into the stands, Jimmy, the popcorn man, caught his eye and motioned him over.

"Hey, Jack! What do you know, bud? How'd you get off for the night? I thought you always had to work on Saturdays."

"Most of the time, I do, but I wanted to see Richard race tonight. Mary Ann said she'd cover for me. She told me to take off for the night."

"Sounds like you work for good folks. You think that'd happen here at the track? Ain't no way. If I was outta here for one day, they'd bring in some snot-nosed kid, and I'd be out of a job."

Once Jimmy got up a head of steam, it was hard to get him to shut up, and Jack didn't want to get into a long-winded conversation with Jimmy tonight. "I'm gonna go get me a seat, Jimmy," Jack said. "It looks like the stands are filling up pretty fast."

"Before you go up," Jimmy said, "Richard was down at the concession stand a little while ago. Said if I saw you, to tell you he needed to talk to you. He said he'd leave a pit pass for you at the gate."

"Did he say what it was about?" Jack asked.

"No. Just that he needed to talk to you if you came in."

Jack spent most of his time making himself invisible, blending into the background. Richard had gone out of his way to engage Jack in conversation since he had begun dating Mary Ann, but to be picked out and asked to come to the pit was a big deal. In all his years around the track, no one had ever asked him to join them in the pit.

Jack stepped up to the guardhouse where the drivers checked in their cars.

"I'm Jack, from Moon's," he said to the young woman in the booth. "Mr. Kyle left me a pass?"

"Sure, Jack, your pass is right here," the girl said, passing the plastic card on a string into the change tray.

The drivers were like kids at the dinner table—everybody had their own seat, and only an outsider would invade their space. Richard's spot in the pit was halfway down the backstretch, under an old gum tree. His car was a 1969 Ford Fairlane, painted cherry red with bright blue bumpers; it was easy to pick out of a crowd.

Jack saw Richard and Art standing around the old Fairlane, and he made his way across the pit area. Art was the first to see him.

"There he is," Art said. "Jimmy must have seen you."

"Yeah, he did," Jack said. "Did I do something wrong?"

Richard smiled. "No, there isn't anything wrong," he said. "We just need an extra set of hands. Joe's under the weather, and we need somebody to fetch and carry. Could you help us out for the evening?"

"Yeah, sure. Of course I can. I don't know what to do, though. I never worked in the pit before."

"That's okay," Richard said. "Art can show you."

Jack was now a part of Richard Kyle's pit crew. Art took him around the area and showed him where everything was—where they kept the various tools, the spare tires, and the extra lugs—and showed him how to work the jack.

Richard revved the big engine in the cherry red car and headed off for his first race. Jack felt his heart rate soar. It was a preliminary heat, and most of the entrants were shade-tree mechanics that only raced from time to time. Richard easily won. For Richard and Art, it was routine, but it was Jack's first victory.

In the semifinals that night, Richard came in second when he got trapped behind a slower car near the finish line.

In the last race, eight cars vied for the five-hundred-dollar prize. After the first eight laps, Richard was in second place. With two laps to go, he surged ahead, and he won by five car lengths going away.

It was a good night for the Kyle team, but Jack felt like the biggest winner— he was now a part of the pit crew. Back at the cafe, he didn't stop talking about it for two hours. Mary Ann, Richard, and Art listened and laughed as Jack rehashed every event of the evening.

CHAPTER 8

strawberries

One Sunday afternoon, as they were closing the cafe, Mary Ann said to Jack, "I know you like strawberries—I've watched you go after the strawberry jam with your biscuits. How about you and I go out to Mule Johnson's farm in the morning and pick berries? Do you remember Leonard? Mule was Leonard's father."

Jack shook his head. "I didn't know Leonard."

"No, come to think of it, that's right ... Leonard was killed the day you came in the door. Anyway, I think you know Mule—he's the old man who runs the farmer's market over by the Ice House. He's opening up his strawberry patch in the morning for anyone that wants to go pick. What do you say? You want some fresh strawberries?"

"I know Mr. Johnson," Jack said. "He's a nice guy. He and his buddies talk to me while I'm cooking on the smoker out back. There's nothing I like better than fresh strawberries, but I never picked berries before. Is it hard?"

"Hadn't thought about that," Mary Ann said. "It's easiest if you get down on your knees, but you could do just about as well sitting on a pickle bucket. I have a feeling that if you get down on your knees, Jack, you won't be getting up. I'll throw a bucket in the pickup before I leave today. We'd better get out there pretty early, or the best stuff will be picked over. I'll be by your house about seven in the morning. In fact, I'll go you one better—why don't I come by about six thirty, and we can stop by Peeler's for breakfast? They got great pancakes."

"That'd be okay. I don't eat much. Don't eat much at all, unless I'm here at the cafe. I eat some popcorn at the track, and, every once in a while, a can of soup at my apartment."

"You mean, you can go for a day or two without eating at all?"

"Yeah, I guess so. I just don't think about eating."

"I wish I could go for ten minutes without thinking about food. Being around you makes it worse." Mary Ann hesitated. "Don't get me wrong—I *love* the way you cook. That's part of the problem. It all smells so good! If you'd rather not, we don't have to go for breakfast."

"No, breakfast is fine."

Early the next morning, Mary Ann pulled into the drive by Jack's apartment. He was sitting on the bottom step with Gracie in his lap. Mary Ann wore a wide-brimmed Mexican sombrero with a string looped under her chin to keep it from blowing off. "Morning, Señor," she said. "Ready for a day of working in the fields?"

Jack smiled, gently placed Gracie on the step, and walked toward the truck. He slid into the passenger seat and closed the door without a word.

"You know, Jack … When I was a kid, I always wanted to have brothers and sisters, but Mama had sworn off men by that time. Having cousins was okay, but not like having other kids in the house. Coming over here, I was thinking that having you around is kinda like having a big brother to do things with. You're like my big brother. What do you think about that?"

After a moment of silence, Mary Ann looked over to see that there was a tear running down Jack's cheek. "Are you okay?" she asked. "Did I say something wrong?"

"No, you didn't say anything wrong. I never had brothers and sisters either, and I didn't have cousins, and I don't hardly remember having a mama or a daddy. I never think about the idea of having a family, 'cause when I do, something deep inside me hurts. I like the idea of you being my sister and Mr. Moon being my brother."

"Now wait a minute, I don't know about asking Moon into this family of ours!" Mary Ann said, laughing.

"He's scared, too," Jack said. "Just like you and me."

"What do you mean, 'scared'?" Mary Ann asked.

"He's scared he's gonna get old. He's scared that the girls are gonna quit coming around. He's scared he's gonna end up broke. That's part of why he acts like he does. He's just a scared little boy who hasn't ever grown up."

"How do you know all of this?" she asked.

"I been around for a long time, and I've seen a lot of men and women just like him. They aren't very happy people, and most of them don't *ever* get happy. Practice just seems to make permanent."

"You said that you and me were scared too. What do you think *I'm* scared of?"

"You don't want to end up alone."

"How do you know that?"

"I don't know. I just do. I also know that you like this place and these people, no matter how much you talk about wanting to get out of here. It's not just your mama that's keeping you here. I get the feeling, when I watch you with Richard that you'd like for him to be the one for you, but the idea of trying to settle down again is scaring you."

Mary Ann chuckled. "Well, now, aren't we the head shrink?"

Jack reached over and put his hand on Mary Ann's arm. "I didn't mean to hurt your feelings. I hope I didn't say anything wrong."

"Jack, you didn't say anything wrong. In fact, you're absolutely right. I *am* afraid of committing to anyone. I've been burned twice, and I don't want it to happen again."

Mary Ann pulled her pickup into the gravel parking lot of Peeler's. The lot was full of empty logging trucks and muddy pickups. Mary Ann and Jack found a table along the east wall, where the early-morning sun was coming through the window.

Mamie Moon was working the room by herself, and she didn't notice the identity of the pair when they came in. "You two want coffee?" she asked without looking up. "I'll be with you in a minute."

"Don't worry about us, Mamie," Mary Ann said. "We'll get our own coffee."

Mamie looked up. "Mary Ann! Good to see you! Yeah, it'd be great if you'd get your own java. And you must be Jack. I'm Albert's mother. Nice to meet you."

Jack nodded.

As Mamie went on serving her other customers, Jack and Mary Ann got up, got cups, and poured themselves some coffee.

Beside the coffee station was a large glass case full of pies. Peeler's was known for its coconut cream pie with thick meringue topping. While Mary Ann poured her coffee, Jack slid back the glass case-front and smelled the pies.

They returned to their table, and, a couple of minutes later, Mamie came around to take their order.

"I'd like a short stack with a side of bacon and some hash browns," Mary Ann said.

Mamie turned her attention to Jack. "And what do you want, my friend?"

"I'd like a piece of that coconut cream pie. Is that okay?" Jack asked.

"Of course it's okay! Old man Peeler says that everything in the place is for sale at any time, day or night, including the chairs and tables."

"I don't want any of the chairs and tables," Jack said. "Just a piece of pie."

"Sure, sweetie, whatever you want," Mamie said. She turned and went back to the service window.

Mary Ann held her coffee cup in both hands and slowly sipped at the dark liquid.

"Jack, you mentioned Richard before, and you're right. He is a real nice guy, and I really do like him. But, before you go off having the two of us getting married, I've got to tell you that he's just about as gun-shy as I am. Worse than that, he's broke. I learned a few years ago that trying to live on love means a starvation diet. I want to ask you something about Richard. I know you've been spending a lot of time working with him on his crew ... I wouldn't want you to break any confidences, but does Richard ever talk about me when you're with him working on the car?"

Jack thought for a minute. "No, not that I remember." He hesitated, then added, "Well, there is one thing he asked a couple of times."

"What's that?" she asked.

"He asked me if you ever talked about him."

"Oh, I see," Mary Ann said, smiling.

Mamie brought their food. Mary Ann doctored her pancakes with butter and syrup, and Jack began eating his pie.

Mary Ann cut into her pancakes and looked up at Jack; he had a contented smile on his face.

"Jack, you're always talking about shapes and colors. If you don't mind telling me, what is it that you're feeling right now?" she asked.

"It's a billowy cloud of round, golden softness. It's kinda what you'd expect. It doesn't have any edges. It's just warm, like the sunshine coming through the window, or that yellow blouse you wear to work sometime. You know, the Chinese like that yellow gold color—it's their royal color. The round taste of yellow is like medicine for me."

"Have you ever told your doctors about the way you hear and taste colors?" Mary Ann asked.

Jack shook his head. "Whenever I tried, they looked at me like I was crazy. You're different; I can talk to you. The doctors would just give me more medicine, and I don't *want* more medicine. So don't tell anybody."

Mamie walked up to the table. "So, how was the pie?"

"Very good," Jack said.

"More coffee?" Mamie asked.

Mary Ann finished the last bite of pancake and put her fork down. "Don't have time. We're heading for the strawberry patch right now. Johnson's opening it up this morning."

"Kinda wish I was going with you."

"You're more than welcome," Mary Ann said. "The more, the merrier! Right, Jack?"

"Sure—I could always ride in the back," Jack said.

"Thanks anyway," Mamie said, "but I got work to do. It wouldn't hurt my feelings, though, if you guys brought me about two quarts."

"Consider it done," Mary Ann said. They got up to leave.

Part of the secret of Jack's gift of smell and taste was the ability to discern layers of taste. He could take a prepared dish and decipher the spices and herbs that had been woven together to create the fabric of flavor. He held up his hand to get Mamie's attention. "Mrs. Mamie, you guys have got a little gas leak somewhere."

"Are you sure?" Mamie asked. "I don't smell it."

"Yes, ma'am, it's there. It's lying right in there with the smell of the burned chicken from yesterday."

"I don't smell it either, Mamie," Mary Ann said urgently, "but if Jack says it's there, I'll guarantee you that it's there."

"Fair enough. I'll get the boys from the gas company to come in and check it out. Thanks, Jack."

Johnson's Berry Farm was in the sand hills east of town, and Mary Ann had been right—cars and trucks already lined the road, and most of the pickers had settled on where they wanted to start.

Mule, a wiry, balding old man with a full, gray beard, liked making a show out of the first day of berry season, and most everyone went along with it. At eight o'clock on the nose, he would fire his shotgun into the air—the signal for the pickers to enter the field. A few old die-hards had even camped out the night before at the end of the row they intended to pick. There was always a prize for the most berries picked, the prettiest berries, and the neatest pickers. Mule was the sole judge, and there was no arguing with his decisions.

Being a good businessman, Mule charged a fair price for every quart of berries picked and a small fee for everyone who entered his little contest—that is to say, everyone who picked on the first day. Jack and Mary Ann stopped at the berry shed and paid their entry fees. They each picked up a hand-crate and six quart baskets.

Once they had their equipment, Mary Ann led Jack around to the north side of the field. The ground here wasn't quite as good, but there was less competition for space. In any case, most years, Mule's field had good berries all over.

When Mule fired his shotgun, the season officially began.

The sandy ground was moist but not wet. The straw that mulched the berries provided a nice cushion for their knees. Soon, Jack had abandoned his pickle bucket and was moving slowly along the row on his knees.

For a while, they said nothing as they just inched their way along the rows. Jack was a quick learner, and he had soon filled the first three quarts in his carrier.

"I need to stand up and stretch," he said. "My knees are beginning to ache."

"Knock yourself out," said Mary Ann. "We aren't in any hurry. You need some help getting up?"

Jack waved her away. "I'm okay," he said.

He leaned over, braced himself on his carrier, shifted his weight to the right, and gave himself a boost. The maneuver almost worked. In mid-effort, the handle of the carrier gave way, leaving Jack with his one good foot in loose sand and the other doing an awkward pirouette in a futile attempt to maintain his balance. Mary Ann looked up just in time to see Jack come cascading down on top of her in a shower of strawberries and sand. When all of the motion was spent, Mary Ann was face down in the sand and Jack was lying on her back, his face to the sky. For an instant, they both lay there doing a survey to make sure all of their parts were in the right place.

Jack was the first to speak. "Mary Ann, are you okay?" he asked.

"Well, Jack, you *are* a little heavy."

Jack immediately began to struggle to get up, which did nothing but cause the two of them to wallow around in the sand. It didn't take long for Jack to realize that the leg that had been stuck in the sand was not working right.

Mary Ann started to laugh. "Jack, you're like a beached whale. Stop! Stop! Wait!" She studied the situation for a minute and then said, "Instead of trying to get up, just roll over. And then, when I get up, I'll help you up."

On the second try, Jack rolled over and off of Mary Ann. Mary Ann rolled onto her back. By that time, they were both laughing.

For a couple of minutes, they lay in the sand, laughing and talking about how funny Jack had looked as he came crashing down in slow motion.

"Are you two okay?" It was the voice of Mule.

Mary Ann looked up. "Yeah, I think so."

"You need some help getting up?" Mule asked.

"I think we're okay," Mary Ann said.

Mary Ann got up and brushed off the sand. When Jack started to get up, it was obvious that something was wrong with his left knee.

"What's the matter?" Mary Ann asked.

"I don't know. My left knee doesn't want to work."

Mary Ann rolled up his pant leg. Jack's right knee was obviously swollen. "Jack, was your knee like that this morning?"

Jack shook his head.

"You stay right there. I'm gonna go get the truck and take Mule up on that offer of help. I think you did something to that knee when you fell."

Jack nodded.

Mary Ann steered her truck down the tractor row and into the field, where she grabbed two teenage boys who were working in the berry shed and got them to help her load Jack onto the front seat of the truck.

Mary Ann pulled up in front of the Green River Clinic. "Jack, you stay in the truck. I'll go in and get a wheelchair. Be back in a minute."

Two minutes later, Mary Ann and the nurse came back out to the truck with a wheelchair. They helped Jack into the chair and rolled him into the clinic.

"Let's go ahead and x-ray that knee," the nurse said. "Dr. Taylor is in the back, burning some warts off of a kid. He'll be out in a few minutes."

After the X-ray had been taken, the nurse returned with a set of forms for Jack to fill out. Jack looked at them as if they were written in a foreign language.

"Here, Jack, I'll see if I can't help you fill these out," Mary Ann said, taking the forms from Jack. "Let's see. What is your full name? I mean, besides 'Jack.'"

"Don't know," he said.

"You got a Social Security card?

"Yeah."

"Let's see it."

Jack reached into his back pocket and pulled out his old, ragged billfold. He slid out a small stack of cards and handed them to Mary Ann. Most of them were business cards. There was also a library card, and, on the bottom, his Social Security card. Below the number on the card was the name Jack Smith.

"I didn't know your last name was Smith."

"It's not," he said.

"But the card says it is."

"That's a name a clerk made up 'cause I didn't know what my name was."

She looked at his Medicaid card—it bore the same name.

"Is that the name you use to get your medicine?" she asked.

"Yeah."

"So I guess that means your name is Smith."

"Yeah, I guess so."

While they were discussing his name, or lack of name, Dr. John Taylor came in with the X-rays.

Mary Ann handed him the forms. "Well, Mr...." He glanced down at the papers. "... Smith—" He looked at Mary Ann, then back at Jack. "Oh, you're Jack the cook. Well, Jack, let's look at your knee. How did you hurt yourself?"

Because Jack was so literal-minded, Mary Ann knew that having much of a conversation with him could take a long time, so she answered for him. "We were picking strawberries, and Jack twisted it when he fell."

The doctor gripped Jack's leg and gently extended it, then he stressed the inside and outside of the knee. When he was through with the exam, Taylor walked over to the view-box and inserted the films. "Well, Jack, there aren't any breaks, but you really have an old-looking knee. It looks like you've put some real wear and tear on it over the years. Do you remember ever hurting it?"

"No. It just gets stiff," Jack said.

"Well, I'll tell you this much—it swelling up so quickly probably means that you've done some internal damage. If you were one of our young athletes, I'd send you to Batesville for an MRI, today."

Jack frowned. "I don't want to go to the hospital. I don't like hospitals," he said.

"It would just be an out-patient test," the doctor said. "You wouldn't have to stay there."

Jack shook his head. "I don't want to go to the hospital for tests."

"Well, Jack, my friend, you sure don't have to. This here is America. Men fought and died so you could do what you damn well please." Taylor turned to his nurse. "Marge, go get Jack a knee brace and a pair of crutches." He turned back to Jack. "Now, Jack, I want you to promise me that if this knee isn't better in a week, you'll come back and let me take another look at it."

Mary Ann spoke for her friend. "He will," she said, and then she turned to Jack. "Won't you, Jack?"

Jack nodded.

After Jack was outfitted with his brace and crutches, Mary Ann insisted that he come home with her, but he would have nothing of it.

"Thanks, but no. I'm going home after work today. Gracie needs me."

"You don't plan on going to work today, do you?" Mary Ann asked.

"Of course I do. It's just my knee."

"Will you at least let me drive you home after work?"

"We'll see."

Despite his stiff-legged walk with the brace, Jack never mentioned the knee again. Whenever Mary Ann would ask about it, Jack changed the subject. A couple of weeks later, he put the crutches in the back of Mary Ann's truck and asked her to take them back to the clinic.

CHAPTER 9

lighting a fire

Jack enjoyed Wednesdays. He spent most of the day at the outdoor cooker that Moon had won in a poker game. With help from the old men at the farmers' market Mary Ann and Jack installed the cooker on the back of the parking lot between the cafe and the old ice house. Mule Johnson and his friends who ran the farmers' market were a delightful group of old men, and they were particularly fond of Jack and his cooking. They never tired of giving Jack advice on each step of the process of cooking. Jack would begin the day by stoking up the outdoor grill with a low-heat fire and slowly smoking peppers over wet woodchips.

After strawberry season was over, Mule was at the market twice a week, every week. He would pull up in his old van and unload all of his fresh produce. He was particular about the fact that everything at the market was grown locally. There were no Texas onions or Iowa sweet corn—it was all homegrown.

"Morning, Jack," Mule said as he began unloading his truck.

Jack smiled and waved, but he didn't speak. The smoke that enveloped him and the cooker contained a symphony of colors, sounds, and tastes. The fresh hickory fragrance was carried up from the fire in tongues of hot steam. The chilies reacted first with knifelike points, but as the skin of the peppers blackened, the points were replaced by rich violet colors and a cloud of reddish orange sound.

There was an old maple tree between Mule's van and Jack's cooker. That was where all of the men would sit when there were no customers. Mule set up his table and a small propane stove, and fixed a pot of coffee.

"You want a cup of coffee, Jack?" Mule asked.

"Yeah, that would be good," Jack replied.

Jack laid down his tools and walked over to the gathering place under the tree.

"How's your knee doing?" the old man asked.

"It's okay," Jack replied.

"Have you seen Moon this morning?" Mule asked.

"No, sir, Mr. Moon won't be around 'til late this afternoon."

"Would you give him something for me?"

"Yeah, sure, what is it?" Jack asked.

Mule got up from his chair, walked over to the passenger side of his truck, opened the door, and pulled out a cardboard box full of papers. He brought it over and set it down in front of Jack.

"What's in the box?" Jack asked.

"It's the sum total of all that my son accomplished in his life, and I guess that was mostly my fault." Mule sat down and sipped his coffee. "When the boy was little, I was fascinated by that P. J. Ives character that came through here. His little blue Nash Rambler ended up at one of the local car lots, and I bought it. When Leonard got old enough to drive, I gave it to him as his first car. Anyway, he got fascinated with Ives and decided to investigate what happened to the guy. Most folks will latch onto something and then, a year or so later, go on to something else. Well, that didn't happen with Leonard. Another problem was that he and Moon had always been friends, and they fed off of each other. Between them, they got the idea in their heads that Ives was the illegitimate brother of Glen Marshall and that he'd been trying to blackmail the family. According to Leonard, Glen and his daddy hired a fella from Batesville to get rid of Ives. They were gonna go talk to this fella in Stone County who knew all the facts but then Leonard got stuck by lightning. There were all kinds of holes in the story they dreamed up, but it didn't do any good to argue with them.

"Anyway, Linda, Leonard's wife, wouldn't allow Moon in the house—they had a history, you know—and she wouldn't let Leonard leave all his P. J. Ives stuff laying around the place, so he built a little shop behind the house, and that was where he did all of his 'research.' After Leonard died, Moon asked Linda if he could have the papers. For spite, she locked up the shop and told Moon he could have them when she got around to cleaning that place out. I think she got tired of putting Moon off, and she finally did a good housecleaning. She burned most of the stuff that was in the shed, and then she called me yesterday to ask if I would bring this box into town and give it to Moon. So here it is."

"I'll give it to Mr. Moon when he comes in," Jack said.

"Thanks. That'll help close a page in our history," Mule said.

Jack went back to his cooking. When the peppers were done, he replaced them with large cuts of beef and pork, which he slow-roasted for hours. At midafternoon, he removed the cooked meat, turned up the heat, and quickly roasted a number of chickens.

While the meat was cooking, he prepared his enchilada sauce—fresh tomatoes, garlic, basil, salt, and a handful of the roasted peppers.

An hour before the evening crowd began to arrive; he packed and rolled the enchiladas with meat or chicken, along with strips of the spicy peppers. On top of the wraps, he placed a trail of his red sauce and a small helping of grated sharp cheese.

There were never any leftovers.

Richard, Art, and Joe sat at one of the back tables, engaged in a friendly game of poker.

Mary Ann was busing tables and grousing about how nasty the Van Austin boys were. "I swear, you'd think those two were raised in a barn. Most of their food ends up on the floor," she said.

Jack came out of the kitchen. "We're out of enchiladas," he told Mary Ann. "You think I should make some more? It won't take but a few minutes."

"I don't think so," she said. "It looks like the rush is over." She turned to the boys at the back table. "You guys want anything else to eat? We're about to start cleaning up the mess."

Richard and Art shook their heads. Joe said, "I don't want anything to eat, but I'd like a beer, when you get time."

"Sure," Mary Ann said.

Moon walked in the side door. He was dressed in a navy blue suit and red tie; his hair, which almost always needed cutting, was nicely trimmed; in place of his scuffed cowboy boots, he had on a pair of nicely shined oxfords. Under his arm he had a book.

Art was the first to notice Moon. "Wow, look what the dogs drug up! Damn, Moon, you clean up pretty good!"

Moon walked toward their table. "I have a date with a lovely lady tonight."

Joe pointed at Moon's right arm. "What's that you got there?"

"If you will reach far back into the recesses of your mind, you just might remember a concept from the distant past called a book," Moon said. "It contains knowledge. It's used to advance your mind. Unlike you hicks, I've decided that I want to improve myself."

"So, what's in *this* book?" Richard said, laughing.

Moon held the book up and moved it back and forth to get it in good focus. "Let's see, the exact title is *God and the Electronic Media* by Paul George."

"What does George Paul know about God and electronics? He didn't even graduate from high school," Art said.

"No, stupid," Moon said, "not George Paul that runs the scales down at the granary. This is Paul George. He's an Englishman or something. Looks to me like he knows a whole lot—after all, he filled up this whole big book."

The meaning of all of this began to sink in on Joe. "Now, tell me, Moon, this wouldn't have anything to do with that pretty little piece of ass from the school you been dating, would it?" he asked.

"You watch your mouth, shithead! She's not just some little plaything!"

"No shitting!" Joe said. "Serious, huh?"

"You bet I am," Moon said. "I never met anybody like her before. She isn't like all these other girls. She's sweet, she's pretty, and she smells wonderful. And she's smart as hell."

Art wasn't sure he was buying the line that Moon was trying to sell. "Yeah, but the real question is: how is she in bed?"

Moon didn't answer this question. "I kinda feel stupid around her," he said instead. "She knows so much stuff. That's why I bought this book. I figure I got to start somewhere."

Jack came out of the kitchen and said, "Mr. Moon, Mr. Johnson, Leonard's father, gave me that box of papers to give to you." Jack pointed at the cardboard box, which he had set on the floor.

"Excellent!" Moon said. "Now maybe we can get this show on the road!"

"What is it?" Mary Ann asked.

"It's the results of the studies that Leonard and I were doing before he died. If all goes well, we should be able to solve the mystery of Mr. Ives once and for all. Some of this stuff, Leonard wouldn't even show me. Top secret! It could blow the lid off this town. Put that box in my office, Jack, and I'll look at it in the morning." Moon walked over to the cash register and opened the drawer. "I'll see you guys later. Kate and I are driving over to Jonesboro tonight to listen to some fella talk about moral decay in America. I never heard of him, but Kate speaks real high of this guy. See you in the morning. Phillips—remember to lock up!" Moon turned and walked out the door.

"Well, ain't that something," Mary Ann said. "Moon's in love!"

"Won't last," Art said. "Don't care how pretty she is."

"Why do you say that?" Richard asked.

"Moon's not ever gonna stay with a woman that's smarter than him. It's not in his nature."

CHAPTER 10

Skinny Dipping

In the middle of the small pasture, under a large red oak, two horses watched as Mary Ann's truck turned off the highway and made its way down the narrow lane toward Richard's shop. Both horses were four-year-olds—beautiful, gentle, and strong horses that seemed out of place in the world of combines and tractors. In many ways, Richard himself was no less a contradiction in terms. Although he studied everything new there was to learn about raising a rice crop, he still listened to the land. Like most good rice farmers—like his father—he always had his ears and eyes open.

"A farmer who lives in town loses contact with the farm," his father would say. "It's hard to put into words, but there's a sense—a knowledge—that you get by standing in the middle of an open field. It's in the way the air moves, the feel of the humidity, the clouds forming and reforming." Year round, winter and summer, his father slept with his windows opened just slightly. "I work out in the heat and the cold," he said. "I don't have the luxury of dictating what the temperature will be when I walk out the back door. With the window open, I live outside all the time. I don't have time to be thinking about how hot or cold it is."

An early summer rainstorm had settled the dust and left a hint of cool in the air. Richard had invited Mary Ann for a late-afternoon ride.

She brought her truck to a stop in the middle of the work-lot. The old shop had originally been built as a stock barn with cattle stalls and wings for storage on either side. These spaces were now filled to overflowing with rusted scrap metal, old barrels, and parts of old tractors. Richard emerged from the shop dressed in cut-off shorts, a pair of leather sandals, and a safari cap with a flap to protect the back of his neck. In his right hand, he held a three-quarter-inch box-end wrench, and in his left was a hammer.

He smiled at Mary Ann as she slid out of the truck. "Glad you're here!" he said. "I'll get the horses. You and I need to go and check out a potential problem." He laid his tools down and reached down into a tub of solvent cleanser.

"What's wrong?" Mary Ann asked.

"Nothing, I hope. But at this time of year, you can never tell. That little storm that came through had some wind to it, and there's always the possibility that it could have washed out some of the levees on the high ground."

"Would that be bad?" she asked.

"Well, it's like this: if one of the sandy upfield lands washes out a levee, then the water goes down to the next land and washes out the next levee, and, before you know it, all the water that I've been pumping onto the fields for the last two weeks ends up in Caney Creek."

"Oh, I see," she said.

"Might involve a little work," he added.

"I'm game," Mary Ann said.

Richard turned toward the pasture and whistled a long, sustained note. The horses looked up from their position beneath the tree and made for the barn at the edge of the field, near the shop.

"You know how to saddle a horse?" Richard asked.

"I've done it once or twice, but it's been a while."

"Maxine is easy. She don't bite, and she don't kick. She likes to have her head rubbed."

"Sounds a little like me." Mary Ann smiled at her own joke and began putting the blanket and saddle on Maxine.

When the horses were ready, Richard secured two shovels to his saddle, and they were off.

Except on the racetrack, Richard was never in a hurry. That was why he still used horses. Most farmers used a tractor or four-wheeler to check their fields, but not Richard. "I'm not rushing through this life," he would say. "Daddy always said that life don't exist in the past or in the future. It's right now. It's this moment—this instant. If you hurry through one chore to the next and then the next, pretty soon, you're through, and your life is over."

For Mary Ann, there was something very peaceful and reassuring about the slow movement along the top of the field—about the blue sky, the warm wind, the horses, and about Richard.

When they reached the point where the first levee intersected with the outside levee, Richard and his horse, George, crossed the outside levee in one step. Richard turned back toward Mary Ann and said, "The water's down about an inch and a half. That's not good. We're gonna have to walk out this levee to find where the break is. When George and I take off, just give Maxine her head, and she'll follow us."

As Richard had predicted, when George began walking in the trough by the levee, Maxine stepped over the outside levee and followed in his tracks.

"I think I know where the break is," Richard said. "There's a low place about two hundred yards out in the field. I've tried to plane it out, but it never works out as well as I hope it will."

The break was just where he thought it would be. "All right, Miss Mary Ann, the free ride's over. We've got work to do. We need to plug the hole in this levee."

Richard dismounted, untied the two shovels, and pulled out three tow sacks. "First, we'll fill the sacks and plug the hole. Then we can build up the levee on top of them."

Mary Ann had never been accused of being afraid of work. In a few minutes, they were topping off the patched levee with a layer of blue gumbo mud.

"That wasn't too hard," she said as they patted down the fresh mud.

"I'll warn you," he said. "That's probably not the last one."

He was right. The next two lands had holes as well, and the fourth land was full of water, with several places looking like they could overflow at any time.

"We need to cut a hole in the outside levee and take the pressure off this land. If we don't, we'll lose every land down the way before the night is over."

They took several bags, filled them with mud, and created a buttress on either end of an area about three feet wide. The bags of mud helped them keep the hole from washing too wide.

When the dam broke, water streamed from the land onto the road that ran downhill beside the field.

By the time the gap was created, Mary Ann and Richard were covered head to toe in mud.

"Real romantic, huh?" he said, smiling at Mary Ann. "This is the first time I've taken a girl out to play in the mud since I was a kid."

"Boy, you really know how to win a woman's heart," she said.

"Come on, let's go check the other lands. By the time we get back, we should be able to plug that hole and then refill the upper lands."

The rest of the levees were in good shape. Mary Ann and Richard circled the field, filled in the gap in the outside levee, and then headed for the pump. Richard threw the switch on the electric motor. The pump began to whine, and, within a few seconds, cold water rushed out of the twelve-inch pipe and filled the holding pond before it streamed out and down the canal to the first land of the field.

Richard and Mary Ann had watched each other as they worked in the field. The heat and humidity had saturated their clothes within minutes of when they started, and soon, their clothes had served as only the thinnest of veneers. Mary Ann's cotton shorts and blouse molded to her contours in a way that accentuated the lines of her form each time she thrust her shovel down into the mud. At one point, as Richard stood holding a sack of mud, Mary Ann leaned forward to loose the shovel from the sticky mud, and her blouse gaped open. Richard stood frozen in place; he had been mesmerized by the vision of her breasts in front of him.

Mary Ann, for her part, had watched as he carried the bags to the hole in the levee and packed them into place. He would throw a bag over his shoulder, and the muscles in his back and shoulders would tense. From head to toe, there didn't seem an ounce of fat on him. His brownish red skin stretched tight over his back, butt, and legs. But there was no artificial bulk—only a perfectly balanced physical specimen who used his body as nature intended.

Richard's father had told him, "We ain't nothing but field animals. We're built to do physical work. If we don't use our bodies, we'll grow weak and break down."

As Mary stood watching the water flow from the metal pipe at the end of the wellhead, Richard walked over to his saddlebags and pulled out a bar of soap. He walked back and climbed up onto the pipe. He threw his hat onto the bank and jumped into the fast-moving stream.

When he came up at the end of the stream, where it abutted the bank, he burst out of the water and screamed, "Damn, that's cold!" He looked up at Mary Ann and laughed. "Join me in the ice water, city girl," he said.

Mary Ann looked around for a way to ease herself into the water. Richard laughed again. "Don't do it the chicken-shit way," he joked. "It's easier to just jump in, all at once."

Mary Ann was not to be made fun of. She eased out onto the metal pipe and then, with a flourish, jumped spread-eagle into the coldwater stream. When she came up, her blouse was filled with a large air bubble.

"Wow," he said, "everything *I* got gets *smaller* in the cold water."

Richard had already shampooed his hair, and he moved to the shallow water, where he soaped down his hands, arms, and chest.

Before she knew what she was doing, and without any prompting from Richard, Mary Ann began to remove her blouse and bra. Richard stood in rapt attention, watching lovingly as she came free from her clothing. Standing in waist-deep water, she reached down, undid her shorts, and threw them, along with her top, onto the grassy bank.

He fully understood the invitation, and he slowly moved to the deeper water where she stood. She noticed that he moved with a fluid grace in the water, that there was no wasted energy in his movement. When he was standing in front of her, she reached out and undid his cutoffs, pulled them down, and threw them to bank on top of her clothes.

There was something perfect about this moment. It was the kind of rare, fleeting moment that people could spend many years trying to recapture. The sun was just warm enough, and the wind blew in a gentle breeze. Richard began to soap her shoulders and chest. He paused to massage each breast before moving on. He turned her around and began to lather her neck and back. When he had finished with the part of her that was above the water, he rinsed off the excess lather, reached around to hand her the soap, and began to kiss her on the neck.

Mary Ann purred. "It's my turn," she said. She turned around to face him and began to massage his chest and neck. "While you were working, I was watching your muscles. They're so well defined—every muscle you have looks strong."

He smiled, leaned forward, and kissed her. She dropped the soap, put her arms around him, and pulled him toward her. "From what I can feel under the surface," she said, "I'd say that you've gotten used to the cold water."

"I'd have to be dead not to respond to you," he said. "Would you like to move to that grassy spot over on the bank? It might be a little more comfortable." He led her toward the water's edge.

On the bank, they gathered their clothes and made a pallet on the soft grass.

The lovemaking act itself was short-lived, but, in both their memories, it would seem like a dream that had gone on forever.

Afterward, they lay back on the pallet of clothes and gazed up at the blue sky, "Richard Kyle," said Mary Ann, "you are one hell of a man, and you have the finest touch I have ever experienced."

"Well, Miss Phillips, I can tell you that you're about the prettiest thing I've ever seen. I haven't enjoyed an afternoon this much in my life. As for my touch, I might do even better, if I had more practice."

"I guess we'll have to see what we can do about that," she replied, and then kissed him again.

CHAPTER 11

adding heat to the fire

Jack didn't need an alarm as long as Gracie was around. Thirty minutes before first light, the cat would leave her position at his feet, circle around to the head of the bed, balance herself on the narrow metal headboard, and stalk back and forth until Jack woke up. Most of the time, she didn't make a sound as she moved around the house, but when it was time to go outside, she would not be ignored. First, she would extend her front claws as she walked across the metal, making a clicking sound. If that didn't work, she would bat at the lampshade on the night table. As a last resort, she would position herself on Jack's chest, purr loudly, and reach out with one of her paws to touch his chin.

"Good morning, Gracie," Jack said, smiling. "Are you ready to go exploring?"

Jack rolled out of bed and headed for the bathroom. While he brushed his teeth and took his pills, Gracie paced back and forth at the bathroom door. If he took longer than expected, she would begin to complain. After Jack finished in the bathroom, he opened a small packet of wet cat food. Gracie licked the moisture from the food, saving the solids for later. While she got her nourishment, Jack put on a kettle for a cup of hot tea.

When the tea was ready, he opened the door and walked to the bottom of the stairs to drink it. Jack enjoyed the sunrise across the delta. Despite her hurry to get outside, the cat didn't stray far, as long as he was at the bottom of the steps.

Jack and Gracie were both creatures of habit, and they had developed a degree of comfort in the order of these little routines.

When the sun began to turn from orange to yellow, Jack made his way back up the steps to take his shower and get ready for the day. Gracie disappeared into a world that only she knew. For both of them, the rest of the day was up for grabs. Gracie was on constant alert for dogs, bigger cats, and the occasional raccoon. Jack dealt with an ever-changing world that caused him some consternation. Mary Ann was a warm, comforting presence in Jack's life. She treated him like a brother but never made demands. Richard and his crew were fun. Jack would stand on the edge of their conversations for hours at a time, listening as they talked about women, sports, and cars. He seldom added anything unless he was addressed directly, but just the thought of not being an outsider felt good to him. It was Moon who added a degree of uncertainty. His wild, exaggerated plans, designed to change the world and forgotten the next day, reminded Jack of people he had known in the clinics that had been a part of his life. Mary Ann was the shield that Jack stood behind whenever Moon went off the deep end. Moon's romance with Kate had muted his manic interludes, but all of their elements were still there.

A recent addition to Jack's routine was a visit to Peeler's each morning. A piece of coconut cream pie with peaked meringue and a cup of hot, black coffee were worth the ten-minute walk down the highway. As Jack walked across the gravel parking lot, loggers were heading out to the timberland across the river. By eight o'clock, the farmers who had taken their men to field returned for one last cup of coffee. At nine, the businessmen from downtown began to gather. In the meantime, Jack would pretty well have the cafe to himself.

Most places had their own distinctive smells, and Jack was particularly sensitive to that form of sense memory. Cafes, with the wide range of foods they served, were like brightly colored, layered paintings that got more complex the closer he looked. Old coffee and the odor of burned food tended to muddy the tastes and colors. Canned vegetables all tended to have the same dull, gray feel, but fresh fruits like apples, peaches, and strawberries injected yellow, red, green, and orange sounds into the mix. Jack could sit for hours in a new place, deciphering the colors and tastes. But it was hard to concentrate when there were a lot of people around, which was one of the reasons he liked Peeler's at this time of morning—that and the coconut cream pie

"Morning, Jack," Mamie said as he walked in and went to his regular table. "You want the usual?"

Jack nodded and slid into one of the booths under the window.

Mamie slid the pie case's glass door open and pulled out one of the pies. She carefully cut a slice and transferred it to a dessert plate. "Here you go, Jack. This is fresh this morning. Let me know how you like it."

Jack nodded, picked up his fork, and cut into the cream pie.

Mamie didn't have to wait for Jack to tell her that he liked it; she could see it on his face. When Jack smiled, Mamie smiled. She started to go back to her work, but then hesitated.

"Hon, can we talk?" Mamie asked. She sat down across from Jack. Not waiting for a reply, she plowed in. "I'm worried about Albert Lawrence."

"Mr. Moon is Mr. Moon," Jack said.

"He just seems different recently," she said.

"I heard him say he was in love."

Mamie smiled. "He's always in love. He's been in love with one skirt or another since he was five years old."

"Ms. Mamie, you know him a lot better than I do, but I think this is different."

"What makes you say so?"

"I heard him telling some of his friends that he was gonna marry this girl," Jack said.

"Are you talking about the schoolteacher? What's her name ... Ellis?"

"Yes, ma'am, that's the one. Her name is Kate Ellis."

"So, what do you think of her?" Mamie asked.

"It's none of my business ... but I think she's a lot like Mr. Moon."

"How do you mean, Jack?"

"Well, it's not any of my business," Jack said.

"Please, tell me. I won't repeat anything you say, and you can't tell me anything about him I don't already know."

"I think this lady knows what she wants, and she'll do anything it takes to get it. Hook or crook," Jack said.

While they were talking, the next group of coffee-drinkers began to filter in. "That's about what I thought," Mamie said. "I heard that some of the parents had complained to the school board about her hanging around down at Moon's place. They said it wasn't a fittin' place for a schoolteacher to be spending her time. Said it was setting a bad example for the students. Bunch of sanctimonious bastards ... but don't get me started on that crowd."

Jack had finished his pie.

She picked up his plate. "Would you like some more coffee?" she asked.

"No, ma'am. I got to get going. I'm barbecuing a side of beef today. It's gonna take most of the day to get everything done. You want me to set aside some ribs for you?"

"That would be nice," she said. "I've heard real good things about your barbecue. I'll pick it up on my way home from work."

There really wasn't any hurry, but Peeler's was beginning to fill up, and Jack felt the need to get out of doors and walk. He left the cafe and cut across the city graveyard. Jack enjoyed the walk through the graveyard; the oak trees were big and old, and they faintly reminded him of his childhood. Most days, if he had time, he stopped, sat under the trees and let his mind wander, searching for clues of his lost youth. There were several places in Gum Ridge that gave him that same kind of feel: the courthouse and its broad lawns, the First Baptist church with its big, wide steps and large columns, the rotating red and white pole at Rooster's Barbershop, the blinking stoplight at the junction of Highway 80 and Main Street and Mr. Kim's store, with the dragons in the front window. The longer he lived in Gum Ridge, the more he realized that his being there was no accident. But, exactly *why* he knew this, he didn't know.

After he had completed his circuit, he stopped at Kim's to pick up the meat he would be cooking. Kim had gotten a good deal on some beef that was slightly freezer burned. Mary Ann and Jack had gone over the day before to see if it would be good enough for barbecuing. They had left it in Kim's food locker overnight.

"Lee, I came to pick up the meat," Jack said to Kim Lee, who was stocking shelves in the back.

"Give me a minute, and I will help you. I've got old wheelbarrow in the back. It'll make much easier to carry meat to grill. You get the wheelbarrow while I finish up here."

When Jack returned with the wheelbarrow, he and Kim wheeled it into the cooler. Kim had cut the meat into manageable pieces, and the two of them filled the wheelbarrow with half of it. They wheeled it over to the cafe, deposited it on Jack's prep table, and went back for a second trip.

Jack was a master at barbecue. For years, he toyed with his sauce, trying to get just the right amount of honey and vinegar, and balancing the garlic, salt, and pepper. He would begin by searing the meat, and then he would dry-smoke it away from the direct heat. He slowly added the sauces, the kind depending on the type of meat. For tougher meats, he added more vinegar; for wild game, more sweetness. Much of this type of cooking had to do with the feel of the meat. Raw meat had a soft, pliable feel, and overcooked meat was hard—he strove for somewhere in between. As for most of his dishes, Jack had no written recipes for his barbecues, and when people asked for the recipe for his sauce, Jack would mumble something about a little bit of this and a little bit of that.

Jack was fully immersed in a plume of smoke and the aroma of singed meat. Unlike the effects of dry roasting, the barbecue manifested itself in a cloud of red and brown shapes. These appeared on a background of summer greens and contrasted against the black, angular harshness of gasoline and hot asphalt that dominated the street. Had he been a painter, he would have been a colorist like Van Gogh, with his visions that contained more than was seen by the casual eye. As the meat cooked, a parade of pickups drove by with their windows rolled down. Each trucker would slow down, turn a solemn face toward the cooker, take in a deep breath, smile, and then drive on.

Mid-afternoon, Mary Ann came out to the cooker with a pitcher of ice tea. "Don't get yourself overheated," she said, handing Jack a glass of tea. Mary Ann circled the cooker, taking in the smell of the dark meat. "Jack, my friend," she said, "I think you've outdone yourself this time. I've never smelled anything *half* that good. For the last two hours, I've been fielding calls from people wanting to know what in the hell you're cooking up. I hope you've cooked enough, 'cause we're gonna have half the town down here for supper. I've already got ten to-go orders for tonight."

"I cooked everything I had. Will that be enough?" Jack asked.

"What if I sent Joy over to the A&P to pick up some extra chicken breasts and unshucked corn? Would you have time to cook them?"

"Sure," he said.

While they were talking, Moon pulled into the parking lot at full speed and came to an abrupt stop in his parking spot near the front of the cafe. It appeared that he was talking to the air. "I'll get your money to you tomorrow," he said. "Right. Yeah, I understand. Noon, no later. Adios."

He got out of his car and walked back to where Mary Ann and Jack were standing.

"Who were you talking to?" Mary Ann asked.

"What did you say? I didn't hear you," Moon said as he removed the phone earpiece from his right ear and a wax plug from his left.

"What's with the earplugs?" she asked.

"If you'd keep up with the times, Phillips, you wouldn't have to ask stupid questions," Moon said. "I'll have you know that this is the latest in electronic gear for the busy businessman on the go. This little black thing ..." He pointed to a quarter-sized lump in the middle of the wire. "... is the receiver I talk into. Kate bought it for me while we were in Jonesboro last week. The problem is that I have to wear an earplug in the other ear to hear, even with the phone turned up as loud as it'll go. I think there's something wrong with the unit."

"Maybe you're going deaf," she suggested.

"Whatever." Moon had already turned his attention to Jack. "All right, Jack, how much did all this cost?" He pointed at the racks of meat in the cooker.

"I think you'll come out at least even," Jack said.

"Look, Moon," Mary Ann said, "we got this meat in a fire sale from Kim across the street."

Jack pulled a small rack of ribs off the fire and put it on a plate.

"These are about done, Mr. Moon. Would you like to try a little bit of it?"

Moon held his hand up. "No, I don't think so. In fact, I think I'm probably going to become a vegetarian."

Mary Ann began laughing. "Moon, this is the silliest shit I ever heard! *You*, a vegetarian? What brought this about?"

"Well, Kate ..."

"I thought so," Mary Ann said.

"Anyway, Kate gave me this book about being a vegetarian. It's about this guy named Gandhi. She says it's wrong for us to inflict our judgment on animals. It don't make a lot of sense to me, but if she wants to do it, I guess we will. We'll probably teach our kids to be vegetarians, too." Moon seemed to be entirely in earnest.

"That might be hard, Mr. Moon," Jack said.

"What do you know about raising kids?" Moon asked.

"It's not that. It is just, well ... the other thing that Mr. Gandhi gave up."

"And what was that, wise guy?"

"Sex. Mr. Gandhi gave up sex. I guess you and Ms. Kate could adopt," Jack said.

"Yeah, Moon, you could adopt!" Mary Ann said, laughing at Moon's dilemma.

"You people are impossible," Moon said. "I've got work to do." He turned and went indoors.

For the next several hours, Jack tended to the cooker. Just as he was finishing the last batch of ribs and chicken, Kate rolled into the parking lot in her yellow Volkswagen. Her parking spot, Moon had painted the sign himself, was right beside Moon's. Kate remained in the car for several minutes, redoing her makeup and combing her hair.

Before going into the cafe, she went out back, where Jack was cooking.

As Kate approached the cooker, Mary Ann came out with a plastic bag full of garbage.

Kate shook her head in wonder. "Jack, that barbeque smells wonderful! Could I have a little taste?"

Jack looked at her. "But, Ms. Kate, Mr. Moon said you were a vegetarian."

"What are you talking about, Jack?" she asked, a look of astonishment on her face.

"Moon said that you both were vegetarians now," Mary Ann verified.

Kate stared at them both. "That's the silliest thing I ever heard! Where did he get that idea?"

Mary Ann took the lid off the trash can and put the bag into the container. "Said he got it from you—something about Gandhi."

"Crap, I really have to be careful what I say around that man," Kate said. "I was only speaking ministerially, like my father."

"What do you mean?" Mary Ann asked.

"You know, like something we should all think about, but that nobody is really gonna do—like a lot of Christianity. Now that *that's* settled, can I have a rib? I'm starving!"

While Kate was feasting on the ribs, Moon came out of the cafe with a yellow legal pad in one hand, a glass of tea in the other, and his telephone earpiece in his ear.

"Well, Moon," said Mary Ann, "it looks like your little vegetarian has fallen off the wagon."

Kate smiled from behind a sauce-covered rib.

"But ... I thought ..." he said, pointing at the rib.

"But they smelled so *good*," Kate said, half-apologetically.

"Okay, never mind. I've got work to do before we leave. Don't eat up all my profits while you wait."

Eager to change the subject, Kate asked, "Where we going tonight, Moon?"

"I don't know. Dealer's choice," he said, disappearing into the cafe.

Kate was in a bind. She'd had visions of dancing the night away with Moon and then holing up in cheap motels for hours of passionate lovemaking, but it just wasn't happening. Her wild child had started showing up in tailored suits. He had traded in his cowboy boots for a pair of Italian leather shoes. All he wanted to talk about was Bill Clinton, George Bush, and the future of the space program. It sounded like he'd been reading an encyclopedia. And now, the idiot had decided he—they—were going to be vegetarians. She wanted to talk about his bookie business and the racetrack hoods with the New Jersey accents. She wanted to hear about the dog track, cockfights, and his secret marijuana crop. But when she asked about any of these things, he changed the subject.

For weeks she had been formulating a plan to get Moon into the sack. The plan revolved around the contents of her handbag and a good opportunity. The handbag was always ready, and Moon had given her the opportunity with his off-hand remark about Dealer's Choice.

Jack finished up the meat, Mary Ann went back to her customers, and Kate went to the restroom to clean up after the ribs. Moon came out of his office, a yellow legal pad full of bets still in his hand. "You know, there ought to be a law," he said, adding up the betting tallies.

"A law about what?" Mary Ann asked.

"A law about those Yankees coming down here and taking all our money back up north."

"What money are you talking about?" Mary Ann knew better than to get him started, but she just couldn't resist.

"Phillips, haven't you been listening to what I've been saying?"

"Moon, you've been locked away in that office of yours for the last two hours. How should I know what you've been saying?"

"Yeah, right, yeah. Well, you see, it's like this: they come down here, open up these casinos and tracks, skim off all the profit, and take it back to New York City. But I think I've figured a way to get a part of the deal."

"So what is it now?" she asked.

"You know those buses that the casinos use to haul folks back and forth? What I was thinking about doing was buying me a bus and hauling people back and forth to the dog track in West Memphis. I can make book over and back on all kinds of things. I could charge fifteen or twenty bucks one-way, but the *real* money's in the gambling. I got a buddy who can sell me crop fuel, and, since it ain't taxed, I could get a break there."

"Sounds like a surefire scheme to lose money to me," Mary Ann said.

Kate came up to the bar. "What scheme?" she said.

"Never mind," Moon said. "It's just an idea I had." Moon could change the direction of a conversation on a dime. "Now, let's get onto to something *real* important!" He leaned over the bar and smiled at Kate. "So, what do you want to do tonight, young lady? You name it."

Kate had waited several weeks for that line. "Road trip," she said. "I want to ride through the Ozarks with the top down in that convertible of yours."

"Road trip it is!" Moon said. "Let me get rid of my papers, and I'll be ready to go."

Soon, they were driving northwest, heading for the foothills of the Ozark Mountains. When they came to the outskirts of Batesville, Arkansas, Kate motioned for Moon to pull into the parking lot of the Bluebird Motel.

She jumped out, went inside, and emerged a few minutes later with a set of keys.

"What's going on?" Moon asked, half guessing.

"Don't ask any questions. I've got a surprise." She led him toward room number eleven, opened the door, and motioned toward the bed. "Just get comfortable. Set yourself down, right there on that bed."

She disappeared into the bathroom. When she reemerged, she looked like a model from a lingerie catalog. In her large bag purse, Kate had squirreled away a thin nightgown that left absolutely nothing to the imagination. Moon, still in his suit and shoes, sat stiffly on the bed.

"What do you think?" she asked.

"You're beautiful … just beautiful."

"Well?" she said.

"Well, what?" he asked.

"Well, get undressed, stupid! I want to make love to you."

Moon didn't move; he didn't say anything; he just sat there. She was the most beautiful thing he had ever seen. He wanted her more than life. He loved her more than he had expected to love anyone or anything … but this just wasn't right. He had been in and out or more beds than most men see in a lifetime, but this was supposed to be different. *She* was supposed to be different.

For Kate, this was to be the fulfillment of a long-held dream. Deep in her soul, she had been sure that if she could get him in the right situation, he wouldn't be able to resist. But she had been wrong, and, through his hesitation, his silence, and his body language, she knew it.

At that moment, for the briefest of instants, Moon could have changed his mind, shifted gears, and had wonderful sex, but the end result would have been the same.

As he looked into her eyes, large tears formed in them, and she turned toward the bathroom. "I'll change, and you can take me home," she said.

The ride home was quiet and dark, with both of them immersed in their thoughts, both trying to figure out where they had gone wrong. When Moon pulled up in front of her apartment, the passenger door was opened before the wheels had stopped turning.

"I'll see you tomorrow," he said.

There was no answer; she slid out of the seat and walked away.

CHAPTER 12

a fortune worth telling

Mary Ann and Jack were finishing the cleanup after Sunday lunch. "You doing anything tomorrow?" Mary Ann asked.

Jack shook his head.

"I'm going down to Sylvia's," she said. "You want to come along?"

"Sure," Jack said. Mary Ann had talked a lot about her friend Sylvia and how good a cook she was.

"I've got some things to do in the morning. How about I pick you up at your house at about one o'clock?"

"If it's okay," he said, "why don't you pick me up here? I've got some prep work to do for Tuesday."

Promptly at one, Mary Ann pulled into the parking lot at Moon's. Jack was sitting on the back step, smoking a cigarette.

"You ready?" she asked from the truck.

Jack nodded, stood up, dropped his cigarette into the gravel, and crushed it with his foot. He walked around and got into the truck.

"You must have been doing some serious thinking," she said. "I've noticed that you don't smoke unless you've got something on your mind. You're not getting ready to wander off again, are you?"

"No, I'm fine. It's just that there are things about this town that I remember. Things about the cafe. Sometimes, at the end of the day—or like this morning, when I'm here by myself—I get the distinct feel that I've been here before. That I know this place."

"Maybe you *have* been here before," Mary Ann suggested. "Have you ever told the doctor that gives you your medicine about this?"

He shook his head. "They're not interested in that kind of stuff," he said. "It's just like the tastes and colors of sounds. When I told them about *that*, they told me I needed to increase my medicine."

"Well, if you do start feeling bad, let me know," she said. "Don't just go wandering off." She reached over and patted him on the leg. "You hear me?"

He looked up at her and nodded.

Sylvia lived in the back of her old cafe. She and her husband had run Sylvia's Cafe and Prince's Liquor Store for several decades. After his death, she closed the liquor store and, eventually, the cafe. After crossing the tracks, Mary Ann kept going straight past the faded sign for Armstrong's Grocery and turned into a narrow alley. Grass grew up around the edges of the alley, giving it an abandoned look. At its end was a closed, rusted gate big enough for a small car to pass through, and beside that was a smaller, wooden gate for humans. Neither was locked. Outside the gates was a world of crumbling brick walls and rotting wood, but walking into Sylvia Prince's yard was like walking into a fairyland—a brightly colored world of fantasy and myth. In place of grass was a blanket of white and tan river-stones. In the far corner, toward the river, was a patch of blue stone surrounded by inverted and half-buried red bottles, and in the middle of the blue garden was a pedestal with a golden-colored gazing ball on top. In the middle of the yard, a large black and silver Harley-Davidson motorcycle seemed to be bolting up out of the ground—it had been half-buried, up to the level of the clutch. In the center of the enclosure was a small peach tree that had been turned into a bottle tree. Hanging from its limbs were the same kind of bright red, yellow, and blue bottles that outlined the small designs in the yard. Nearest the house, on the far side, was a raised bed featuring a variety of different shades of green. From this plot of green emanated a world of wonderful herbal fragrances.

By the wall nearest the gate was a brightly colored wagon—a gypsy *varda*. It was a bow-topped affair as ornate as a carnival wagon, decorated with red and brown horses, winged serpents, and tongues of red and yellow flame. The rear of the wagon had been connected to the house, and its front appeared ready—with traces, breast choke, halter, and reins in place—to accept a large horse and be pulled away from the house.

Wind chimes swayed gently in the afternoon breeze. As Mary Ann and Jack walked toward the back porch, a thin older woman came out the house. Her long, black hair fell on her shoulders like a beautiful mane. Her red cotton dress, accented with yellow and a touch of purple, clung to her body as she moved. She carried a broad-brimmed straw hat and a small basket. She was followed by a brown and white puppy that playfully bit at her long skirt. Unaware that she had company, Sylvia knelt down and began playing with the dog.

"Sylvia," Mary Ann said quietly.

Sylvia looked up. "Mary Ann, sweetheart, I didn't see you standing there."

"It looks like we caught you at a bad time. You seem to be heading some-where."

"Nowhere important," Sylvia said. "Snuffy and I were just going down to the river to look for rocks."

"We could come back at some other time, if you want," Mary Ann said.

"Oh, my goodness, no. The rocks will be there tomorrow. I haven't seen you in a while. Where have you been?"

"We've been real busy down at the cafe. Mostly because of Jack, here." She turned and pointed at Jack, who was standing several steps behind.

"Hello, Jack. I'm Sylvia. Welcome to my home. Your reputation precedes you. Mary Ann speaks highly of your cooking. I guess I'll have to come down to the cafe and try it sometime."

When Jack made no move forward, Sylvia stepped off the porch and approached him. Expecting a handshake, Jack extended his arm, but Sylvia surprised him by enveloping him in her arms as if she had known him for ages. "Welcome to my home," she said. "There are no strangers here."

Jack smiled. There was something very familiar about her fragrance—a hint of angelica in her hair, a scent of lavender in the warmth of her cotton shirt, and the soft feel of jasmine and almond in her gentle touch.

"I think I need to sit down," Jack said. He had been overwhelmed by the sense of this place and this woman.

"Are you all right?" Sylvia asked, backing off a step.

Mary Ann walked toward him. "You okay?"

"Yeah, I'm okay. It's this woman and this place."

"Yeah, I bet. All the smells and bright colors. I hadn't thought about that. Let's sit you down."

There were several pieces of wicker furniture on the porch. Mary Ann guided Jack into one of the chairs.

"Can I do anything?" Sylvia asked. "Would you like a glass of ice water?"

Jack nodded. "That would be nice."

When Sylvia returned with the water, Mary Ann asked Jack, "Would you mind if I told her your secret? She'd never tell anyone."

Jack nodded, and Mary Ann began to explain about the tasting of colors and shapes.

Sylvia nodded knowingly. "Have no fear—your secret will be safe with me. When I was a child, one of my cousins had something like that. It can be a heavy burden—I know that it was for him. He began drinking, and, by the time he was thirteen or fourteen, we'd lost track of him. The funny thing is a lot of people have gifts that they never even know about. Sometimes, it takes some looking to find out what they are. Most people are so concerned with doing the 'right thing'—with being accepted by other people. The idea of standing out in a crowd scares them to death. They never see their gifts; they never know they exist. Sometimes, they get a glimpse, but it's fleeting. Are you beginning to feel better?"

"Yes, I'm better," he said.

"Good. Let's go inside."

Sylvia's living room was full of overstuffed, brightly colored sofas and padded chairs. Mary Ann and Jack both sat down on the large sofa by the window. Sylvia sat cross-legged on a big red pillow on the floor.

"What brings you two down to this side of the tracks?" Sylvia asked, smiling.

"It's like this …" Mary Ann started, "… I've met this guy."

"Oh, I see," Sylvia said. She had heard this story before.

"And you know I haven't had the best track record."

"Well, that's one way to look at it."

"I think it's time to read the stones."

"This must be serious," Sylvia said.

"Maybe, maybe not."

"Let's have some tea, and then we can get to the stones."

Sylvia eased herself up from the pillow and made her way into the small galley kitchen that separated the apartment from the old juke joint. While Sylvia put the water on to boil, Mary Ann got up and walked around the living room

"When I was a teenager," she said to Jack, "my friends and I spent a lot of time down here. It was the only place where we could hear live music. There was a band every Friday and Saturday night—most of the time, this place was jumping! We weren't old enough to be in the big room—when they got to drinking, the crowds could get a little rough. Mama didn't like it much that we came down here, but she knew that Sylvia and Melos would take good care of us and not let us get into any trouble.

"Jack, do you need sugar for your tea?" Sylvia asked from the kitchen.

"No, ma'am," he replied. "Just plain."

She soon came out with a tray holding three cups of chamomile tea. She handed one of the cups to Jack and another to Mary Ann. She smiled at Mary Ann. "This should put us in the right frame of mind for the stones to fall well," she said.

"Jack," Sylvia said. "There's something very familiar about you. Do we know each other from somewhere?"

"I don't think so," he said, "but there are a lot of things I don't remember."

When they finished their tea, Sylvia said, "Come with me, Mary Ann. We'll go to the *varda*."

Mary Ann looked at Jack. "Jack can come with me," she said. "I don't have anything to hide from him."

"I think it would be best if Jack stayed here," said Sylvia. "He has a force about him that might distort the stones. He can come in after we've finished. Trust me, it's best."

"Will you be okay?" Mary Ann asked Jack.

Jack nodded.

This wasn't the first time Mary Ann had sought out Sylvia's assistance. There had always been a bit of mystery to the juke joint south of the tracks, and there had always been a bit of mystery to Sylvia. On a half-dozen occasions, Sylvia had thrown the stones in order to help Mary Ann find an answer. Each time the questions had involved men, the answer was always the same—drop him like a hot potato and stay away. Usually, Mary Ann had ignored the stones.

Around her neck, Mary Ann wore a small locket that Sylvia had given her when she was a teenager. In the locket was a small white stone. Each time Mary Ann came to have the stones thrown, Sylvia would ask for the stone hung around her neck.

They walked from the living area through the bedroom, down a short hall, and up three steps into the back of the brightly colored wagon.

Sylvia's whole life was contained within her *varda*. Nothing that happened in her life was left out of the wagon. The throwing of the stones, the reading of tarot cards, the reading of palms—all were done in the *varda*.

Sylvia lit incense, and the two women sat and waited for the room to prepare itself. While they waited, Sylvia assembled the cloth and stones that would help to answer the questions that were on Mary Ann's mind.

"Is Richard the one?" Sylvia asked.

"Yes," Mary Ann replied.

When Sylvia was satisfied that the room was ready, she laid out the circle of Mary Ann's life. She took the *putshe*—a small purse—from her waist and opened the drawstring.

"Reach into the *putshe*," she said, holding out the purse. "Choose one of the stones and remove it."

Mary Ann did as she was instructed.

"Now, take your stone out of the locket and put it into the *putshe*."

As Mary Ann obeyed, Sylvia explained. "Your stone has absorbed the energy of your life. Now, it will have a chance to speak." She closed the drawstring and jostled the nine stones around inside the sack.

"The incense and the aroma that is distinctive to you have prepared the room. The stones have lain together and are warm with the energy of your life. You come to the circle as an earnest seeker of the truth. Now, it is time to ask the stones what it is that you want to know."

Mary Ann looked into Sylvia's eyes. "I think that I'm falling in love with Richard Kyle," she said. "He's a nice man. My question is: Is he the right man for me? Should I let this continue? I really don't want to get hurt again."

Sylvia rolled the stones out of the bag into the circle. When they came to rest, she pronounced it a good throw

"Look … that your stone has landed on the centerline means that you will have a good future. The line to the left indicates a long life on a true course. There is money in your future. See the square off to the side of the line? That is your man, Richard. The line points toward your choice. The combination of the three-stone line and the square is strong magic. The stone off on the edge of the circle is the only worry—it represents an unknown factor that can go in any direction. It means that there is risk in anything you do.

"Now, Mary Ann, take your stone and put it back in the locket. When you go to the other room, I will gather the stones. It is bad luck for me to disturb or touch them until you have departed the *varda*. Go and check on your friend. I'll be out in a minute."

Sitting in the living room with Snuffy asleep in his lap, Jack was stroking the puppy and staring out into the backyard. He didn't seem to have moved since they left.

Mary Ann walked into the kitchen area and poured herself another cup of tea. "Jack, would you like more tea?" she asked.

Pulled out of his private world, Jack looked at Mary Ann and said, "No, thank you, I'm fine."

"Isn't this a delightful place?" she asked as she sat by him on the sofa.

"I remember this place," Jack said.

"You mean ... you've been here before?"

"No, it's not that. It's more like I've been someplace *like* this. The colors sound so rich and warm. The movement of the red and blue bottles on the tree has a cinnamon feel."

Sylvia had entered the living area in time to hear this last comment, and she walked over to Jack's seat. "Jack ... you said that you have problems remembering your past. Sometimes, that's for the best. There are often things in one's past that are just too painful to remember—deep in our souls, we choose not to remember them. I know that is true for me."

Jack looked into Sylvia's eyes, and said, "I remember the smell in your hair—the angelica. I'm not sure where it's from, but I do remember it. I want to say that it's from my childhood—maybe my mother. I don't remember her, but I do remember the wavy form of angelica and the billowy cloud of lavender."

Sylvia got up and went to her bedroom. She returned with a small locket similar to Mary Ann's. "Jack, this is a moonstone—one of my favorites. It aids in memory and collects tidbits from your past. Wear this around your neck. If you ever want me to help you remember, bring it back, and we'll use its stored energy."

"There is one thing I'd like to do, Mrs. Sylvia," Jack said.

"What's that?" she asked.

"I'd like to come here and eat sometime."

"Jack, my friend, you can come here and eat anytime you want."

CHAPTER 13

the aftermath

It was a hot afternoon, and it hadn't rained in two weeks. The dust on Border Street, just east of the cafe, billowed up each time a truck passed. The fine, powdery dust found its way into every nook and cranny, and it made the air feel gritty. The air conditioner on Moon's back wall was working overtime and barely keeping up.

The track was closed for a couple of days, so Mary Ann convinced Jack not to cook a big meal, in order to cut down on the heat. It was just as well, since only the regulars showed up on a day like this.

"Jack, did Moon come in while I was at the grocery store?" Mary Ann asked.

Jack shook his head. "I haven't seen Mr. Moon since the weekend."

"I've got some checks he needs to sign. These suppliers aren't going to wait forever for their money. You know, since he got that little phone of his, he hardly shows up. It was a pain in the ass listening to that answer-phone all day, with all of his bettors, but at least he had to *be* here, so we could get some business done."

"You think Ms. Kate has anything to do with it?"

Mary Ann smirked. "He's got himself a dose, all right," she said. "I've never seen Moon fall for someone like he has for that little girl."

Jack pondered for a minute, then asked, "If they get married, you think Ms. Kate will come to work here at the cafe?"

"Lord, I hope not! First of all, I don't think they're gonna get married. There's something about those two that just don't ring true. And second, that girl is a shit-stirrer. She'd have everybody around here fighting all the time."

The side door opened, and Moon walked in. His button-down dress shirt and chino kakis, which had looked so clean and freshly starched when he had put them on several days earlier, were now dirty and stained. His hair was disheveled. If neither Mary Ann nor Jack had spoken, Moon would have walked right past them and into his office.

"Damn, man," Mary Ann said, "you look like you've slept in those clothes for a week!"

"I've been a little preoccupied, I guess." Usually, when Moon talked, you could hear him clearly across a crowded room, but, this afternoon, he sounded more like Jack—quiet and mumbling.

Mary Ann went behind the counter and put her hand on his forehead. "Do you have a fever?" she asked. It would have been natural for Moon to brush her hand aside, but he didn't.

"I'm not sick. At least, not like you're thinking."

"Well, what's wrong with you then?" she asked.

"Kate and I had a fight. Well … it wasn't really a fight. A fight might have been better, actually. It's more like we had a misunderstanding, and now she won't talk to me."

Mary Ann led Moon around the bar and sat him down at one of the tables while Jack poured him a glass of tea.

"What did you guys fight about?" she asked.

Jack set the tea down in front of Moon. "Was it about being a vegetarian?" he asked.

"What?" Moon looked up at Jack. "What the hell are you talking about?"

"Jack," Mary Ann said, "I doubt very much that this had anything to do with eating meat or not eating meat. Don't worry, honey, you didn't cause this." She turned back to Moon. "What *did* it have to do with, Moon?"

"I'd rather not say. It's just … a real important subject that we don't see eye to eye on."

"Well, maybe you can work it out."

"That's the problem," he said. "If I could get her to talk to me, I'm *sure* that we could deal with this and move on! But I've been parked in front of her house or at the school for the last five days, trying to get her to talk to me. She just stares right past me like I wasn't there. I don't know what to do."

"You want a burger?" Jack asked. "I could fix you a burger and some onion rings."

Moon shook his head.

"You know, Moon, Jack's right," Mary Ann said. "Knowing you, you probably haven't had anything to eat in days. It'll make you feel better, even if you aren't hungry."

"Okay, sure, whatever," Moon said. "But I don't want to eat it out here. I don't feel like talking to people right now. I'm gonna go into my office. Bring the burger back there. If anybody calls, I'm not here. Unless it's Kate."

Moon trudged into his office and shut the door.

"Wow," Mary Ann said, "I've known him since we were little kids, and I've *never* seen him like this. He's *really* got a dose."

"Do you think he might hurt himself?" Jack asked.

"You mean … commit suicide?"

Jack nodded.

"Why do you ask that?"

"That's what they always ask me when *I* get sick."

"I guess he could do something that stupid—anything's possible. But, with Moon, I think that it's really unlikely. He may love this girl, but he loves himself more, and I can't see him doing anything that final."

"Maybe food will help," Jack said.

"Couldn't hurt," said Mary Ann.

Richard, Art, and Joe came in and ordered a round of beer.

"I thought you guys were going to be working on the car till after midnight," Mary Ann said.

"I just couldn't stand the idea of spending another evening away from you," Richard said.

"What a crock of shit!" Art said, laughing. "The air conditioner at the garage was out, and it was too hot to work, so we called it a night."

Richard smiled. "Well, that too, but …" His voice trailed off.

"That's one of the things I like about you, Mr. Kyle," Mary Ann said. "You're such a smooth talker, and you think well on your feet, too! I'll get the beers."

Mary Ann was cleaning the most recent layer of dust from the top of the bar when H. T. Lincoln came in.

"Evening, boys," he said, touching the brim of his hat. He turned toward Mary Ann. "Evening, Ms. Kitty." H. T. was stuck in the days of the old west.

"Evening, Marshall Dillon," Mary Ann said in an affected western accent. "Want a shot of red-eye?"

"Thanks, but no thanks. I'm looking for Moon. Is he around?"

"Sure, he's on the phone back in his office. I'll get him for you."

Most people didn't seem to affect Jack one way or the other, but policemen were an exception. When he noticed H. T., he made an excuse to go to the store-room.

Mary Ann knocked on the door to Moon's office.

"Moon, H. T.'s out here. He wants to talk to you."

"Yeah, I'll be out in a minute!" Moon shouted.

When Moon appeared, he seemed to be a better mood. "Hey, fat boy," he said to his friend H. T., "what do you need?" H. T. wasn't fat, but he and Moon had a running gag about which of them would chunk up first.

"I need to talk to you, buddy."

"Go ahead, shoot," Moon said.

"Not here. In private. How about your office?"

Moon shook his head. "It's too small," he said. "Come on, let's go out front." They went outside and stood beside H. T.'s car.

"Moon, you know that schoolteacher you been dating?"

"Yeah ... did something happen to her?" Moon didn't like the sound of this.

"No, that ain't it. She come down to the station this morning and said you been following her and parking in front of her apartment. She said she knew her rights, and to tell you that, if you don't quit, she's gonna file charges against you. And I got the feeling she was serious. I asked the prosecuting attorney, and he said she could file stalking charges. She might not make 'em stick, but she could sure make your life hard. It looks to me like you ought to stay away from her. She wasn't kidding."

Moon had had some real scares in his life, and he'd even been sad a few times, but he'd never been utterly, completely rejected.

"Sure, whatever, H. T.," he said. "I don't want to cause any trouble. You tell her I understand." He was lying. He didn't understand. He'd been told that what women really wanted was for men to respect them—to treat them like ladies, to cotton to their whims, to speak nice and soft about things of love—and look what it got him. Today and forever, he would remember his love for Kate, but he would never understand.

CHAPTER 14

cook like magic

Jack opened the gate and walked into the backyard; he was spellbound by the fragrances of Sylvia's dreamland. A light but unmistakable green cloud hovered over the herb garden, spilling out like a low-lying fog onto the white rocks. The bottle tree, with its red, yellow, and blue glass, had the flavor of confectioner's sugar and cinnamon. The old motorcycle emerging from the ground gave out a silent roar that was blue and red with purple edges. The red and gold *varda* with inlays of lightning bolts and charging horses had an earthy aroma—like a good, full-bodied wine, it left a taste of blackberries and oak in his nose.

Sylvia sat on the back porch with Snuffy in her lap. From his first visit to her, Jack and Sylvia each knew that the other needed few words. Jack walked around the yard absorbing the kaleidoscope of colors and tastes; Sylvia watched and stroked the puppy.

Jack completed his walk and sat down on the edge of the porch, near Sylvia's feet. "I brought the stone back," he said. He removed the moonstone necklace from around his neck and started to hand it to Sylvia.

"You hold on to it 'til we're ready to let it do its work." She pointed to the backyard. "Tell me, Jack, what do you hear and feel in this yard?"

Jack explained the mix of tastes and colors that the place conjured up.

Sylvia smiled. "I remember," she said, "that when I was a child, my Cousin Vaness had something like this—he could see and feel music. When he was four, he picked up his father's fiddle and began to play as if he had studied for years. The problem was that he got obsessed with hitting the right note. He played the same note for hours at a time. He would go for days without sleeping or eating. It took over his life. The only way he could get relief was with alcohol. Anyway, he ended up dying real young, but that boy could conjure up a spell with his fiddle. They buried him with it." She stood up. "You want to go fishing, Jack?" she asked.

"Sure, I guess so."

"There are a couple of poles rigged up in the shed at the back of the yard. Why don't you go get the poles and tackle while I get my shotgun?"

Jack got up and walked to the small shed at the back of the lot. On his right as he entered the shed was a wooden workbench, and on it was a tackle box. He picked up the box, two rods equipped with hooks, sinkers, and red and white bobbers, and a dip net.

As he left the shed, Sylvia came out of the house with a small single-barreled shotgun under her arm. She went over to the herb garden and picked up a small shovel.

"We'll dig up some worms down at the river. While we're down there, I'll see if I can kill a rabbit. If I do, I'll fix you a pie. You'll like that. My husband always liked my rabbit pie."

The distance from Sylvia's place to the river was a little over half a mile. They followed the tracks to the river, where a small footpath veered off to the south. A hundred yards downstream was a small sandbar. On the south side of the bar, water eddied out into a deep hole where Caney Creek flowed into the river.

Sylvia laid her shotgun on an old stump and motioned for Jack to leave the fishing equipment and follow her. She scampered up the steep bank and watched while Jack struggled up the incline. They walked into the woods until she found a rotten log. She brushed the leaves aside, and had soon unearthed a treasure trove of earthworms and grubs. They quickly collected enough bait for the evening. She re-covered the site with rotting wood and leaves, and they returned to the sand bar. Soon, she and Jack had baited their hooks and were waiting for the first fish to come their way. Sylvia noticed that the eddy current had washed Jack's cork into shallow water, and that the cork was lying on its side. As she was about to instruct him on the finer points of fishing for crappie and catfish—to tell him that the float must be upright—Jack's bobber disappeared under the water. The line snapped taut, and the reel began to whine. Jack looked at Sylvia. "What do I do?" he exclaimed. "What do I do?"

"Set the hook, Jack! Pull back hard and fast on the rod, and keep the tip up. You got a big one, and it looks like he's heading for that log up in the mouth of the creek. Don't let him do that! There's a bunch of limbs back in there, and you won't ever get him out."

"Here, you take it!" He handed the rod to Sylvia.

Sylvia realized that Jack had no idea what to do with a fishing line. She took the rod, set the crank, and pulled back abruptly on the rod, setting the hook in the mouth of the fish.

"That's a big fish you got there, Jack! You want to bring him in?"

"No, you do it. I'll just watch."

It was a good-sized catfish, and he was heading for a series of holes in the soft bank just beyond the fallen tree. If she pulled too hard, the fish would break the line, but if she gave it too much line, it would be under that tree and into a hole.

She waded out into the water, leading the fish away from the bank. She gave him a little line and then took back more than she gave. By the time she and the fish had battled for about three minutes Sylvia had waded about ten feet out into the water and was buried up to the middle of her calves in sand and mud.

"Bring the net, Jack! I'm going to need your help!"

Jack was mesmerized. He wasn't quite sure what he was supposed to do.

"Look, Jack, get the net and bring it out here. I'll guide the fish around to where you're standing, and you put the net under him and lift up."

Soon, Jack was standing far enough out in the water for Sylvia to direct the fish close to him. Finally, the fish tired, gave up, and swam into the net.

"Hold him up!" Sylvia said. "Let's take a look at the catch of the day."

Jack raised the net up out of the water. The weight of the fish caused him to lose his balance, and he went over backward into the water.

Sylvia laughed. "Hold the net up, Jack! Don't let him get away!"

The harder Jack struggled, the more awkward he became. By this time, the fish had become so tangled in the net that it could never have gotten away. While Jack struggled, Sylvia stood in the water laughing and Snuffy ran back and forth on the beach.

Before long, Jack and Sylvia were back on shore with the catfish secured on a stringer. "That should be enough fish for you, me, and Snuffy for supper," Sylvia said. "Now, let's go and see if we can rustle up a rabbit. There's a soybean field with some open brush and a windrow just on the other side of this patch of woods. I bet we can find a nice, fat rabbit along the edge of that field. Do you want to carry the gun?"

"No … I don't know how to hunt."

"I could tell you didn't know a lot about fishing," she said. "Have you ever done any hunting or fishing at all?"

"I don't think so. Most places I been in the last twenty years were cities."

"What about when you were a kid?"

"Mary Ann and I talked about that," Jack said. I don't remember much, but it seems like it was in a town or a city."

Sylvia and Jack walked away from the riverbank, following Caney Creek back toward the bean field. When they emerged from the woods, Sylvia called Snuffy, picked him up, and handed him to Jack. "You and Snuffy wait right here. This won't take long."

She slowly circled the field in a half crouch. Then she quickly stood up, leveled the barrel of the gun, and fired. Jack and Snuffy both gave a start, Snuffy whined, and Jack froze. Sylvia turned and looked back at them. "You can let the dog down now," she said.

She walked over the edge of a brush pile and picked up the rabbit. "Let's go home now," she said. "We've got enough for today and tomorrow."

As they walked back to the house, Sylvia said to Jack, "When I was a kid, we moved from place to place in our wagons. Wherever there was fruit to be picked or cotton to be chopped, that was where we would stop. Since we traveled around, we never had a smokehouse or a root cellar, so we just kept enough food for one or two days."

"We lived in a pretty town," Jack said.

"I thought you said you didn't remember."

"I don't … But it was pretty," he said.

Sylvia and Jack walked by the abandoned sawmill and up the alley behind her backyard. With a deft hand, Sylvia nailed the catfish and the rabbit to the back wall of the shed, and skinned and gutted them both. "Jack, hook up the hose and turn on that faucet, will you?" She washed down the fish and the rabbit, and then cleaned up the mess.

"I don't cook much anymore," she said. "But it's always fun for me to cook for someone who appreciates good food—someone who really understands cooking and eating. If you're hungry, I fixed some olive bread this morning. I'll fillet the catfish and make some soup stock. This rabbit will make a great pie. He isn't too fat. Why don't you debone the rabbit while I work on the stock?"

They went to work preparing the ingredients for their meal of catfish soup and savory rabbit pie.

The smell of onions and garlic cooking in olive oil on the gas range was followed by that of the fish head and bones, carrots, vegetable stock, and celery simmering in a large pot.

Once the rabbit had been deboned and the meat shredded, it was sautéed in butter, red wine, garlic, and savory. Sylvia added a small amount of chicken stock to the mix, along with a handful of browned rice. This she simmered for thirty minutes, and then she added to it a blend of milk and eggs. She poured the mixture into a piecrust, which she then set to cook.

While they waited for the soup to simmer and the pie to bake, Sylvia suggested that they adjourn to the *varda*. "Jack, the stone around your neck has had time to absorb some of those forgotten memories that make you who you are. Do you really want to remember who you are and what brought you here?"

"Yeah … I think I do," Jack said, nodding.

"If at any time you get uncomfortable, we can stop. Okay?"

"Yes."

"Okay, let's go." Sylvia led Jack into the brightly colored wagon.

She set up a circle and asked Jack to sit in the middle. When he was comfortable, she lit a candle and set it right in front of him. Sylvia took the moonstone from Jack using a clean white cotton cloth, and put it in a small bowl of blue water.

"Now, Jack, wet your face and hands with the water from the bowl, and I'll do the same. Let's you and I see if we can call to mind your past."

She reached into the bowl, wet her hands, and then her face. "Now, Jack, you do as I did."

Jack did as he was instructed.

"There's nothing magical about the moonstone. Most of who you are—of what you do, say, and feel—never enters your conscious mind, but it surrounds you and penetrates all that you are. We are like an onion—one layer on top of another. All the moonstone does is pick up on those layers—it catches a glimpse of who and what you have been. The color blue and the water help to release those energies. By bathing in the essence of these energies, you coax them to the surface. Now, I want you to close your eyes and tell me the first thing that you sense."

Jack closed his eyes, and, soon, his shoulders slumped. The slight worry lines around his eyes began to smooth, and his breathing slowed and softened. Sylvia watched as Jack immersed himself in the moment.

"Angelica," Jack said. "It's wavy, soft, flowing, and yellow."

"Is the angelica from my hair?" Sylvia asked.

"No, it's someone else. A young woman who isn't very happy."

CHAPTER 15

a troubled mind

Saratoga Springs,1940

The strong scent of angelica filled the bedroom, and a Glenn Miller tune emanated from the radio on the bedside table. Clare Currier sat on the bed, holding her face in her hands and silently crying as blood ran down her arms and onto her dress. The razorblade with which she had inflicted the wounds was lying on the floor.

Paul J., her son, opened the front door of the duplex, unaware of the drama being played out in the back of the house. He dropped his book satchel on the sofa in the front room and headed directly to the kitchen. "I'm home, Mom," he said. "What are we having for supper?"

There was no reply from the bedroom.

"Mom, are you back there?" he said a bit louder to make himself heard over the radio. There was still no reply.

It wasn't unusual for his mother to be asleep when he came home in the evening. She had explained to him that, sometimes, it was the only way she could escape from the way she felt.

Pauly reached into the cabinet, grabbed a glass, and retrieved the milk from the icebox. He poured himself a glass of milk, and then rummaged through the icebox for something to eat. On the second shelf from the bottom, he found a half-eaten bologna sandwich wrapped in wax paper. He unfolded the paper and sniffed the sandwich. His sensitive nose assured him that it was still fit to eat. Milk and sandwich in hand, he walked into the narrow hall that separated his room from that of his parents. The door to their bedroom was slightly ajar.

"Mom, are you in there?" he asked.

Again, there was no reply, but this time, he could hear her sob. It was then that a feeling of dread came over the ten-year-old boy. "Mom, are you okay?" he asked, nudging the door with his foot. The door swung open all the way, and the dread that had begun just a moment ago was confirmed. His mother was sitting on the edge of the bed in an enlarging circle of blood.

"Mama!" Pauly screamed, dropping his milk and sandwich.

Clare dropped her bloody hands and looked up at her son. There was no sign of recognition. "Help me," she said. "Help me."

For an instant, Pauly was frozen—he simply couldn't move. The only thing that went through his mind was, *This can't be happening.* It was then that he thought of Mr. Jarvis, the old bachelor who lived on the other side of the duplex. Pauly ran out the back door of their apartment and threw open the door to his neighbor's. The old man was sitting at his kitchen table. "Come quick, my Mama's been hurt!" Pauly cried. He turned and ran back out of the kitchen.

Jarvis pulled himself up from his chair and followed the boy into the Currier home. Jarvis quickly appraised the situation.

"Go to the bathroom and get some towels," he instructed Pauly. "I'll see if I can get the bleeding stopped."

Jarvis laid the poor little woman down on the bed and cleaned enough blood off to see the extent of the wounds. She was bleeding heavily, but there weren't any arterial cuts, so he went to work trying to create a bandage to stop the flow. When Pauly returned with an armful of towels, Jarvis tried to reassure the boy. "Your mom is going to be all right. A little bit of blood goes a long way. But I still think she needs to go to the hospital. Call the telephone operator and tell her we need an ambulance. Are you all right, son?" Pauly had been staring at his mother and crying.

"Yes, sir, I'm okay," Pauly said. "But we don't have a phone."

"Go over and use mine, and be sure to give them the address. After you call for the ambulance, call your father at the hotel and tell him what's happened."

"I can't do that," Pauly said. "They won't let him take personal calls at work. Dad says we're not to interrupt him at work, no matter what! He said it would get him in trouble."

"I bet he'll make an exception this time. Now, get to it!"

Jarvis was right about Clare not having done herself any major physical damage, but the problem went far deeper than a series of knife wounds on her wrists. This wasn't the first time that Clare had tried to take her own life, but each time before this, Paul Sr. had been able to shield his son from the knowledge.

Paul Currier and Clare Holts had met in 1920, when both worked for the Grand Union Hotel in Saratoga Springs, New York. He was a veteran of the Great War and she a young French German immigrant from Alsace-Lorraine. If either had family, neither spoke of them. Paul began his career as a bellman at the hotel. He took to his job and was quickly promoted to assistant head bellman. The men and women who frequented the Grand Union were quite wealthy, and many were public figures. One requirement of a good bellman was the ability to keep his own counsel, and Paul understood this. By the midtwenties, he had a second job as one of the racetrack accountants. He loved horses, and his reputation for keeping his mouth shut was a valued commodity at the track—it meant that he could be trusted.

Clare worked in housekeeping at the Union. She was a slender woman who wore her black hair in a severe bun. Her delicate facial features were laid out on a background of high cheekbones and a dark complexion. By ordinary standards, she was not pretty, but she carried herself proudly.

Their courtship and marriage was a no-nonsense affair that culminated in a civil ceremony at the hotel. A brief spell of joyful marriage was followed by long years of hell. An early miscarriage in 1925 resulted in a round of severe depression for Clare. Their lives were punctuated by her fits of rage and hallucination, which were followed by deep troughs of despondency. Paul and his young wife were left grasping at straws. Traditional medical doctors were of little assistance, so the couple resorted to an herbalist and aromatherapy. With time, the depression lifted. Clare became convinced that she had been cured, and she became a devotee of aromatherapy. For every complaint, real or imagined, there was a remedy. The Currier apartment was always filled with the scent of eucalyptus or lavender or rosewater. There was always a pot of herbal tea—chamomile or mint—steeping in the kitchen. The essence of clary sage or castor or lipsop emerged from the window of the small bathroom, where Clare kept her pharmacy. She spent every spare cent the two of them possessed on her hoard of aromatic supplies. In the late twenties, she announced her intention of quitting her job at the hotel and working full-time as an herbalist. Even though Paul had serious doubts about the effectiveness of her purported cure, it was hard to argue with success.

All went well until the birth of their only child, Paul Jr. A pretty baby, Pauly was quiet and seldom sick. Even as an infant, he made few demands on his mother. The problem was with Clare. After the birth of her son, she began a slow descent into madness. The landmarks of Pauly's childhood were measured in terms of his mother's mental health and the fragrances that filled the house.

Despite Clare's problems, a bond formed between her and her son. She was the one person who understood Pauly's confusion regarding shapes, smells, and colors. They would immerse themselves for hours in books that displayed the paintings of Van Gogh and Gauguin—men whose art blurred the borders between the senses; men who didn't feel constrained by the bounds of ordinary reality. Pauly understood that, and so did his mother. The blues of Van Gogh's skies melted into the radiating sun; the bright yellow sunflowers and red poppies absorbed the light of southern France and refracted it like a magnifying glass. The dark bodies of Gauguin's women—their breasts and faces that seemed larger than life—would be Pauly's first introduction to the sexual nature of his existence. Pauly added to this visual mix a taste and feel that rose out of the pictures and blurred their margins even more. After the incident on the baseball field, he told his mother about the butterscotch taste that had overwhelmed him. She smiled and hugged him.

"You really have a special gift," she said. "But if you try to tell others about it, they will be like your friend, Billy—they simply won't understand. You would probably do better just to keep it to yourself." Pauly understood; it would be their secret.

Following Mr. Jarvis's instructions, Pauly was able to summon an ambulance and call his father. Jarvis accompanied Clare and Pauly to the hospital, and Paul Sr. met them there. When Paul Sr. arrived, Jarvis explained what had happened, then excused himself, leaving Pauly and his father alone in the waiting room. After what seemed like an eternity, a young doctor came out and told them that Clare would survive, but that she would have to stay overnight, at least. He then asked to talk to Paul Sr. in private. The two men went into a small office, leaving Pauly alone in the waiting room.

After about fifteen minutes, the door to the office opened and Pauly heard his father say to the doctor, "Well, sir, you make whatever arrangements you feel are necessary. We'll do as you ask."

"Good," the doctor said. "I really think it's for the best. We may be able to move her as soon as tomorrow, but that will depend on what happens overnight. We need to make sure that she's medically stable before we move her."

"Sure, that makes sense," Paul Sr. said. "Can we see her now?"

"You probably shouldn't. We have her sedated, and it might really agitate her."

"We'll be back in the morning then. Is that all right?"

"That's fine. We'll see you then."

On the way home from the hospital, Pauly began to cry.

His father turned to him and asked, "What's the matter, son?"

"What's going to happen to Mom?" the young boy asked through his tears.

"She's going to have to go to a special hospital for people who are sick like she is."

"What do you mean, 'special hospital'?" Pauly cried. "You mean, you're going to send her away? When can I see her? I don't want her to go away!"

"Son, your mother has got to go somewhere where she can't hurt herself. She's had spells like this before. They eventually pass, but until this one does, there's not much we can do. It's for her own good. You understand that, don't you?"

"I guess so. But I don't want her to go away."

"I understand, son, but there isn't anything we can do about it for the time being. It's just the way things are." Paul Sr. looked at his son, his own face dark with sadness and tears. He had cried all the tears he could for Clare, and there were none left. Living with Clare had long ago become a sad movie, one for which there was no good ending. The tears he shed now were for his son.

Despite his father's reassurance that Clare's committal was only "for the time being," she never came home again. For the next thirteen months, she made repeated attempts at suicide, and she finally succeeded in hanging herself with her own bedclothes.

The last keepsake of his mother that Paul would carry with him was a photo his father took at the State Hospital in Albany. In the picture, his mother was sitting in an old wooden chair on the hospital lawn, and Pauly stood beside her, his arm on her shoulder.

Like all fathers, Paul Sr. had dreams for his son. Secretly, he wanted him to be a jockey, but he abandoned that notion as Pauly reached puberty and began to spread out into his adult form. He never would be tall, but he was stocky, built close to the ground.

During the summer racing season, Paul Sr. and Pauly would get up well before dawn, have a light breakfast, and be at the track early enough to watch the trainers work their horses.

When Pauly was old enough, his father got him a job as a "hot walker" at the track. This was a fancy name for a stable boy, but that didn't matter to this specially gifted young man. Images of these giant thoroughbreds standing in the early-morning sun after a hard workout, steam rising from their backs, would linger in the recesses of his mind throughout his life. The track was alive with the natural force of these great horses. He would watch as the jockeys pushed the large, graceful animals to their limit, their shod hoofs pounding the track. Pauly would position himself at the last turn coming into the homestretch. As they approached his position along the rail, he would sense a rolling mass of gray-black clouds sweeping past him like a tidal wave. There would also be the distinct taste of vanilla. He stood as fixated as he had been that day with the baseball glove.

In the spring of 1948, Pauly graduated from high school and prepared to go to Albany in the fall. A small college had offered him a scholarship and a job.

Late one afternoon, he came home from his job at the track and found his father sitting at the kitchen table smoking a cigarette. "Sit down, son. There something I need to talk to you about."

Paul Sr. tapped a fresh cigarette out of the pack and lit it off the one he had in his mouth. "Son … I'm dying," he said. "I have lung cancer."

CHAPTER 16

happy birthday

"Morning, Sunshine!" Mary Ann said as she came in the back door. "What are you cooking? It smells great!"

Jack was putting the finishing touches on a chocolate-lavender cake. It was a sponge cake laced with lavender and unsweetened chocolate. For Jack, the bitter taste of semisweet chocolate, with all its sharp edges and powerful movement, was paired with the smooth quietness and encompassing warmth of lavender. The cake was shaped like a stock car. "It's a birthday cake for Richard," Jack said. "I heard you mention that this was his birthday."

"That's awful nice of you, Jack! He *really* likes chocolate," she said. Mary Ann walked over and kissed Jack on the cheek. "You're a great guy, Jack Smith."

Jack looked up from his work. "My mother was a very sad lady," he said.

"What are you talking about, Jack?"

"My mother—she was very sad."

"I thought you didn't remember anything about your parents."

"I don't, really … but I went to Sylvia's yesterday. Something about her made me remember my mother."

"What is it you remember?"

"I remember all the smells. It was kinda like Sylvia's. The bathroom in our house was full of little bottles of oils that had these rich smells. Her hands and hair always had these rich scents."

"But you said she was a sad woman. Why do you say that?"

"I don't know, but I vaguely remember that she had to leave, and she never came back. She must have left real quick, because she didn't take her oils with her. I kept her bottles. I guess I must have thought she would come back for them … and for me."

Mary Ann stuck a finger into his bowl of red icing. She tasted the icing and smiled. "This icing is wonderful," she said. "What about your dad? Do you remember anything about him?"

Jack shook his head. "I don't remember much, except that he really enjoyed the ponies. I remember that we spent a lot of time around the horse track when I was little."

"What happened to him?"

"I guess he left too," Jack said in an offhanded manner. "I don't remember."

Mary Ann leaned over and smelled the cake. "There's something unusual about that cake—I don't recognize the smell."

"It's fresh lavender. I found it at the flower shop."

Moon came in early in the afternoon. For the first time in months, he looked like his old self. He wore tight jeans and a western-cut shirt, his hair was slicked back, and a piece of hammered gold hung around his neck. His crocodile boots were slightly muddy, and he sported a giant silver belt buckle he had won in a poker game.

"Phillips, pour me an ice tea and bring it to my office," he said.

"Yes, sir, Captain, sir," Mary Ann said, saluting Moon as he disappeared into the office.

Joy sat at the bar folding rollups. "Looks like the boy's back in form," she said.

"Yeah, it does, doesn't it? In some ways, that's not all bad. You know, if it wasn't for Moon, this place might get a little boring. At least he adds some entertainment."

From the office, Moon shouted, "Phillips, quit yapping, and get my tea!"

Mary fixed the ice tea and took it to his office. "Here you are, Your Majesty," she said, putting the tea down on his desk.

Moon was staring at a photocopy of an old photograph, and didn't acknowledge her presence.

She walked behind him and leaned over his shoulder. "What's that?" she asked.

"See this guy?" He pointed to a figure wearing an old-style hat. "Do you recognize him?"

"No," she said. "Should I?"

"*That* is P. J. Ives himself. This is the same picture that Leonard enlarged to make that poster in the front window. It was taken at the Old Fashion Day parade the fall that he was here. Let's see ..." He pointed at the newspaper heading at the top of the photo. "Yeah, it was September, 1957. It's the only known photo of the illustrious Mr. Ives."

"Was there anything else in that box you got from Leonard?" she asked.

"No, Linda must have cleaned out everything important; everything in the box is old news."

Mary Ann patted him on the shoulder. "Are you okay?" she asked.

"Yeah, I've just about given up on the Ives thing. It seems like everywhere I turn is a blind alley," Moon said without looking up.

"That's not what I'm talking about. I'm talking about Kate."

Moon sighed. "There's more than one fish in the sea," he said.

Mary Ann had heard him use that line many times, but the old confidence was missing now.

"Life goes on," Moon said, again without conviction.

"Well, it's nice to have you back," she said, turning to leave.

This time, Moon looked up. "Thanks," he said. "It's nice to be back."

By evening, the usual crowd gathered around the TV at the front of the bar to watch the running of the Mid-South 500, the biggest stock car race in the region.

As the green flag dropped, Art pointed at the bright red car that held the pole position. "That could be us in a couple of years! Richard at the wheel, and me, Joe, and Jack in the pit."

They all looked at him, but no one bothered to reply.

On the first lap, as the cars entered the backstretch, one of the hotshot rookies tried to bolt out into the lead. The front of his car clipped the back of the lead car, and both cars began to pitchpole. In midair, the cars came apart in a dramatic shower of metal parts, wheels, and smoke. The lead pack had no time to avoid the two leaders, and the race soon came to resemble a demolition derby.

Mary Ann set a beer down in front of Art. "Yeah, right, that could be Richard in the middle of that disaster."

Art nodded, but he didn't say anything.

No one had mentioned Richard's birthday, and he was beginning to think that they had forgotten. He wasn't one to make a big deal of birthdays or holidays. Since his wife left, he had immersed himself in the regularity of everyday life, and special days did nothing but throw him out of his routine. Nonetheless, he would be disappointed if Mary Ann didn't at least say *something*.

Without warning, the overhead lights went out. The only lights left shining were the orange Cock's Crow sign in the front window, the TV screen showing a rerun of *The Andy Griffith Show*, and the kitchen lights at the end of the bar. One of the girls at the front table giggled. Richard realized that something was afoot.

"Happy birthday to you, happy birthday to you, happy birthday dear Richard, happy birthday to you!"

Mary Ann had started the song in the kitchen, and she and Jack came out carrying the chocolate-lavender cake with the bright red, yellow, and blue icing. The cake was covered with a whole box of candles, since no one knew Richard's exact age. By the time they reached Richard's table, everyone in the bar had joined them in song.

"Happy birthday, sweetie," Mary Ann said. "Now, blow out the candles."

Richard blew out the candles, and Jack handed him a knife. The knife slipped through the surface of the cake as though it were a light, fluffy cloud. Richard took a fork, raised a small bit of cake to his mouth, closed his eyes, and smiled. When he opened his eyes, he looked up at Jack. "Jack, I'll tell you what," he said. "That is the best piece of cake I ever had. In fact, I think I could get high on that stuff. I remember eating a brownie one time that tasted kinda like that. You didn't put anything illegal in that cake, did you?"

Everyone looked at Jack. The idea of Jack doing something illegal or dishonest was so far beyond the pale that it was humorous.

"No, no, no," Jack said. "There's nothing bad in the cake—just cake and lavender and chocolate."

Richard smiled. "Well, Jack, you could bottle this taste and sell it. Thanks."

After Mary Ann had discovered Jack's cake earlier in the day, she called all the regulars and informed them of an impromptu party for Richard that night. While Richard ate his cake, a series of gifts began to appear on the table. Richard was in the process of opening Art's package when Moon came rushing out of this office.

"All right, people, I have some really great news for all of you!" He stopped short, realizing that he was interrupting something. "What's going on? Who died?"

"No one died, Moon," Mary Ann said. "It's Richard's birthday."

"Okay … good. Good for you," he said, nodding at Richard. "Now, let me tell you people my news. This is really important!"

"Don't tell me—you've figured out who P. J. Ives was!" Joe said.

"Shit, no, this is *real* news! Something that's gonna make a lot of money."

"So what is it, Ace?" Art asked. "What new scheme you got now?"

"It's not one of my ideas, but I plan on taking advantage of it. If this works out, I'll be a rich man, and anybody who wants in on it will share in the treasure!"

"So … tell us!" Mary Ann said.

"The Streak is coming!" Moon announced.

"What are you talking about, Moon?" Mary Ann asked. "What streak?"

Moon looked disgusted. "No, Phillips, it's not *what* it is. It's *who* it is!"

"Well, excuse me," she said. "Who the hell is it?"

"The Streak's a kid from Mississippi who races stock cars," Richard said.

"That's right," Moon said. "And this kid is a phenom! He's won forty races in a row. They say he's the biggest thing to hit the track since Petty's early days. Anyway, the boys over at the track are going to announce tomorrow that this kid will be here for the Green River Festival in September. A little bird told me that, if all works well, he should be racing for his fiftieth win that Saturday night. When *that* happens, one of the big companies is going to offer him a big, fat contract. This is going to put this little town on the map!"

The Streak coming to town was a big deal, and it would draw the crowds, but how it would make Moon a rich man was beyond Mary Ann. "So, what's in it for you?" she asked.

Moon shook his head. "Think big, Phillips! This'll bring a bunch of high-rolling rednecks to town looking for a place to put down some money. We don't want these Yankees from across the street walking off with all the cash. The deal is: you guys come up with a couple thousand bucks, I'll match it, and we'll put it all on the Streak's nose. If we play our cards right, we'll be rolling in the dough! But remember—it takes money to make money."

"Right. That's what I thought you meant," Mary Ann said. "Count me out. In fact, Jack, Joy, and I want to be paid in full before you get too involved in this scheme."

Moon turned to Joe and Art. "What about you two?" he asked.

Joe reached into his pockets and turned them inside out. "Nothing here," he said.

"Now, see?" said Moon. "There you go again, thinking small. I've heard you two talk about the retirement plans you got at that steel mill. You could borrow on that! Double, maybe even triple your money in a couple of weeks!"

Art and Joe looked at each other and smiled. They both looked back at Moon and shook their heads.

Jack whispered something to Mary Ann, and she began to laugh.

"What are you laughing at?" Moon asked.

"Jack wants to know if he can bet on Richard in the big race."

CHAPTER 17

a sure thing

"Welcome, friends, to the Green River Racing Festival! I'm Albert Lawrence Moon, your track announcer, and I'd like to personally welcome you to the Green River Speedway and Gum Ridge!"

Cars were beginning to drift into the parking lot in front of the track. The security guards, hired for the evening, were there early to make sure that the cars were lined up in neat, even rows. Moon was standing on the catwalk along the back of the press box above the stands. He was dressed in his white Kentucky Colonel suit with a white top hat, a large cigar in one hand, and a microphone in the other.

"Admission is eight dollars for adults, six dollars for all you seniors, and the little kids under twelve get in free. For those of you wishing to get into the pits, there's a twenty-dollar charge.

If you want a closer look at the cars and drivers, they're lined up west of the track, checking in right now. Go on over, talk to the men, and look at their cars!

We have the coldest beer in town, fresh popcorn, pizza, and sandwiches. So eat up, drink up, and get ready for a night of dynamite racing!

Tonight's feature race is the Street-Stock Championship featuring D. J. Thompson—The Streak! He'll be going for his fiftieth win in a row tonight!"

*   *   *   *

Moon had been right—the Streak had attracted a huge crowd. The Circle K campground down by the river was full, Moon's and Peeler's had waiting lines out the front doors, and Main Street was bumper-to-bumper traffic. But Moon still had a problem—he'd lost his edge, and it was all the fault of Mary Catherine Ellis. All his life, he'd always the first one in the water. While others hesitated and held back, he jumped in with both feet. Games of chance were only partly luck; the skill was in knowing when to get in and when to get out—when to hold out for an inside straight and when to pass and wait for the next hand. When Kate walked out of his life, something happened—he lost his touch. At first, he went to bars where no one knew him, and he drank alone. That succeeded only in getting him drunk, and when he woke up, he found himself no better off. After that, he began to call old girlfriends, trying to find someone who would take his mind off of Kate. That didn't work either—after the first ten minutes, he'd remember why they'd broken up in the first place. The next strategy was to immerse himself in gambling. This worked out better, but he still had trouble making decisions. The first night of the Racing Festival had earned him a clean thousand dollars in the fourth and fifth races. This was the stake he needed, and it provided a light at the end of the tunnel.

Between his work for the Harris brothers at the track and his bookie service, Moon hadn't been spending a great deal of time at the cafe. When he did stop to think about it, which wasn't very often, he had to admit that Mary Ann had become more than just a waitress—she was the manager, and he was the absentee owner. It was like the Bozeman family and their landholdings—you hire somebody you trust, give them a title, pay them as little as you can, and drop in once in a while to collect the money. For Moon, this was the ideal way of doing business. He thought that he would soon have to give her a title that fit her new status, but he wouldn't do that till she demanded it.

At midday, he checked in on Mary Ann and Jack to make sure that the cafe was running smoothly. The parking lot was full, and there were knots of people waiting outside the door. Mary Ann and Jack had roped off part of the side-lot, set up tables they had borrowed from the school, and were serving outside, by the cooker. Mary Ann had enlisted the assistance of her friends Jenny and Crystal, Mary Ann's mother, and Sylvia. Mary Ann was running the cash register and serving beer at the bar when Moon came in.

"You need any help?" he asked.

Mary Ann thought for a minute. "To tell you the truth, Moon ... I don't want to hurt your feelings, but you'd just be in the way. I think we got everything under control." Mary Ann went back to her customers.

Moon had important business he needed to be doing, but her comment had indeed hurt his feelings. What did she mean; he would be in the way? This was his restaurant, and it was his money that was buying all the food! Next week, after the rush was over, he was going to have to have a talk with that woman and let her know who was boss.

Moon went into the kitchen to see if Jack could use some help. When he walked through the double doors, it was obvious, even to Moon, that Jack and Sylvia were working efficiently as a team and that one more person in the kitchen would be too many.

He went back to the bar, poured himself a glass of tea, went into his office, and closed the door. Moon had a big decision to make. His phone had been ringing since early morning, and, if there were no big surprises, the vigorish—the bookie's slice on all the bets—would bring in a minimum of six or seven thousand dollars. The big question was how much he should bet on the Streak. While he moped over the loss of Kate, Moon had made several trips into Mississippi and Tennessee to watch this boy race. There was nobody in the area that could come near this kid. Richard might be almost as good a driver, but he didn't have the car, and he certainly didn't have the kind of mechanic that Thompson did. So ... how much money should he bet? The biggest bet he had ever dropped had been five thousand dollars in a high-stakes poker game, but then, he'd been playing with the house's money. He'd thought he had a hand that couldn't be beat, but the guy across from him had proved him wrong, and Moon had gone away empty-handed.

Moon stewed for an hour trying to decide what to do. He repeatedly called the Harris brothers' number to learn the fluctuating odds on the race. Early in the week, the Streak had started at six to one; since Friday, he'd been stuck at five to two.

"Damn that woman!" Moon said out loud to himself. "I can't make up my mind, and it's all her fault. Shit!" Despite his reassurances to Mary Ann, Moon still thought about Kate day and night.

It was time for him to go home and change into his white linen suit. He picked up his pad and phone, got into his car, and headed for home. As he pulled into his driveway, it came to him—ten thousand dollars. He was going to bet ten thousand dollars. If he was ever going to get out of this dead-end town, Moon was going to have to start thinking and acting big, and today was the day. He showered, dressed quickly, and headed for the track.

Moon pulled up in front of the Harris's trailer. When he reached up to switch off the ignition, he realized that his palms were sweating. He rummaged around on the floor and found an old T-shirt. *Can't let these boys see me sweat,* he thought. He wiped off his hands and neck with the shirt and straightened his tie. He took a couple of deep breaths and got out of the car.

The Harris brothers had had a small, covered porch built at the door of their trailer. They never asked or allowed anyone inside. All of their business was carried out on the porch.

Moon rang the doorbell and waited. When no one came, he rang again. "Hold your horses," said a vaguely familiar female voice. "We hear you."

The trailer door opened to reveal Kate Ellis looking out at him through the screen door.

"Hey, Moon," she said. "What do you need?" Kate was dressed in a thin house gown, and on the ring finger of her left hand was the biggest diamond Moon had ever seen.

He couldn't speak. He just stood there, staring at Kate and her ring.

"Well, Moon, you gonna stand there all day? What do you want?"

"Oh, yeah, uh … I need to talk to Jerry."

"Jerry's taking a shower, and John's working. Anything else?"

From the darkness behind her, Moon heard, "Who is it, Katy?"

"It's Moon," she said over her shoulder. "He wants to talk to you."

"I'll be out in a minute. Tell him to wait on the porch," Jerry shouted.

"He wants you to wait on—"

"Yeah, I heard him," Moon said.

"I'm closing the door. We're letting all of the cool air out." She didn't say "nice to see you," "adios," or "good-bye"—she just shut the door and left him standing on the small porch.

Moon found it difficult to move. The surprise of seeing Kate had taken him aback. Up until that moment, he'd harbored the faint hope that, somewhere along the line, he'd find a way to get back in her good graces. Seeing her standing there at the trailer door had caused him to realize that it was over, once and for all. Much to his surprise, his predominant emotion was relief. It was over—he didn't have to think about her again.

For what seemed like an eternity, Moon waited for Jerry to come out and take his bets. He could hear Jerry and Kate moving around inside, talking and laughing. Finally, Moon raised his hand to the door again, just in case they had forgotten he was there. But before he could knock on the door, Jerry came out in a silk bathrobe.

"Moon," he said.

"Jer," Moon replied.

"*Jerry*, Moon. My name is Jerry. 'Jer' sounds like some slobbering idiot. Call me Jerry."

"Sorry. I heard your brother call you Jer."

"You don't know me that well," Jerry said

"Right. I understand."

"What you got for me?" Jerry asked, reaching out for Moon's legal pad.

"I got three pages of bets that are a little on the heavy side for me. I need you to pick them up. The phone's been ringing off the hook."

Jerry looked over the list of names and bets, looking for deadbeats. When he was satisfied with the list, he nodded. "Got anything else? I got to get dressed."

"Yeah, I thought I might put down a bet myself."

"Yeah? How much?" Jerry had a pen in his hand, ready to make a note of Moon's bet.

Kate walked up and put her left hand on Jerry's shoulder.

Moon looked up at Kate and the big ring on her finger. Before he knew it, he had blurted out, "Twenty-five grand on the Streak"

Jerry looked up from the pad. "Moon … You got that kind of money?"

"Of course I do. What do you take me for, a rookie?"

"Wait a minute." Jerry turned and went back into the trailer. Through the open door, Moon could see John working at a computer screen. Jerry and John conferred for a minute, and then Jerry came back to the door.

"Well, my friend, you got yourself a bet," Jerry said. "But you're jumping in there with the high rollers. You'd better be sure you can cover it."

"Look, boys, if your people can't handle my bet, I can always take it elsewhere."

Jerry put his hand on Moon's arm. "We'll cover your bet, friend. You just make sure *you* can."

"Don't worry about me. I'm a big boy. I can take care of myself."

"Remember, Moon," Jerry said, "General Custer was confident just before the Indians attacked."

When Joe and Art left the cafe after lunch, they walked by the kitchen. "See you at about five thirty, over at the track," Joe said.

"Yeah, five thirty," Jack said.

Mary Ann walked into the kitchen with a tub of dishes. "Did you put any money on the race?" she asked.

Jack smiled and shook his head.

Sylvia looked up from the plate of meat loaf she was putting together. "How about you?" she asked Mary Ann.

"Of course I did! Fifty bucks. Had to bet on my honey," Mary Ann said.

"Wow," Sylvia said, "it sounds to me like you and that boy with mud between his toes have stepped it up another notch!"

"Why do you say that?" Mary Ann asked.

"Well, you're putting down real money on him, and against the odds, to boot."

Mary Ann smiled. "I guess I really *am* falling in love with him."

"That's good," Jack said.

"Why do you say that?" Mary Ann asked.

"'Cause you need somebody to love," Jack said.

"But I don't want to fall in love with him if he doesn't love me," she said

"Can you do that?" he asked.

"What?"

"You know ... only fall in love with somebody who loves you back."

She had no reply to this. She supposed that she loved her rice farmer, one way or the other.

"Are you going to fix something for supper before you leave for the track?" Mary Ann asked.

"I was thinking about it. What do you think I ought to make?" Jack asked.

"How about a meat pie that's full of surprises, just like you?" she said.

"Meat pie it is."

For the rest of the afternoon, Jack and Sylvia trimmed and cleaned the meat, cooked the potatoes and vegetables, made the pastry dough, and fashioned the pies. As the time drew near for him to leave for the track, all that remained was to bake the pies. Starting at four o'clock, Jack began looking at the clock every twenty seconds or so. Sylvia noticed Jack's agitation.

"Go on, Jack," she said. "I can handle to rest of this. You go on, and have a good time."

When Richard pulled his truck and trailer into the parking lot of the track, Jack was already waiting for him at the sign-in table. Even though he had a pit pass that identified him as a crew member, Jack never entered the area when Richard wasn't there.

"Jack," Richard said, "you seen anybody come through the gate we weren't expecting?"

"Mostly, it's been folks who are here every week," Jack said. "The Thompson car is set up back along the middle of the backstretch. Kincaid's under the trees behind the scales. Browning's just inside the gate, up in the corner."

"Anybody in our regular place?" Joe asked.

"No, but it's filling up fast."

"Well, we better get our ass on the road before somebody beats us to our lucky spot," Richard said.

At the beginning of the backstretch, along a fencerow, was an open spot that Richard liked best. A lot of traffic came by on their way to each heat and it gave him a chance to look at and listen to the competition as they prepared to race.

It didn't take long for the Fairlane crew to get everything set up and ready to race. As they finished up their last-minute details, Richard said, "Jack, old buddy, you want to go out and run the packing rounds with me?" If anyone rode along on the packing rounds, it was usually the chief mechanic, but, since Richard was his own chief mechanic, he usually went by himself. Richard had seen how excited Jack got that first night, and had decided several weeks before to let Jack ride shotgun in the warm-ups.

Jack just stood there, looking at the car.

"What do you think, Jack?" Richard asked. "You want to go out and test out the car with me?"

"Yeah, sure. I'd really like that."

"Now, while we're out there, I want you to listen to the motor and let me know if you see or feel anything," Richard said. "I'll goose it a few times to see if I can make it act up."

When the race director called out their heat to run the track, Richard handed Jack a helmet. "Jump in! Let's go for a spin, old buddy!"

Richard carried a special wooden box he'd built for a passenger-side seat. When it came to the hot laps, he would take it out to cut down on weight.

After some awkwardness, they managed to wedge Jack's less-than-nimble body through the roll cage and get him secured on the wooden box.

Jack hadn't been prepared for the sensations that awaited him as the Fairlane climbed the dirt-incline ramp and merged with the twelve other cars circling the track. The fluid motion, compounded by the strobelike effect of the banked track lights, created a seizure of sensations that nearly overwhelmed him. A collage of cold, loud blues and yellow-tinged roars from the engines combined with the speed to come out tasting like vanilla.

The next day Jack would try to explain the experience to Mary Ann. "You can stand as close to the track as you want and not realize how fast things are happening. It's like a tornado—everything is caught up in the force, but in the center, it's still. A few yards off the track, everything goes on like normal. Once, when I was a kid, I had the same feeling watching a horse race. It was like a rolling, gray-black cloud that tasted like vanilla. Not like in ice cream, but like you took a vanilla bean and chewed on it. The smell was so strong at one point on the far curve, when Richard punched the car; I thought I was going to pass out."

When Richard and Jack pulled off the track, Jack was so weak that he couldn't get out of the car by himself. It took all three of the men to maneuver him out of the car and into a folding chair by the trailer.

"Are you okay?" Richard asked.

"Yeah, I'm fine. That was really something." Jack smiled feebly.

Soon, the call came for the hot laps. Art, Joe, and Jack went and sat in the metal stands along the backstretch and watched as Richard put the car through its paces. When he came out of the near curve and stepped on the gas, the car took off like a rocket. After Richard finished his run, the four men went to work putting finishing touches on the car.

*   *   *   *

"Welcome, my friends, to the Green River Racing Festival! You are about to see some of the best street stock in the world, right here on this track!

We've got fifty-two cars looking for a spot in the final. There will be four qualifying heats, two semifinals, a losers' race, and a final. Five cars from each semi and two from the losers' race will advance to the final.

The winner of the final gets a check for fifteen thousand dollars!

For all of you not familiar with our track, you will see that all of the drivers have moved down to the scales, where the race director is giving them the rules."

The race director stood on the scales and looked out at the drivers and their crews. "All right, boys, listen up," he said. "Here are the rules. I don't want no crybabies. If you get bumped in a curve, don't come whining to me. If I catch you jamming someone over the edge, I'll black-flag your ass. You pass on yellow, you go to the rear. You spin out over the edge, you go to the back. If you get lapped, you're out—no losers' bracket, no nothing. Standard rules for challenge—if you challenge the winner, we tear down the motor. If everything is in order, then you pay for it. Everybody clear?"

All the drivers nodded.

"Good," he said. "Everybody have a good race."

Richard, Jimmy Kincaid, and Larry Browning were the three best local drivers, and if anyone was going to stay with the Streak it would be one of them. Kincaid won the first heat going away, Browning came in third in the second heat after getting boxed in on a curve, and Richard won his heat, lapping all but three cars.

When Richard pulled into the pit area, he was shaking his head. "There's something not right about this car."

"Well, you couldn't tell it from that race," Joe said. "You kicked some ass out there!"

"Maybe so, but it just doesn't *feel* right," he said. "Let's go watch this Thompson kid—see what makes him so good."

When the green flag dropped, Thompson was on the third row inside. It took him a lap to work himself outside for a shot at a clear track. By that time, a pack of three cars had separated themselves from the rest. For the rest of the race, Thompson took it high and wide; with each straightaway, he would pass another car and make up time on the leaders. With two laps to go, he put his gas pedal to the floor and passed the leaders like they were standing still.

As Thompson took his victory lap and passed Richard and his team in the backstretch stands, Richard turned to Art and said, "I can beat this guy."

Art was startled. "Richie, did we watch the same race?" he asked.

"No, we didn't. I saw how powerful that car is, and he's a pretty good driver, but he's got weaknesses."

"Like what?"

"You'll see."

The semifinals went pretty much as expected, with Richard coming in a distant second to the Streak. As Richard pulled off the track and headed for the pit, the Fairlane backfired, and a giant cloud of blue smoke boiled up from under its hood. The car rolled to a stop, dead.

Moon announced:

"Did you see that folks? It looks like Little Richard just blew himself an engine! Don't look like we'll be seeing him for the rest of the evening."

"Shit," Art said.

"Well, it looks like that's it for us tonight," said Joe.

"Maybe not," Jack said.

"What do you mean?" Art asked.

"Been around tracks a long time," Jack said. "Saw it before, down in Florida. That's what Richard was feeling earlier. He was losing a little compression, but not enough to throw any oil. If we got a gasket, it'll take about forty-five minutes to fix."

When the wrecker pulled the car into the pit area, Joe and Art were already assembling the necessary tools.

Richard was impressed. "You guys are getting pretty good! How did you know it was a valve gasket?"

Art pointed at Jack. "The pit boss knew what was going on in about five seconds," he said.

"Well," Richard said, looking at his watch, "let's get to work. We got a race to run in about an hour."

While Richard and his crew feverishly worked against the clock, the sprint cars got their qualifying runs out of the way. Then came the losers' bracket, which took twice as long as any of the other races, because each of the participants knew that it was their last chance for the night. Because of accidents, the yellow flag came out five times in the first six laps. Two cars spun out in the infield and couldn't get restarted. Three others went over the edge. By the time the race was over, there were only six cars left, four of which weren't in the running for anything but a long week in the shop.

*　　*　　*　　*

"*This is it, folks—fifteen laps for the whole enchilada! The winner of this race goes away with fifteen thousand dollars and automatically qualifies for Batesville next week. Let's look at the field as they assemble in the pit area. As expected, D.J. Thompson will have the pole position and is the odds on favorite. Paul Browning out of Batesville fills out the front line. Jimmy Kincaid from Jonesboro starts in the second line, along with Junior Parker from Augusta. It looks like our local boy, Richard Kyle won't ... no, wait a minute, someone just handed me a note saying that his car is fine, and that he'll be in the final!*"

The official lap car led the racers onto the track, with Thompson leading the pack. After two warm-up laps with the cars jockeying back and forth for space, the lap car left the course on the back turn. When the lead cars hit the back-stretch, they bumped up the power, and everyone behind followed their cue. They hit the straightaway and jumped it up another notch. When they passed under the green flag, they were at full power.

Richard's strategy depended on Browning running true to form. Richard knew that he wouldn't let the kid take the lead by himself, and Browning tended to crowd people in the curves. Through the first half of the race, Thompson and Browning ran neck and neck on the straightaways and fought it out on the curves. Richard's car was running perfectly, and he had soon worked his way up into fourth place. With four laps to go, he found himself on Thompson's bumper. Browning sat on Thompson's outside shoulder. Each time they went into a curve, Richard fell in behind Browning on the last lap, coming out of the back straight, Browning made a move. He nosed in on Thompson to cut him off. Thompson let up for a split second, then floored it, bumping Browning's car. Using the draft from the car in front of him, Richard ran wide at full power and pulled slightly ahead of the other two cars. When the cars came out of the turn, with the checkered flag ahead, Richard, Browning and Thompson were running one-two-three, and they all barreled down the straightaway.

Had it not been for flash photography, no one would have been able to tell who won the race.

Over the crowd noise came the voice of the race director on the PA system:

"Get somebody up here! This asshole Moon has passed out! Hell, he might be dead for all I know. Who cares? We got a race to call. Shit the mike is keyed!"

For a moment, there was silence. Then, a more controlled and even voice came over the loudspeaker.

"My friends, you've just seen the finest race you'll ever see. It's a photo finish, and we'll have a result for you in about three minutes!"

The medics arrived and administered oxygen to Moon. He was slowly coming around. "Who won the race?" he asked.

The race director keyed the microphone again, cleared his voice, and said:

"As you know, there's been a photo finish for first place in the street stock championship final. We've had photos before, but never between three cars in the championship race! Before I announce the winner, I'd like to congratulate all three of these men and their teams.

Now on to the results. The third place finisher, by less than a foot, is D. J. Thompson!"

It only took a split second for the crowd to realize that one of the local boys had broken the streak, and they went wild. In that same instant, Moon saw the twenty-five thousand dollars he had bet on this race—money that he didn't have—go sailing out the window. He fainted again.

Richard, Joe, Art, and Jack were sitting on the Fairlane in the infield, along with the other two cars.

Richard turned to Art. "I told you I could beat that kid," he said.

The announcer continued:

"The result of tonight's race ... is an absolute dead heat! We have a tie for first place between young Mr. Browning and our own Richard Kyle. Barring challenges and weights, these two will split the proceeds and be declared cochampions!"

Most of what he'd said had been lost in the roar of the crowd. For most of these folks, this was as close as they would ever get to the Indianapolis 500, the Super Bowl, or the World Series. Despite the rules against such behavior, the fans flooded onto the track and the infield. Soon, Richard, Browning, and their crews were being carried around the track on the shoulders of the crowd.

While they waited for the race director to validate the victory, Richard and the boys moved back to the pit area and began packing up. A well-dressed man in a western-cut suit came up to Richard.

"Mr. Kyle," he said, "I'd like to congratulate you on one of the finest pieces of racing I have ever seen—and I see a lot of races." He reached into his breast pocket, pulled out a card, and handed it to Richard. "My name is Roland Reagen. And no, we aren't any kin—the spelling is different. I work for the Big Boy Smokeless Tobacco Company Racing Team. My job is to recruit drivers and manage the team. I saw what you did with that piece-of-shit car of yours—you've got a great future in racing! Right now, here and now, I'm offering you a job. I'll pay you a thousand dollars a week, plus expenses and ten percent of your winnings. We provide you with everything, including the car. Or, if you happen to be a risk-taker, you can have thirty percent of the winnings if you cover your own personal expenses. I been doing this long enough to know that you'll come out ahead for the first year on a guarantee, but, one way or the other, you'll take home about a hundred grand a year. It don't make a lot of difference which choice you take—you can change your mind next week, if you want to."

"When do you want me to start?" Richard asked.

"Monday morning."

"Where?"

"Batesville Speedway," Reagen said.

"It sure does sound inviting," Richard said seriously. "But I got my farm to think about."

"Well, I'll tell you what, son—I guarantee you'll make more money driving for me in a year than you'll ever see from that little old farm of yours. But it's up to you. Now, go enjoy your victory. If you show up on Monday, I'll assume you want the job. If you aren't there, I'll assume you don't."

As they finished up their impromptu meeting, the race director declared both winning cars legal and certified the race results. In a brief ceremony, the results were declared official and each team was given a check for seventy-five hundred dollars.

CHAPTER 18

life is full of hard decisions

Once the Fairlane had been secured back at Jacob's car lot, Richard and the boys returned to the cafe. Someone had gotten his hands on a copy of the videotape, and they were playing the race over and over again on the big-screen TV. Each time the three cars made the final turn, the crowd in the bar was out of their chairs, shouting and screaming.

The crew came in the side door in the middle of one of the replays. Everyone was so glued to the video that they didn't notice the arriving heroes. The boys said nothing and joined in watching the tape—it was the first time they had seen it. At the conclusion, when the three cars crossed the line neck and neck, they realized how incredibly close it had really been.

In the midst of the repeated celebration, Mary Ann noticed Richard, Art, Joe, and Jack standing behind the patrons.

"Ladies and gentlemen," she said, "I present to you our own champion, Mr. Richard Kyle!" She ran out from behind the bar and engulfed Richard in an all-encompassing embrace, accompanied by a kiss that seemed to go on forever. In the meantime, Art, Joe, and Jack were swallowed up by the crowd."

Eventually, Jack disappeared back into the kitchen, and Mary Ann followed him.

"Are you okay?" she asked.

"Yeah, I'm fine, "he replied.

"This is an awful lot of excitement for you in one day," she said. "You think you can handle it?"

Jack nodded. "I'll just take a little extra medicine." He began putting on his apron and cap.

"What are you doing?" she asked.

"Somebody might want something to eat. By the way, have you heard anything about Mr. Moon?"

"You mean about him passing out?" Mary Ann asked.

"Yeah."

"He's okay. He came through here about thirty minutes before you guys came in. It was obvious that he wasn't in a particularly good mood. He had a little cut on his head and blood all over his Kentucky Colonel suit. Anyway, he was in and out of here in about five minutes."

The party went on for several hours, and then everyone began to filter out, until all that were left were Art, Joe, Jack, Mary Ann, and Richard.

As Art and Joe were leaving, Art turned to Jack. "You need a ride home, bud?" It was the first time that any of the regulars had offered Jack a ride.

"Sure, that would be nice," Jack said, "if it's okay with Mary Ann."

"Yeah, I'll close up," she said. "You go on."

Richard stuck out his hand to Jack. "Thanks for your help," he said.

Jack shook Richard's hand and nodded.

Mary Ann locked the front door behind the three men. "You want another beer before I close things up?" she asked Richard.

"No. I want you to sit down here with me. I have something to ask you."

He explained the offer that Mr. Reagen had made. "I don't think I'll have a chance like this again. I'm never going to make any money farming, no matter how much I love it. Anyway, Mary Ann ... I love you very much, and I want you to marry me and go with me on the road."

For the longest time, she sat there without saying anything, and then big tears welled up in her eyes. "Richard, I love you more than you know," she said. "Before tonight, I'd decided that if you didn't ask me to marry you, *I* was going to ask *you*. But I can't marry you and go away with you. I know me, and I know what I'd be like moving from one hotel to another. I've had my fill of life on the road. It wouldn't be a pretty picture. And, most of all ... I just can't watch you race—it scares me to death!"

"You do understand," he said, "that this is a chance I just can't pass up."

"I know," she said, "but I still don't want to see you go."

"I really need to give it at least a year."

"I'll tell you what, cowboy," she said. "I'll be here when you get back. Just please don't leave me sitting on the fence too long. If you get out there and meet some cute little honey, just send me a telegram and tell me straight away. Don't make me sit around and guess. When are you leaving?"

"He wants me in Batesville on Monday morning."

"What are you going to do about your rice crop?" she asked.

"It won't cost me much to get Pete Carlisle to do the harvest," he said.

"What about the farm?"

"Well, I renew the lease at the first of the year, so I don't have to make a decision about that until January."

Mary Ann got up and walked around behind his chair. "Can I go home with you tonight?" she asked, putting her arms around his shoulders.

"I wouldn't have it any other way."

Sunday morning was a blur for Mary Ann and Richard. They had fallen asleep in a tangle of arms and legs that seemed like so many parts of a jigsaw puzzle. They had hoped that they would awaken with an answer to their problem.

The cafe had been the last thing on Mary Ann's mind when she drifted off to sleep. When the bright morning sun flooded the bedroom, she rolled over and glanced at the clock on the bedside table. It was nine forty-five.

"Shit," she said as she untangled herself from Richard's arms.

"What's the matter?"

"I'm late. I've got to open up in fifty minutes. It takes at least two hours to get ready for the Sunday lunch crowd."

"Can't Joy and Jack handle it?" Richard asked. "What about Moon?"

"The way Moon looked last night, I don't think we'll see him for a day or two. As for Jack and Joy, I guess they *could* take care of things, but that's a big load to put on them, and the crowd today is going to be bigger than normal, 'cause of the races."

"How about if I came by at around noon and pitched in?"

"That would be great," she said.

She slipped on her blouse and skirt and grabbed her purse. She walked up to the bed and pulled back the sheet. "Damn, you're a good-looking man! And I do love you …" She leaned over and kissed him on the cheek. "But I've got to go."

When Mary Ann pulled into the lot behind the cafe, Joy and Jack were sitting on the steps.

"Damn, look what the cat drug up!" Joy said. "Looks like you haven't been to bed."

150   WE ALL HEAR VOICES

"Almost haven't," Mary Ann said. "Can you guys handle this place for an hour while I go home and put my face on?"

"Sure we can, and if you gave one of us a key, you could phone in your distress call and not put us through this sight," Joy said.

Jack hadn't said a word.

"You need anything from the A&P, Jack?" Mary Ann asked.

"No, I got everything I need. Are you okay? You don't look good."

"Yeah, I'm fine. Just didn't get much sleep. It's a long story, I'll tell you about it later."

Jack and Joy set up for lunch. The special of the day was rosemary chicken. For Jack, rosemary was the spice of remembrance. When a few sprigs of the fresh herb were placed under the skin of a bird and roasted rapidly, the aroma drew forth from the cubbyholes of his long-term memory an ancestral knowledge that went far beyond individual experience. For Jack, raw chicken was full of sharp points, but, as the rosemary and chicken blended in the cooker, these points melted away. When the last of the points were gone, the chicken was done.

Mary Ann got back right before the lunch rush.

"Jack, I can smell that chicken three blocks away," she said. She noticed that he had on a new cap. It was black with gold scrambled eggs across the bill. On the front it read, in an arch, "Green River Street Stock Champs." In a straight line underneath the arch, it said, "Pit Crew."

"I like your new hat," she said.

"Yeah, me too," Jack said.

"Everything going okay?"

"Yeah, sure."

"You need anything?"

"Don't think so," Jack said. "Joy and Richard are inside getting the potatoes and green beans ready. You might ask them."

"You mean *my* Richard?"

Jack nodded and went back to his birds.

She walked through the side door to find Richard rolling up silverware and napkins at the counter. He looked up. "Wow, don't you clean up nice!" he said. "And it didn't take long, either. You look good enough to eat."

When word got around over at the track that Richard was at Moon's, the lunchtime crowd got even bigger.

By two thirty, they had run out of food. As the last of the customers paid their bills and were on the way out the door, the sound of the rescue-squad siren began. It was faint at first, but when it passed the front door of the cafe, it drowned out all conversation. Everyone walked outside to see what was going on. There was always one ambulance on hand during the races, and something bad must have happened for them to need a second.

As the second ambulance negotiated its way into the track, the first one came careening out of the gate. It headed east on Highway 80, toward the hospital in Clear Lake.

In a few minutes, stunned spectators began to drift into the cafe, and the staff was able to piece together the story of what had happened. One of the sprint-car drivers had jumped up to a late-model car, and, on the third lap of the second heat, his car went airborne over the edge and landed on another car, which had just topped off with fuel. Both cars exploded, killing their drivers. The explosions sent debris flying like shrapnel. There were at least fifteen people injured, some seriously. Helicopters were on their way from Batesville and Jonesboro. The least seriously injured were being taken to Cooper County Hospital.

Mary Ann turned toward Richard as they stood watching the first of the helicopters land on the drag strip north of the track.

"Honey, that could just as easily have been you, and that's exactly why I can't go with you," she said.

He put his arm around her shoulder. "I know," he said. "I know."

CHAPTER 19

a change of heart

Since the day Richard left, Mary Ann had not been in a good mood. The staff and customers at Moon's began talking about taking up a collection to buy Richard a farm of his own, so he could give up the road, come back, and marry this woman. But nothing anyone did was good enough. Even Moon was on his best behavior around her. The only time she was happy was when Richard called.

It was a Friday afternoon, and Richard was scheduled to race in Greenville, Mississippi. Mary Ann was checking the weather, hoping for a rainout, and Jack was putting together quesadillas for the happy-hour crowd.

Jack wandered into the bar area, looking for his favorite spatula. While he was rummaging through the utensil drawer, he dropped a large potlid. Instead of falling flat onto the floor, it rolled like a top; he couldn't have made any more noise if he had tried.

Before she realized what she was doing, Mary Ann let loose with a tirade that rivaled one of Moon's. "Dammit, Jack, would you be quiet? I'm trying to listen to the weather!"

Without comment, Jack got his spatula and returned to the kitchen.

He was spreading cheese over the flour tortillas when Mary Ann came in. "I'm sorry, Jack," she said. "I didn't mean to lose my temper."

"It's not anything I did, is it?"

"No. I just haven't slept in a week. Every time I *do* go to sleep, I have these odd, god-awful dreams. And I've lost weight. Not that I didn't need to lose some, but I'm beginning to think there's something really wrong with me."

"Well, there *is*," Jack said.

"And what might that be, Mr. Doctor?" she asked.

"You're in love, and you're depressed."

"Of course, I'm depressed! But I mean something more—some kind of physical illness."

"Same thing," he said.

"What do you mean?"

"Well, most people think that the things that go on in their head are somehow different from the things that go on in the rest of the body. That's wrong. It all works together."

"Where did you learn that?" she asked.

"Don't you understand?" Jack said. "I've lived with this all my life."

Mary Ann thought for a minute. "You just gave me an idea, Jack." She picked up the phone and dialed a number. "Sylvia," she said, "can you come down and help Jack and Joy for the evening? Good. Wrong? No, nothing's wrong. I'm just going to Greenville to see my honey."

She started laughing as she walked out the door. "I already feel better," she said to her co-workers. "I'll see you whenever."

Two hours later, Jack, Joy, and Sylvia were in the midst of the dinner crowd. Jack had taken a bag of trash out back and was coming back in when Richard's new pickup came sliding to a stop on the lot.

"Hey, old buddy, how you been doing?" Richard asked as he got out of the truck. In his left hand, he had an envelope addressed to Mary Ann.

"I'm doing fine," Jack replied, "but Mary Ann's not doing so well."

"I think I know how to fix that," Richard said. "Don't tell her I'm here. I got a surprise for her."

"I hate to tell you, but she's got a surprise for you, too," Jack said.

"Has she got a new boyfriend already?"

"No, nothing like that."

"Well, what is it?" Richard asked.

"She's not here," Jack said.

"Where is she?"

"In Greenville."

"Why?" Richard asked.

"She came looking for you."

"When did she leave?"

"About two hours ago."

"Damn! I must have passed her on the road. Come on, let's go inside. I'll see if I can reach her."

Using the telephone behind the bar, Richard called the track in Greenville and described Mary Ann to the girl at the gate. All he told her was that it was an urgent call from Moon's cafe in Gum Ridge, and that Mary Ann needed to call back before she did anything else.

Richard hung up and turned to Sylvia. "I got something I want you to read to Mary Ann when she calls." He handed her the letter. She opened it, looked it over, smiled, and nodded.

Two beers later, the phone rang; it was Mary Ann. Joy handed the receiver to Sylvia. "Honey, I got this letter this afternoon addressed to you. It reads, 'Cowgirl, get off of the fence—there's a former stock car driver, a rice farmer in Gum Ridge, who wants to marry you. Signed, The Cowboy.' Now, I think you're really going to like the delivery man." She handed the receiver to Richard.

"Woman, what in the hell are you doing in Greenville?" He hesitated for a few seconds, then smiled. "What do you mean, what in the hell am I doing in Gum Ridge? I came looking for you! I want to marry you and make a respectable woman out of you. In front of all of these people, I'm gonna ask you agai … What? Good. I love you, too. Now, if you're not too tired to make another drive, I've made reservations at the Peabody in Memphis."

CHAPTER 20

black

No one in the cafe knew that there was a problem except for Moon. Ever since the day of the big race, Moon had made himself scarce, but there wasn't anything unusual about that.

The Harris brothers and Kate Ellis came in and seated themselves at table seven.

Jerry Harris, the oldest, motioned to Mary Ann.

"What can I get you for you folks?" Mary asked.

"We don't need anything," John said. "We just want to talk to Moon."

Kate grabbed Jerry by the arm. "I'd like a cold beer," she said.

"We're not going to be here that long, so cool your jets. I'll get you something later."

Mary Ann sensed that the trio wasn't in a good mood. "I haven't seen Moon, but I'll check to see if he's in his office."

Mary Ann walked behind the bar, knocked on the office door, and let herself in. "Moon," she said, "there's a couple of guys out here looking for you."

"Who is it?" Moon asked.

"Those two friends of yours from the track."

"Tell 'em ... let's see ... tell 'em I'm not here."

"No, siree, not on your life. I ain't lying to *that* pair. You got two choices. You either go out there, or I'll tell them where you are."

Moon had dreaded this encounter. He slowly got up from his chair, slicked back his hair, forced a smile, and headed out the door.

"Evening, gents," he said. "Can I get you something to drink? A beer, maybe a shot of scotch?"

"No thanks, Moon. This is a business call."

"Well, tell me, boys, what can I do for you?" Moon asked.

"You know damn well what we're here about," John said. "The boss wants his money, and he wants it now."

"And he's gonna get it, no doubt about it! The problem is: that's a lot of money to come up with on short notice." Moon had begun to sweat.

"The boss don't think that a month is short notice," Jerry said

"Has it been that long? Well, I can understand why he'd be anxious, then."

"You don't understand, Moon—the boss ain't anxious about the money," John said. "He knows he's going to get it, and soon."

"Man, you don't understand," Moon said. "It's gonna be hard to come up with that kind of money."

"Once again, I'll tell you—it's *you* who doesn't understand. You don't have any choice."

"But twenty-five thousand dollars is a lot of money. Where am I gonna come up with that much cash?"

John leaned forward in his chair. "That ain't our problem, and, by the way, it's *thirty* thousand dollars now. You know, interest and all. You got two weeks to come up with it, and if you don't, we're gonna take your skinny little ass and bury you in that swamp across the highway—so deep that they'll never find you."

"I could deed the bar over to you," Moon said. "It's worth three times that much, and the deed is free and clear."

"Listen, Moon," Jerry said. "We ain't bankers. We don't give loans. We ain't real estate agents, and we don't want this rathole of a bar. We want our money. Two weeks from today. Period. End of story. Do you understand?"

"Yeah, I guess so," Moon said. "What I don't understand is how the Streak lost that race. He was at forty-nine wins and hadn't lost in six months."

"That's why they call it a race," Jerry said. "Somebody wins, and somebody loses. You bet the wrong car, and you didn't cover your bet. Face it, Moon, you made a rookie mistake. You got greedy. A smart bookie wouldn't do that. Now, it's time to pay. Don't mess with us—we're not bluffing. If we don't get our money, you're dead. Nothing personal—we just can't let you get away with it. We do that, then *everybody'll* try it."

As the party got up to leave, Jerry said, "You got two weeks from today, five o'clock. You got it?"

"Yeah, I got it."

"Good," Jerry said. "I kinda like you. I'd hate to kill you, but you know how it is."

Kate and the two men got up and left. Moon sat at the table with a blank stare on his face. Mary Ann walked over with a tea pitcher in her hand. "Want a refill?" she asked.

"What I really need is that bottle of scotch in my office."

Mary Ann turned back to the bar and said, "Jack, get that bottle of scotch under Moon's desk, and bring it over here, will you?"

She sat down at the table with Moon. "I only caught part of that, but it doesn't sound good. What did you do?"

"A bet went wrong. I lost a bit of money," Moon said.

"How much is a bit?" she asked.

"Thirty thousand."

"Thirty thousand! Moon, you fool, how the hell could you bet that much on one race?"

"Well, I only bet twenty-five, but the meter's been running for the last month. Anyway, it was a sure thing! The Streak hadn't been beat in six months," Moon said. "Forty-nine races straight, all on dirt, and then Richard comes along and screws it up. It was fixed—I *know* it was. Richard has never liked me. He did this to personally humiliate me!"

"That's stupid, Moon. Richard was just the better driver that night. Still, how did you lose thirty thousand?"

Jack came over with the scotch. He looked first at Mary Ann, then at Moon, then back at Mary Ann.

"Is that what those guys wanted?" Jack asked. "One of the guys over at the track pointed those two out to me and told me to stay real far away from them. He said they weren't good people. If they want money, you better give it to them."

"Great advice, Einstein" Moon said. "I would if I had it."

"How did you lose that much money at one time?" Mary Ann asked again.

"Well, I bet all I had. Plus, I figured how much I'd bring in just making book. All told, it came out to almost twenty-five thousand."

"So, you bet money you didn't have?" she said, shaking her head.

"Technically, yes," he said.

"Damn, Moon, my first husband was stupid, but he wasn't *that* stupid."

"Well, thank you for the advice. I'll have you criticize all my bets from now on."

Mary Ann had passed from the surprise stage into anger. "Look here, Albert Lawrence Moon, I know that this is your cafe, but the truth is that this place would have gone belly-up months ago if it wasn't for me and Jack. *Especially* Jack! Now you've gone and got those hoods mad at us. Hell, Moon, they're liable to burn this place down, just to show you that they're serious. What are we gonna do now?"

Moon was slumped in his chair. "I don't know. I don't know what I'm gonna do. I *do* know that those guys are serious and that I've got to find a way to come up with the money."

From the back of Mary Ann's head, Jack heard, *"Okay, you fool, they've found you. They know who you are. It's you that they are after. It's not Moon they want—it's you!"*

Jack mustered his courage. "Mr. Moon … did they ask about me? Was it something I did?"

Distracted from his self-pity, Moon shouted, "Hell, no, Jack! It was *my* damn bets. It had nothing to do with you."

"But did they mention me?"

"No, they didn't mention you. Now, will you go back to your cooking? I don't have time to deal with your craziness right now!"

"Moon, leave him alone," Mary Ann said.

She turned to Jack. "Come sit down, Jack. Listen," she said. "Moon is in trouble, and it has nothing to do with you. He owes those guys a lot of money, and they're gonna hurt him if they don't get it."

"Oh," Jack said. He visibly began to slip into his shell.

The voice from Mary Ann's head began again: *"They've caught you! After all these years, they know where you are—they know about you and your secret."*

From across the room, in a loud booming voice, the vent hood spoke: *"Yeah, you shithead, you've screwed up somebody else's life again. It's your fault he lost all that money. You* made him bet on the Streak, with all your thinking about racing, when you should have been spending your time cooking. If you'd been a better cook, he'd have the extra money today."*

From the back of Mary Ann's head, he heard, *"Jack, it's time to move on. They've found you. Don't let them hurt these people."*

From deep inside, Jack heard a third voice: *"These are my friends, and I like it here. There's something special about this place. I want to stay. I don't want to go away."*

As the war for Jack's soul raged, the world around him went on as if nothing were happening: Mary Ann returned to waiting tables, Moon proceeded to empty the bottle of scotch, and Jack's body went back to the stove. For a while, he went through the motions of cleaning and preparing for the next day, but, soon, the voices had been joined by colors and smells. Red streaks of light issued forth from the stove; they had the feel of diesel exhaust in his nose. There was a dull, dirty yellow halo around the lights that pulsated with fear. At his feet was the color black—an unwelcome intruder who came often in times of terror to stalk and dominate Jack's world. It was the black that stopped him. Soon, it would progress up his legs and hips, and then to his stomach. By the time it reached his neck, he would become immobile, overwhelmed by the feeling of helplessness.

When the black began, Jack knew that it was time to find a quiet place and wait. This was the last the outer world would see of Jack for a couple of days— not by design on Jack's part, but because he had waited too long to seek refuge. Had he left the bar earlier, he would have made it home to the apartment and his bed, but that was not to be. He made it as far as the Legion Hut down by the river before the rain and the blackness in his soul consumed him.

By the time Jack made it that far, his gait had been reduced to a shuffle. Soon, there would be no motion at all. As Jack moved along, he felt a deep, heavy pain in his chest. At the same time, there on the dark street, was a vision of a very angry God. The vision didn't speak; it didn't seem to want anything. This was new to Jack; God had never shown himself to him before. For a minute, Jack stood and stared—through the pain and haze, through the noise, through the voices—and wondered, *What does he want? Why is he so mad?* There was no answer, but at least, for that brief time, there were no voices. There was only the rain, Jack, the pain, and the face of God.

And then, there was nothing but black.

CHAPTER 21

it's a small town

When Mary Ann pulled into the parking lot the next morning, Sylvia was pacing back and forth outside the front door. She was dressed in a thin cloth coat. After the storm passed, the skies had cleared and it turned off cold.

"What are you doing here?" Mary Ann asked. "What's wrong? Are you okay? How did you get here?"

"Yeah, I'm okay," Sylvia replied, "but there's something wrong with Jack."

"What do you mean?"

"I mean, there's something very wrong. Last night, during the storm, I began to sense that something wasn't right. Something strange. Something bad happened last night."

"Well, there was a big blowup at the cafe last night over a problem that Moon has, but Moon's always got problems."

"What about Jack?"

"He left early, during the storm. With one of the guys, I think."

"Did you actually see him leave?" Sylvia asked.

"No, I didn't. I just assumed he went home."

"Mary Ann, it's awfully cold this morning. If he's lying out there under a tree, he could be real sick!"

"Yeah, you're right. Come on in," Mary Ann said. "I need to find some help to open up the cafe. Maybe I can get hold of Moon."

She dialed Moon's mobile phone, but there was no answer. She called Joy and asked her to open up the cafe.

When Joy arrived, Mary Ann and Sylvia got into the pickup and began making the rounds of all the regular places where Jack might be. There was no sign of him.

"You know, Sylvia, Jack's done this before," Mary Ann said, pulling into the pecan orchard for one last look.

"Yeah, I know, but there's something different about this. I can't explain what I feel, but I know that something about Jack changed last night. There's more to him than meets the eye, you know."

"Yeah, I know," Mary Ann said.

"When he told me about his parents, it was as if he wanted to go further, but he just couldn't. There was something that scared him."

Mary Ann nodded.

"And there's one other thing," Sylvia added.

"What's that?"

"I know Jack from somewhere. We've met before—I *know* we have. There's just something about him."

They assured themselves that he wasn't in the orchard and went back to the truck. Driving back into town, they heard a siren and saw Pollard's ambulance heading toward Taylor's Clinic on the north edge of town. The two women looked at each other. Mary Ann did a U-turn and followed the red and white flashing lights.

The American Legion Hut down by the river hadn't been part of Jack's routine. He could have lain there for days if it hadn't been for the Hut's janitor. Thursday night was bingo night at the Hut, and it was his job to set up the tables and clean up the place. Because of the cold, he decided that it was time to get the building ready for winter. When he went out back to check on the pipes and make sure the doors were secure, he found Jack lying under the screened-in porch that faced the river. He thought that Jack was a drunk sleeping one off.

"Hey, mister, get on out of here! We don't allow no drunks here," he said.

Jack didn't respond, so he poked his arm with his broom. When Jack still didn't stir, the janitor turned him over and put his hand over Jack's face. He was breathing, but his body was ice cold. The janitor ran back upstairs and called the ambulance.

The ambulance pulled into the loading dock behind the clinic and parked near the back door. Lloyd, the driver, jumped out and ran inside to find Marge, Taylor's nurse. Mary Ann and Sylvia pulled in right behind the ambulance. Mary Ann got out of the truck and opened the back door of the ambulance, where Jack lay on a stretcher with an IV in his right arm and a heart monitor off to his left.

The EMT had a bag over Jack's face breathing for him. He looked up and noticed her standing there. "Mary Ann, you better stay back," he said.

Dr. Taylor rushed out. "Hey, folks, what we got here?" he asked.

"Found Jack down behind the Legion Hut," the EMT replied. "Well, *we* didn't—the janitor found him. His temperature is ninety. He looks pretty sick, and he's not responding. He's kinda blue, and just barely breathing."

The doctor climbed into the ambulance. He pulled back Jack's eyelids, listened to his chest and heart, poked around on his belly, and tested his reflexes.

"Mary Ann, does Jack take any drugs?" he asked.

"You mean, like the drugs he gets at the mental-health center?"

"No, I mean like stuff he'd get off the streets."

"I don't think so," she said. "I know he doesn't drink."

"What medication is he taking?"

"I don't know, but I'll go to his room and see if I can find it."

"Don't bother—we'll just call over to the clinic," Taylor said.

"Is he gonna be all right?" Mary Ann asked.

"Don't know yet," Taylor responded. He stepped out of the ambulance and put his hand on Mary Ann's shoulder. "Mary Ann, has Jack ever said anything to you about being put on life support? Whether he'd want it or not?"

"What do you mean?

"I mean … like putting him on a ventilator to breathe for him, that kind of thing."

She shook her head.

It dawned on her that this might not be one of Jack's normal spells. "Doc, you know he's done this before, right?"

"Mary Ann, Jack's only a step away from not being here. He's a real sick fella, and I can't help but think that this time is different from the others. The other problem is that we don't know what's going to happen when we start rewarming him. He's not a young man, and there's no telling what's happened to his heart, brain, and kidneys."

"Do anything you can to help him," she said.

Taylor looked up at his nurse. "Call med-flight in Jonesboro; tell them we got an emergency. Tell them to step on it." He looked back at Mary Ann. "Jack is way too sick for me to keep him here."

Thirty minutes later, a blue and white helicopter rose up from the pad, carrying Jack to Jonesboro. Mary Ann and Sylvia stood in the cold morning air and watched as their friend flew away. One of H. T. Lincoln's men drove up with his siren blaring and lights flashing. The nurse walked up and put her arms around Mary Ann's shoulders. "I called H. T. and told him to send somebody to drive you two to Jonesboro. The hospital's going to need family to help make decisions and fill out the paperwork. Is there anybody you want me to call?"

"Call Richard on his cell phone. He can call everyone else," Mary Ann said. "Remind him to call Pete, Sylvia's grandson, and tell him that she's with me."

"Will do," she said.

At six that evening, a young doctor came into the cavernous ICU waiting room. He carried a metal hospital chart. He looked across the crowded room and said, "I need to speak to the Jack Smith family."

When he said Jack's name, most of the people in the waiting room got up and walked toward him. In addition to the people that Richard had called, H.T,'s deputy had started a chain reaction on his way back to Gum Ridge. He had called the dispatcher, who proceeded to tell the whole town.

The doctor smiled. "Looks like Mr. Smith is a pretty popular man."

They all nodded, and Mary Ann stepped forward. "Jack doesn't have any blood family, but he's kinda like a brother to me."

The young doctor stuck his hand out. "I'm Dr. Bailey."

"I'm Mary Ann Phillips. Jack and I work together. We're best friends. How is he?"

"Nice to meet you, Ms. Phillips. Let's have a seat over here and talk about Mr. Smith." He motioned to a small, private glass-walled room near the door.

"Can some of the others join us?"

"Sure, if you think Mr. Smith wouldn't mind."

Mary Ann motioned for Sylvia and Richard to join her and the doctor.

When they were in the room, the doctor said, "Your friend is very sick. He's tried to die on us three times. Once, in the helicopter, his heart went into what we call ventricular fibrillation, and they had to shock him. It happened again right after he got to the unit—that time, we had to shock him twice. We slowly started to warm him up, and, about an hour ago, he began to have seizures. We have that controlled for the time being, but it's hard to know what's going to happen next. We're doing everything we can, but your friend might not make it through the night. Even if he does, it's hard to know if he's going to wake up."

"Can I see him?" Mary Ann asked.

"Sure you can. When you're ready, just punch that button over by the door, and the nurse will let you in."

"When will you be back?"

"One of us will be here all night, but I'll be back for sure in the morning to let you know how he's doing."

"Do everything you can," Mary Ann said. "He's very special to us."

"We will."

Mary Ann walked into the glass-walled cubicle that held Jack's bed. It was hard to recognize her friend. Multiple tubes and machines breathed for him and monitored his heart. Three or four clear plastic lines ran from Jack's arms and chest to bottles of IV fluids. She moved over to the bed and touched his arm. It had a cold, clammy feel. A nurse came in to check one of the monitors.

"Can Jack hear anything I say to him?" Mary Ann asked.

The nurse shook her head. "I don't know, but I don't think so," she said. "We've given him a whole lot of drugs. If he wakes up, I don't think he's gonna remember a whole lot of this."

"Can I stay for a while?"

"Sure. He's been stable for an hour or two."

The nurse left, and Mary Ann pulled a chair over to the bed and sat down. *Jack,* she thought, *you may not come back from this one, and I really will miss you if you go.* Her thoughts were interrupted by the sound of an alarm from the monitor above and to the left of the bed. She looked up at the screen. A few minutes earlier, it had been dominated by a line of regular spikes; it was now filled with a ragged, irregular series of spikes and wide troughs. She heard the nurse who had just walked out shout for help just outside the door. "Smith, in Room Three, is back in V-tach! Get the defibrillator in here!" Within a few seconds, a half-dozen people had descended on the room.

"Miss, you need to go out to the waiting room," the nurse said to Mary Ann. "We'll let you know what happens."

Mary Ann backed out of the room while the nurses prepped Jack to be shocked. She was crying when she walked into the waiting room. Richard and Sylvia were the first to see her.

"What is it?" Richard asked.

"Jack's heart is trying to stop. They're shocking him right now. I'm so scared that he's not going to make it."

Sylvia put her arms around her friend. "He's a tough bird. Don't count him out yet."

The nurse came to the door. "Ms. Phillips?"

Mary Ann looked up. "Is he—?"

"He did okay. He converted, and he's back in normal sinus rhythm."

"What does that mean?" Mary Ann asked.

"It means that his heart is beating like it's supposed to," the nurse said. "He's doing better."

Mary Ann grabbed the nurse's hand. "You call me if he wakes up, okay?"

The nurse nodded, then went back into the unit.

Richard guided Mary Ann back to their chairs. "Honey, why don't you go to the motel and get some sleep? One of us will stay up, and I promise we'll call you if anything happens."

"No. I need to be here if—when—he wakes up," she said.

Jack didn't wake up that night, and Dr. Bailey's news the next morning was mixed.

"The good news is that he's had no more seizures or V-tach since early last night. The bad news is that his kidneys aren't working well, and it looks like he's had a heart attack."

Mary Ann moved forward in her seat. "Has he woken up yet?"

The doctor shook his head. "But that really doesn't tell us much. We have him pretty well doped up for the seizures and to keep him from fighting the ventilator."

"When will you see if he's going to wake up?" Sylvia asked. "I mean, when will you let up on the medicine?"

"If he does well for the next twenty-four hours, we'll start trying to wean him off the ventilator. But ..." He shook his head. "I wouldn't get my hopes up too high if I were you. I'm sorry."

The rest of the day passed slowly. Except for Mary Ann, Sylvia, and Richard everyone else had gone back to their lives. The next morning, when the doctor came out into the waiting room, he had a big smile on his face.

"Mr. Smith is waking up," he said. "We gave him a little extra medicine to keep him from fighting the breathing tube, but he is definitely coming around."

"Can I see him?" Mary Ann asked.

"Sure," he said. "It would probably be a good idea for him to see a familiar face while we're trying to get him off the breathing machine. Sometimes, folks are real wild when they start to wake up."

Mary Ann followed the doctor back into the unit. When she first looked into the room, Jack looked no different than he had the day before, but then she noticed the fingers of his left hand moving—it was as if he was trying to feel his fingertips.

She leaned close to his face and, in a soft voice, said, "Jack, it's me. I'm here. There's nothing to worry about."

Jack opened his eyes and looked up at her. There was no sign of recognition in his gaze.

"Jack, it's me ... Mary Ann."

Jack continued to stare through her.

One of the nurses was working an IV. "He might not be real clear about who you are," she said. "Just keep talking to him—pretty soon, it'll dawn on him."

Mary Ann kept talking. She explained how he had ended up in this strange bed, in this strange place. She explained how all his friends had come to the hospital to see him and how worried they were. She talked about how he'd had a heart attack and seizures, and how, for a while, they were worried that he wouldn't make it.

Soon, Jack was following her with his eyes and trying to listen. Every few minutes, one of the staff would come in and make an adjustment to one of the machines.

"Ms. Phillips," the respiratory therapist said, "you need to step out to the nurses' station for a minute. We're going to take out his endotracheal tube. It may be a little uncomfortable for Mr. Smith."

A few minutes later, the tube had been removed from his airway, and Jack was easily breathing on his own. The staff cleaned up and allowed Mary Ann back into the room.

"Morning, Jack," she said. "I bet it feels good to have that thing out of your throat."

He looked up at her, but he didn't speak.

Mary Ann laid her hand on his arm, but he pulled it away.

"Are you okay?" Mary Ann asked.

"Who are you?" he asked with a raspy voice.

"I'm Mary Ann, Jack. Don't you remember? I work with you at the cafe."

"What cafe?"

"Moon's," she said.

"I don't know anything about any cafe, and I don't know you," he said in a voice that didn't sound like Jack.

She decided not to push it.

"Well, Jack ..."

"Why do you keep calling me Jack? My name's not Jack."

"Okay," she said.

Mary Ann could tell that this conversation wasn't going anywhere, so she stood up to leave the room.

"One other thing," the man in the bed said. "Get me whoever's in charge in here. I want out of this place. It's dangerous to be here."

Mary Ann went to the nurses' station and told the charge nurse about the conversation she had just had with her friend. "I need to talk to Dr. Bailey now, if I can. Jack is really acting strange."

The nurse picked up the phone and paged the young doctor. He returned the call and told the nurse to tell Mary Ann to come up to the fourth floor, where he was making rounds.

"Jack is really acting odd," she said to Bailey at the fourth floor nurses' station. "He doesn't know who I am, he doesn't remember the cafe, and he tells me that he isn't Jack! The worst part is that he is demanding to get out of here."

"He's probably just scared and disoriented," the doctor said. "It happens sometimes, after injuries like this. Then again, you must remember that Jack has had a whole lot of trauma to his brain. He may end up not being the same guy you knew before all this. I'll give him some medicine and see if we can calm him down."

The medicine relaxed Jack, and he stopped demanding to leave, but he still wouldn't talk to Mary Ann. When she went back to the waiting room and told Sylvia what had happened, Sylvia took her to the cafeteria for a cup of coffee.

"I hope you will understand what I am about to tell you," Sylvia said. "All the things that Jack has been through, now and in the past, may have been just too much for him. I may have a clue as to what's going on with him and what this all means. As good a friend as you are, I don't feel that I can tell you what I'm thinking. I know some things about him that *he* doesn't even know. I'm going home tonight, and I'll be back in the morning. It may take a jolt to bring Jack out of this."

The next morning, the doctor moved Jack from intensive care to a regular room. Mary Ann and the doctor stood in the hall outside the new room.

"Your friend is doing well," the doctor said. "All the tests are normal. The heart damage was minor. Even his kidney problem has cleared up."

"But, Doctor, there's something really wrong with him. He doesn't even sound like the same person," Mary Ann said.

"You need to understand that your friend has had quite a lot of trauma to his whole body, including his brain. It may take him a few days to come around. He certainly is calmer today than he was yesterday." The doctor made a notation in Jack's chart, handed it to the nurse, and walked off.

Mary Ann went back into the room. Sylvia was sitting in the chair by the bed. She had a large straw purse. Jack lay with his eyes closed.

"Jack?" Mary Ann said.

The man in the bed opened his eyes, but didn't answer.

"The doctor says you're doing well," Mary Ann continued. "He even said that, if you keep improving, you'll be ready to go home in a few days."

"My name's not Jack," he said.

Sylvia sat up and looked at him. "What *is* your name, if it isn't Jack?" she asked.

"I can't tell you," he said. "For all I know, you work for *them.*"

"For who, Ja—, I mean, for who?" Mary Ann asked.

"Don't you understand? It's all about the money. They want their money."

Mary Ann shut the door and pulled a straight-backed chair over to the bed. "Jack, are you talking about Moon's money?"

"It's *their* money," he said.

"The men from the track?" Mary Ann asked.

"Yes, the men from the track."

"But, Jack …"

"Why do you keep calling me Jack?"

"If your name isn't Jack, what is it?" Mary Ann asked.

"You have to promise you won't tell anyone." He looked over at Sylvia. "You too."

"We won't tell anyone," Sylvia said. "We're your friends."

"My name is Currier. Paul Currier."

"Are you sure?" Sylvia asked.

He looked at Sylvia but didn't reply.

"Well, Mr. Paul Currier," Sylvia said, "for the last year or so, you've been living in Gum Ridge, Arkansas. How did you come to be in Gum Ridge?"

"I can't tell you. They'd come after all three of us."

"Those guys at the track aren't interested in you and me," Mary Ann said. "They're after Moon."

"I don't mean *those* guys."

Mary Ann was beginning to get a little frustrated with this conversation. "Now, stop it, Jack! This is goofy! What in the hell are you talking about? First, you tell us you're not Jack, and now, you're talking about somebody else's money. Who are you?"

Sylvia reached into her straw bag, pulled out an old cigar box, and handed it to Jack.

Jack opened the box and looked through its contents. He pulled out a picture of a young boy and his mother, who sat in a chair in front of a 1940 Ford sedan. As he looked at the picture, he began to cry.

"What's this all about?" Mary Ann asked Sylvia.

"These pictures are the key to who he really is," Sylvia said.

Sylvia looked at Jack. "Paul, you can tell us who you are. We won't tell anyone. We promise."

"I'm Powhatan J. Ives."

"Right, sure you are, Jack," Mary Ann said. "You're the guy with all of the money, and I'm the Queen of England. Jack, my friend, I think you got some brain damage, lying out there in the cold." Mary Ann stared at him. "Look, Jack, if you're P. J. Ives, why didn't you say so before?"

He thought for a minute. "I guess—I didn't know," he said.

"How do you expect me to believe this?"

"I don't know that either," Jack said.

CHAPTER 22

confusing soup

Saratoga to St. Louis Train, 1948

Powhatan J. Ives has a nice ring to it, Paul J. Currier thought as he sat staring out the open window, watching the cornfields as the train headed west for East St. Louis. The warm fragrance of the young corn flooded through the window. Next to him, on the seat, was his mother's canvas bag, and at his feet was a locked leather satchel. The contents of the satchel were why Pauly was on the train.

Two weeks before, his father had revealed that he had cancer and wouldn't live long. In the same conversation, he had instructed Pauly to go to the bedroom closet and retrieve a leather satchel that lay hidden under an Indian blanket. When Pauly returned and placed the case on the kitchen table, the elder Currier pulled out his keys and opened the latch. He grabbed the accordion folds and flipped the bag open. To Pauly's amazement, the bag was full of money—a lot of money.

"Whose money is this, Dad?" Pauly asked. The Currier household had never had any extra money. It had taken all that his father could earn just to pay the rent and keep food on the table. Pauly remembered being a young child and listening to his mother and father fight about money and how much she spent on oils and perfumes.

"It's yours," Paul Sr. said.

"That's not what I mean. Where did it come from?"

"Let's just say that some people at the track have been generous to me over the years—even if they didn't know it at the time."

"I don't understand. Did you steal this money?" Pauly asked.

"Absolutely not," his father replied. "The folks at the track have been good to me. I would never steal a penny of their money."

"Where did it come from?" Pauly asked again.

The elder Currier took a drag off of his cigarette and then coughed. "Part of my job at the track is to take care of the people who haul the beer and clean up the trash. The track always paid extra to keep everything going smooth. It was my job to make sure that the money got paid. It didn't take long for me to realize that those idiots had no idea how much they were supposed to be getting. So, every day, I skimmed a little off the top. As far as I can tell, they never knew what I was doing. The hardest part was keeping it a secret from your mother. She was a good woman, but she would have spent every cent."

"We've got to give this money back, Dad!" Pauly spoke to his father as if he were chastising a wayward son.

"Can't do that, son. The owners of the track wouldn't take kindly to the fact that I've been setting aside a little for my retirement. And, as far as the other folks, I wouldn't know who to give it to. Besides, they'd kill me and you on the spot if they thought I'd been stealing from them."

His father's health and the money in the bag had triggered a deep-seated fear in Pauly that smelled of sulfuric acid.

There was an awkward silence, and then Pauly asked, "What do you want me to do with it?"

"I want you to take it and leave. Get as far away from here as you can. You'll have nothing to keep you here, and when they discover that there's money missing, someone will come looking."

"But what about you, Dad? I can't leave you here like this. Someone's got to take care of you!"

"Bullshit! I can take care of myself," his father said. "You take the money and leave. And don't call or write—I won't be here to get the message, but *they* might."

Paul Sr. was insistent. Pauly must leave, change his name, and never come back. The leaving would be hard, but not the change of name. As a child, Pauly had spent many hours alone with imaginary playmates. The most beloved of these illusory friends had been Powhatan J. Ives. The Powhatan Jay had been his mother's favorite bird, and Currier and Ives was his father's brand of aftershave. When he boarded the train in Saratoga, Paul J. Currier was left behind, and Powhatan Jay Ives—P. J. for short—was born.

As the train neared the outskirts of East St. Louis, the sweet fragrance of the cornfields was replaced by city smells.

On the south edge of town, there was a chemical plant with the serrated edge of malathion; the heavy, oily feel of burning kerosene; and the almond-tinged bite of chlorine. For P. J., this harsh combination was raw with irregular black and violet points that seemed to go off into space and crowd out the sun. It gave him a headache.

As it neared the station, the train passed the stockyards. On a building just to the west of the yards, someone had painted a large makeshift sign that read, "East St. Louis—The World's Largest Hog Market." Unlike the grating chemical odors, this was the smell of life and death—a complex, layered fragrance of survival.

P. J. became lost in this soup as the train slowed and then stopped at the platform. He stepped from the train, the sum of his life contained in his two bags. In a floral-print carpetbag, he carried a change of clothes and a cigar box full of mementos. In the leather satchel, of course, was the money. He was plagued with thoughts of self-doubt and recrimination: *Your father stole this money for you. He gave up his honesty for you. You always wanted more, and he knew it. The strain on your mother was too much for her to bear. If it weren't for you, she'd still be alive. What a selfish shit you are!*

No matter how hard he tried to force these thoughts from his mind, they were always there.

His first stop was the YMCA—a quiet place, a clean room, a shower, and a chance to get his bearings.

For days, P. J. roamed the streets, exploring the neighborhoods. East St. Louis was an easy place to get lost in. As long as he didn't speak, he didn't stand out. Like in most cities, there were nice, comfortable middle-class neighborhoods where everyone spoke English—where people could trace their ancestries back for generations in the same house. But there was another side to the city—a side of impermanence, of temporary, old-country-style ghettos. He was quick to pick out the areas it was best to avoid. The Negro sections of town were clearly demarcated, as were the Italian areas. The people there made it clear—if you were not one of them, stay out. Northeast of downtown was Goose Hill, a Russian Jewish community, and, beyond that, the Fairmont racetrack. At Seventh and Exchange, above the Home Stretch Bar and Grill, was the Bachelor Hotel for Men, which was clean and inexpensive. He asked for and got a corner room on the top floor, and soon he was engrossed in establishing a ritual, one that he would repeat for years.

How can I best secure the money?

Banks were out of the question. "Son," his father had said, "banks are built by and for rich people. Steer clear of them."

Luggage storage at the train station just wasn't secure enough.

Eventually, he bought a small safe. He purchased additional locks for both inside and outside the door to his room. He always kept the windows shut and locked.

P. J. was beginning to understand the relationship between things and people. Things had their own way of communicating. Money had knowledge that was beyond human thought; it was an entity that demanded recognition, and it spoke in no uncertain terms:

"You have responsibilities to me," it said. *"Count me and verify that every penny is here. You will be judged on your stewardship. I am here for a purpose. You are not smart enough to understand this purpose. Just do it."*

He spent a certain portion of each day counting the packets of money. He developed his own accounting system and code, for which there was no key except in his brain.

His next step was to find a job. His meager finances, aside from his father's money, were quickly running out. He soon found that any job beyond dishwasher in the cafe on the ground floor of the hotel required proof of who you were. That could pose quite a problem, since P. J. Ives didn't exist. One evening, as he was sweeping out the kitchen downstairs in the cafe, he overheard the cook talking to his nephew. The young man had run afoul of the law and needed a new start.

"Son, you need to talk to Nat Perkoff, the Russian grocer on Bowman," the cook said. "He knows about such things."

Perkoff's Grocery and Deli was a converted stable that was packed to the rafters with long strips of sausage, slabs of salted beef, kegs of pickles and cabbage, and dry bins of potatoes, corn, and flour.

Nat Perkoff always stood behind the raised counter, directing traffic through this maze of aisles, blind alleys, and occult lofts. He was a big man with a long, black beard, and he shouted orders to his wife, who stood behind him. He spoke in a mixture of Russian, Yiddish, and English, the words interspersed with peals of laughter.

P. J. was immediately attracted to the world of Perkoff's. It seemed as though every hunger could be met here, every appetite whetted within these walls. There were the round tastes of cooked meats, the violent passion of pepper, fennel, and garlic that seemed to leap out in flaming tongues, and the billowy, cloudlike feel of raw corn and wheat. Tightly woven in and around and through all of this was the musty odor of human activity.

P. J. timidly approached the counter. "Mr. Perkoff?" he asked.

Nat looked around in mock disbelief. "Mr. Perkoff? Do I look like an old man to you?" he asked. "Do I look like a man who can't get it up at night? I am *not* Mr. Perkoff! I am Nat. Mr. Perkoff is my father. He is an old man. Do I look like an old man to you?"

"No, sir. I'm sorry to offend you, Mr. Nat."

"What's with the Mr. Nat? It's Nat, like the little bugs on peaches. Nat! Nat!"

"Yes, sir, Nat," P. J. said.

"So, what do you want, boy? I'm busy. Can't you see that I've customers?"

From the large wooden prep table behind him, Anna Perkoff shouted to Nat in Yiddish. "Two orders up, and I need a break! I'm tired," she said.

Nat turned and shouted back, "If we all took a break when we were tired, we would be broke! What do you want me to do, your job *and* mine?" He turned back to P.J., smiled, and threw his hands up in the air. "Women! What can I say? Now, what do you want? You want a Reuben? We got good corn beef. You want soup? We got flankin-in-a-pot. We got fresh lox."

"No, sir, I'm not hungry, thank you," P. J. said.

"What are you wasting my time for? I've got business! What is it? You like to look at my face?"

"I need to talk to you about some papers."

"Well, I got papers: cigarette papers, writing paper, butcher paper, wrapping paper. What kind of paper you want?" Nat asked.

P. J. hesitated.

Nat smiled. "Oh, you want *that* kind of papers. Look, son, I'm busy now. We close at nine tonight. You come back at ten."

"I've been told not to be on these streets after dark."

"You tell them you are coming to talk to Nat Perkoff, and no one will bother you. They better not."

That evening, at the appointed hour, P. J. knocked on the glass-front door, causing the venetian blinds inside to rattle. There was something black about these streets at night, and it seemed like an eternity before any sound or movement emanated from the store. Mrs. Perkoff peered out through the blinds, silently opened the door, motioned him in, and closed the door behind him. Then, like a ghost, she slowly moved through the store with P. J. in tow. In the back of the store, he could see a light shining around a pulled curtain. She drew the curtain aside and motioned for him to enter. The doorway opened into a tiny apartment, cluttered with the paraphernalia of life. In the corner sat a silent old couple. P. J. thought that the old man must be Mr. Perkoff. In the back was a small kitchen with a hutch table in the corner. Nat leaned over a stack of papers.

"Come in, come in." He waved P.J. into a chair across from him. "So, what can I do for you?"

"I need papers."

"I know that, but what for? You are obviously not one of us—your English is too good. You sound American, so why do you need papers?"

"I want to get a job," P. J. said.

"You can get a job without papers."

"Yeah, but not a *good* job. I can't get an education without papers."

"Are you running from something?" Nat asked.

"Sorta, and sorta not."

"Have you broken the law?"

"No, sir, absolutely not," P. J. objected. "I've done nothing wrong."

"Then why not use your real name?"

"I can't—it would endanger other people."

"Okay, son, I'll get you some papers, but it will be expensive."

"How much?"

"Two hundred dollars," Nat said.

"That's a lot of money."

"This is not an easy job. Well, what do you say?"

"Okay, but … will anybody be able to trace me? Anybody?"

Nat shook his head and then added, "No system is foolproof, but our work is about as close as it comes. We borrow names and create a life."

"When do I pay you?" P. J. asked.

"Oh, you don't pay *me*, son. I have something for you." He reached into an accordion folder and handed P. J. an envelope. Inside was a bill for $205.48 from the Southside Mercantile to Anthony Lorenzana. The bill detailed a quantity of flour, vegetables, beer, and wine.

"My friend owes this amount at the Mercantile," Nat said. "I'd consider it a great favor if you would pay it. Then, next Friday, go to the Central Post Office in downtown St. Louis. There will be a package for you in general delivery. It will contain everything you need, with instructions on how to apply for all the other necessary documents."

Just as Nat had promised, on the appointed day, there was a large manila envelope addressed to P. J. Ives waiting at general delivery. The envelope was postmarked in Chicago and bore no other identification. In the packet was a black document with white print that appeared aged and worn around the edges. In white print was the name Powhatan Jay Ives, born December 12, 1930, to John and Mabel Ives in Duluth, Minnesota. The baby weighted 8lb. 6 oz. at birth; the delivering physician was Dr. Sam Enderlin. Also in the packet was a diploma from Duluth Rural High School from 1947. A third piece of paper in the envelope had a brief message: "Here are the lost documents you requested. Use the birth certificate to get your replacement Social Security number. Good luck."

With Nat's help, he got a job as a librarian's assistant at the public library. One morning while taking a coffee break, he was looking through a magazine. On the back cover was an advertisement for a diploma college in South Bend, Indiana. He mailed off the ad, and, in two weeks, he received a packet of materials from the college. Among the courses offered was a correspondence course in the law. The pamphlet explained that several states did not require the completion of law school, but only a thorough, working knowledge of the law, plus evidence that you'd completed a certified course. In Illinois, this course was certified.

P. J. sent in the completed application and fee, and, in two months, he was studying to become a lawyer. Unencumbered, he would have completed his studies in three years and been ready to begin his apprenticeship, but, on several occasions, his well-laid plans were disturbed.

With no explanation or reason, life would begin to overwhelm him. At night, he experienced rage and fear. The rage was a bright red and yellow cloud of bitter regrets that tasted of bile. The fear was a wall of sharp points that roared of freshly plowed wild onions, pungent and eye-opening. In the midst of this sensory storm, the money demanded attention. There were days on end spent counting and recounting each packet. The relief of completing a cycle was short-lived. He would awaken the next day to meet the demons again. These spells would go on for weeks before they slowly subsided.

P.J.'s free time was spent haunting the municipal court of East St. Louis. There, he would observe trials regarding the theft of a loaf of bread, a Saturday-night stabbing in a drunken brawl, a man beating his wife, a wife beating her husband, a parent beating a child—at times, the contrast between legal theory and the practical application of the law troubled him. What he most enjoyed was watching a good judge work the system. That's what he really wanted to be—a judge who knew how to make the system serve justice.

As he neared the end of his course of study, P. J. returned again to Nat Perkoff. This time, he did not come empty-handed. "Nat, I need someone to help me with my apprenticeship. If you help me with this, I promise I'll be there for the people of the community. I owe you and your people a debt, and I will repay it."

Nat arranged for him to be apprenticed to Dr. Bob Kornstol, chiropractor and lawyer. Dr. Bob wasn't particularly good at either profession, but he gave P.J. the firsthand knowledge necessary to pass the bar. P.J. worked hard, and within two years he was building a steady practice. Often, the payment for services was indirect. It could be an envelope delivered by a stranger, or a clothing store might notify P. J. of a credit. Sometimes, work was done for free, but nothing ever went unpaid in the community.

All went well for P. J. until one night in 1957, when Perkoff's grocery exploded in flames. The "accident" was reportedly caused by Jocko Vincent, Nat's Italian counterpart on the other side of the tracks, the result of a recent dispute between the two men. No one could say for sure—the Italians had made certain of that. Nat and his family were killed in the blast. Two days later, a second blast occurred, this one killing two of Vincent's sons. The war was on, and P. J., clearly associated with the Perkoff family, found himself right in the middle of it.

For days, P. J. worried about what to do. He didn't eat; he just sat. He sat and counted the money, over and over again. He feared sleep and dreaming—he never knew when the nightmares might become real. After several days, the money began to speak: *"All right, stupid, do I have to tell you everything to do? Shit, Paul, you realize this is all your fault. I've been telling you for years to get out of this place. What do you think all those dreams were about? The Perkoffs were doing fine until you came along and fucked everything up. If you weren't such a selfish asshole, you wouldn't have put their lives on the line. Think about it—you're alive, and they're dead. But don't worry, it won't take long for Jocko and his men to find you. When they do, you'll be dead meat."*

"Now, you ignorant fool," the money continued, *"you've got two options: you can sit here and wait for them to shoot your ass, or you can get the hell out of here."*

The safe was a complication. It made riding a train or a bus impossible, so he decided that a car was in order. Around the corner from his hotel was a small used-car lot. When he walked onto the lot, he knew right away which car he wanted. In the back, next to a wooden fence, was a boxy little sedan, two-toned with aquamarine on top and white on the bottom. The salesman assured him that it was in top-notch shape and would last him forever. The price was one hundred dollars. P. J. purchased it on the spot.

Before dawn the next morning, he loaded the safe into the passenger seat of the tiny car, put his two bags on the floor, and headed out of the city. He had no idea where he was heading.

As the sun set, P. J. crossed the Missouri-Arkansas border. He hadn't slept in days, and the mountain driving made the fatigue worse. Just after dark, he was awakened when the front wheel of his car left the road and began to bounce around in the loose gravel. He had dozed off, and the car had drifted across the highway. When the car finally came to a stop, he decided that he needed to find a place to pull off for the night. At the top of the next long incline was a roadside park. P.J pulled off the road, parked the car, locked the doors, and went to sleep. He woke up the next morning as the sun was rising over the horizon. There in front of him was a broad expanse of delta cloaked in a blue-green haze of humidity. Running south out of the mountains was the Green River, and crossing the river was a tall steel-framed bridge. The ribbon of highway that extended out from the opposite end of the bridge followed a ridge that angled northeast like an arrow on a compass. After the highway came off the ridge, it ended in a quiet patch of woods and houses that was the town of Gum Ridge.

For the first time in weeks, he felt calm, and the money didn't speak. It was a good sign.

P.J. made the looping drive down to the bridge, crossed over the river, and drove into town. There were a few small businesses and an old movie theater where *A Face in the Crowd* was playing. The grocery store next to the theater smelled of freshly ground coffee. Farther down the main drag were a clothing store and the bank. Just beyond the bank was a barbershop with a revolving red and white pole. The highway then turned abruptly to the left, and, within two blocks, it was obvious he had entered "colored" town—all the roads that fed into the highway were gravel or mud, the houses weren't painted, and the stores all seemed in disrepair. At the edge of town, on the corner of Highway 80 and Border Street, was a small storefront building with a "For Rent" sign in the front window.

P. J. pulled his little sedan up to the building and jotted down the address of the owner from the sign.

He found Marshall Properties and Agricultural Company in an office at the back of the bank building on Main Street.

When he entered, Glen Marshall, heir to the family fortune and manager of his father's properties, was working on the day's receipts.

"May I help you?" he asked.

"I'm interested in your building on Highway 80 and Border Street," P. J. said. "I'd like to rent it."

Glen walked around the counter with his hand extended. "My name is Glen Marshall. I don't think we've met."

P. J. shook his head and tentatively put out his hand. "P. J. Ives."

"What kind of work do you do, Mr. Ives?"

"I'm a lawyer."

"Excellent! We can always use a good lawyer in town," Marshall said. "Now, Mr. Ives, you *do* realize that that piece of property is down in the middle of 'colored' town? I've got some nice space available right here on Main Street and anything you'd pay extra in rent you'll get back five times over in exposure."

"How much is the place down on Border Street?" P. J. asked.

"Well, let me see ... ordinarily, it rents for seventy-five dollars a month, but since you're new in town ... how does fifty dollars sound?"

"That's fine," P. J. said.

"Now, you do realize that you will be responsible for the utilities and any remodeling that needs to be done?"

"Okay, that's fine."

"Do you want to go and look at the building?" Marshall asked.

"No."

"When would you like to occupy it?"

"Today," P. J. said.

"Oh, okay. Let me get one of our standard contracts. It's a six-month lease, and we need a one-month deposit."

"Sure."

P. J. leaned over the counter and signed, "Powhatan Jay Ives."

"That's an interesting name."

"My mother liked the sound of it."

"Where are you from, Mr. Ives?" Marshall asked.

"Here and there," P. J. said.

"You got family?"

"No, just me. They died in the war."

"Oh, I'm sorry to hear that," Marshall said. When Ives offered no further explanation, Marshall dropped the subject.

"Well, Mr. Ives, if there's anything I can do to help you, let me know. Rent is due on the first of the month. I'll come by and pick it up."

P. J. left to occupy his new home.

That night, out on the gravel bar under the bridge, in his brand-new convertible, Glen told Mamie, "I rented the old Polish grocery to a strange little fellow this morning. Talks funny—Northern, or Jewish. Calls himself Powhatan Jay Ives. He's a lawyer. He rented that building even after I told him it was in 'nigger' town. Well, actually, I said it was 'colored' town. You know, come to think of it, I'd better keep my eye on this guy. Could be one of them Yankee agitators. He did seem awful nervous."

Mamie smiled at Glen and slid a little closer. "Talk about nervous! You're the one who sounds nervous. One day, you think that the governor is a communist, and the next, you think that this new fellow's an agitator. Let me see if I can't help calm you down a little bit." She reached out, put her hand on his thigh, worked it up toward his crotch, and gave him a little squeeze. "You need to get rid of a little steam," she said.

While Glen and Mamie were absorbed in their pleasure, P.J. surveyed his new kingdom. At the back of the store, he found an old wooden desk and a couple of chairs. He put his safe behind the desk by the east wall. What legal books he had fit nicely on one of the old bread racks. At the mercantile, he purchased an old army-style cot, some wool blankets, a hot plate, and a coffeepot. He tied a rope across the store and hung up one of the wool blankets, effectively separating the space into an office and a bedroom. P.J. was satisfied. The voices and distrust had calmed. He would have to go to Little Rock to settle the problem of a law license, but that was just a technicality. For the time being, he could settle into a quiet life, at least for a time.

In the interest of good business, Glen threw some legal work P. J.'s way—mostly black folks in trouble with the law. It wouldn't hurt Glen even if P. J. didn't do a good job.

In the next few months, the people of Gum Ridge saw very little of Mr. Ives. Most of his time was spent locked away in his storefront office, counting the ever-present money. Each day required that he account for every penny that had been entrusted to him. With each day, his system of accounting became more complicated. Soon after moving to Gum Ridge, the system of checks and balances began to grow, and, within months, it occupied all of his waking hours. It was then that the voices returned. Despite every effort on his part, nothing could quiet the money. No matter how he counted or recounted, no matter what refinements he made to his system, it consumed more and more of his day. Soon, he was counting the money around the clock. And then, one very cool November evening as he sat counting another packet of twenty-dollar bills, it happened. The combination of fatigue, the voices demanding that he count the money once again, and the fear that one of Jocko Vincent's men would come walking in, caused his connection with reality, as he knew it, to break. The associations of life and family and history—the thread that wove through his being—unraveled. He rose from his chair, free from fear for the first time in years. He walked out the door, across the street, and into the swamp. He never returned.

Two days later, Glen, on his rent-collection rounds, found the money and the safe, but no P. J. For weeks, the State Police and the FBI searched for Powhatan Jay Ives. They couldn't find him. He didn't exist. Except for his law license and a birth certificate, every trail was a dead end. There was a box of mementos that ended up in a safe at the Marshall Company. Conspiracy theories multiplied and grew in complexity. One theory was that P. J. was an alien and that the invasion had begun, another explanation concerned mobsters, Governor Orval Faubus and the NAACP. The theory most of Gum Ridge loved best was that Ives was Glen Marshall's illegitimate brother who had come back to claim his share of the family land and money. Glen, naturally, had him killed and buried his body in the Little P swamp.

While the world searched in vain, P.J. wandered through the swampy forest of the Le Petite River bottomland. Had it not been a warm November, he certainly would have died there.

For weeks, P. J. moved about the swamp with no particular direction. At times, he heard the voices of squirrel hunters as they stalked their prey. He hid, although he wasn't quite sure why. When he got weak, he ate pecans and persimmons. When he got thirsty, he drank the murky swamp water. A month later, he emerged on the other side of the river bottom, thirty miles east and twenty miles south of where he had gone in.

It was early morning when he walked out onto State Highway 128 and started walking east. He walked east because that was where the sun was coming up.

Fats Armstrong was hauling a bob truck of rice to the big granary in Memphis when he saw this fellow walking on the side of the road. Fats pulled over, stopped the truck, and looked down at P. J. What he saw was an odd-looking little man who seemed like he'd been wallowing around in the mud for a couple of days.

"Mornin', friend! You look a little worse for wear," Fats said.

P. J. nodded.

"Where you headed?"

P. J. shrugged.

"Well, I'm headin' for Memphis. If'n you want a ride, you better git in, 'cause I'm leavin'."

P. J. walked around and stepped up on the running board. He opened the passenger door of the old truck and slid in beside Fats.

Fats clutched the truck and worked his way through progressively higher gears as the inertia of the rice load was overcome.

"Boy, you sure do smell bad! What you been doing, wallowing around down there in that swamp?"

P. J. just looked ahead.

"Don't say much, do you? What's your name, Jack?"

P. J. repeated this last word. "Jack."

"Oh, so Jack's name is Jack! Well, at least I know you can talk. You want a cup of coffee? There's an extra cup in the glove compartment. If'n you want some really good soup, there's a hot jar down there on the floor. My wife fixed me two this mornin', 'cause I'm haulin' all the way to Memphis."

The idea of cooked food hadn't occurred to P. J. in weeks. He unscrewed the Mason jar's lid and took the rubber-sealed cap off. The smell that emanated from the jar stuck with him for the rest of his life—it was a succotash of corn and rice and beans and chicken and cheese that he felt to his core. For the longest time, he just sat and smelled the jar of food. As he did so, a flood of sunlight, warm and yellow, invaded his being. The smell of the food, the sunlight, and the purring sound of the old truck felt soft, like a warm blanket on a cold evening.

"Well, Jack, you gonna eat it or just stare at it?" the black man asked with a grin. "Wife's cookin' does that to folks. She can cook up a spell. When I walk in the back door of the house, sometimes, I think I done died and gone to heaven, it smells so good. By the way, Jack, they calls me Fats."

Jack looked at the man, and then down at his stomach. His old gray work shirt was two sizes too small and straining at the buttons and the seams.

Jack turned back to the jar. He ate all of the solids and then drank the pot liquor at the bottom.

"You want the other one?" Fats asked. "Go on, eat it—I got plenty stored up!" He patted his belly and laughed.

Jack piled into the second jar, and was soon sipping on his second cup of coffee. Waiting. Waiting for the next question for which he had no answer. In truth, he didn't know who he was, where he was going, where he had been, or even *if* he had been. This was the first moment of his life. But, from somewhere beyond the glove compartment, beyond the side mirror, a tiny voice was saying to him, *"Keep up your guard, there are people out there who don't like you."* He wondered *what* people, and why they didn't like him, but there was no answer.

By midday, they were crossing the big bridge over the Mississippi River into Memphis. When the traffic thinned, Fats pulled the truck over.

"I'm headin' south of town to Presidents Island, and there ain't nothin' down there that you'll be needin'." Fats pointed north and said, "If'n you cross the road, go under that dry dock, and turn right about six blocks down, you'll find a mission. They'll give you a place to sleep and some food. All you got to do is listen to a sermon. They're pretty nice folks. Memphis is a pretty good place, as long as you're careful. Nobody'll bother you. You ain't got nothin' they can steal. Be careful about the police—they don't like bums. Bein' white and all, they won't give you much trouble."

"Anybody in here know how to cook?" the big black man with the short gray beard asked, looking into the barracks of cots in the mission dormitory. "The Crystal Palace is looking for a short-order cook. They'll pay you regular, and you get all the old burgers you can stomach."

No one came forward.

"Now, don't all you bums rush up here at once," the man said.

Jack got up off his cot, patted down his new clean trousers, and walked over to the big man.

"What's your name?"

"Jack."

"Can you cook?"

"I can eat."

"Good enough. It don't take a brain surgeon to flip burgers. Here, take this slip of paper over to the manager at the Crystal Palace at the corner of Fourth and Union. You'd better shave before you go. You got any ID?"

Jack shook his head.

"Don't matter much—they'll pay you under the table anyway."

The manager at the Crystal Palace was a young kid—about five years younger than Jack. "Are you a wino?" the young man asked.

Jack shook his head.

"You got any horrible diseases?"

Again, he shook his head.

"All you got to do is prep the lettuce, tomatoes, and onions. You understand? If you do okay with that, we'll let you slice potatoes. Do you understand? You work from seven to seven, and we don't pay overtime. Do you understand? You eat a burger, you pay for it. You drop a burger, you pay for it. You complain, we'll fire you. You don't get here on time, we'll fire you. You smell bad, we'll fire you. The police ask about you, we'll fire you. Do you understand?"

Jack nodded his head. He had a job.

It pleased Jack to be busy with his hands, slicing the tomatoes, onions, and pickles just right, tearing the lettuce just right. Each day had its little rituals. Jack came in early, on his own time, to sharpen the knives. He had found an old whetstone in a drawer in the storeroom. Every day, Jack could be found at his prep table precisely at six, his whetstone to the left, his three knives neatly hung on the wall behind. The cutting board was washed and free of clutter. Further down the line was Jake Fullington's worktable. He did the potatoes and some of the burger assembly. The way Jake went about his job worried Jack—there was so much waste. The manager emphasized again and again that wasting food was wasting profit, and the Palace couldn't survive waste. When his job was done for the day, Jack cleaned up his mess, counted his tools, and swept up.

Each morning when he worked at the Palace, Jack hurried back to the mission to help Lemuel of Massa. Lem, as everyone called him, was the cook at the mission. His name was really Lemuel Mason. He had migrated to Memphis from Atlanta, with stops (and marriages) in New Orleans, Meridian, Shreveport, Jackson, and Little Rock.

"You want to help me cook, boy?" Lem had asked him.

"Yeah, sure," Jack replied.

"Well, you keep me in sharp knives. There's a whetstone in the drawer over by the table. I'll teach you a thing or two about cooking. Most people don't think about what they put in their mouths. They just eat what's put in front of them. You need to smell your food. You need to taste your food. Eat slow, cook slow."

So now Jack had two jobs. By day, he was Lem's assistant, and at night, he was the prep man at the Palace.

After the first couple of weeks at the Palace, the manager passed little manila envelopes out with their pay. Jack took his, put it in his pocket, and left.

Just outside, on the corner, there was a stoplight. As Jack stood waiting for the light to change, he heard a voice from the headlight of a 1956 station wagon: *"They know you've got money, be careful."*

Jack reached into his pocket, pulled out the envelope, and threw it into a trash can. When he did, the voice stopped.

A few weeks later, Lem was slicing a ham. "Jack, when you gonna get you some fresh clothes? Those are beginning to get a little rank."

"Where do you get clothes?" Jack asked.

"Salvation Army, down the road. They got plenty, and they're cheap. Take some of that money you been making down at the Palace, and buy yourself some clothes."

"I can't."

"Why can't you?"

"I lost it."

"All of it?"

"Yeah, all of it," Jack said.

"Wait a minute … You puttin' me on! You been workin' two months, and lost all four paychecks?"

"Yeah."

"How?" Lem asked.

"I don't know."

"You need somebody to hold on to your money for you."

"How about you? Would you?" Jack asked.

"No, sir, I don't think that would be a good idea. Demon rum would come calling on me real quick. Then we'd both be in trouble. No, why don't you get Amos, the head cheese here at the mission, to hold it for you? He's done that before. There used to be this deaf and dumb boy that worked the collection plate in the chapel—he couldn't keep anything straight either."

This seemed to solve the problem for a while. Amos kept the money, and when Jack needed something, Amos bought it for him.

Late one afternoon, Jack was sleeping in the back when he was awakened by Amos. "Jack, wake up. I need to talk to you."

"Did I do something wrong?"

"No, you didn't do anything wrong. I need your help. It's Lem—he's gone. We got to have somebody to cook. Will you help us?"

"Where's Lem?"

"We don't know. I think he's probably somewhere drunk. Can you help us?"

"Yeah, sure. Do you think he'll be back? I hope so. I really like him."

"Yeah, we do too, but he's gone now, and my bet is that he's gone for good."

"Well, I've done parts of meals, but I've never done a full one."

"Can you try?"

"Yeah, I guess so. Will you talk to the people at the Palace? They been real good to me," Jack said.

"Sure."

Lemuel never came back; the demon had found him.

Jack walked around the mission kitchen, opened and closed the cabinets a few times, and walked through the big walk-in pantry lined with all types of canned goods. He looked into the chest freezer and surveyed its contents. His only question was, "What do I want to eat today?" His taste and smell guided his cooking: ham with honey-glaze sauce, burgers with onions, sausage with eggs, pork chops with pineapple, potatoes with cheese. In a brief period of time, word had spread that the food at the mission had taken a quantum leap forward. The price of a meal was to sit through one of the mission sermons, but Jack's food made it well worth it.

One of the regulars at the mission was John Allen St. Clair. He'd been a drunk—still was—but he'd been sober for six years. John Allen had a knack for making money and a lust for the finer things of life—pretty women, fast cars, and good whiskey. "I can sell ice to Eskimos, bracelets to Indians, and fried chicken to black folks." And he did just that. He won every fight but one. In the end, whiskey landed the knockout punch. It had taken fourteen rounds, but when he hit bottom, there was nothing left. What crawled into the mission that night was still human, but just barely. There was an AA group that met at the mission, which Amos strongly encouraged all the residents to attend. Well, the cure took, and John Allen never forgot it. From time to time, he returned, as he liked to say, "to the place and people of my rebirth." He came by regularly for a meeting, or just to shoot the bull. There was always somebody new to hear his story.

One evening, after John Allen had spoken to the men, he and Amos joined the serving line.

"J. A., I think you're gonna like our new cook," Amos said. "Lem disappeared, like we all knew he would."

"What are we having?" John Allen asked.

"Chicken-fried steak, mashed potatoes, purple hulls, and fresh bread."

"He's gonna have to go some to outdo Lem."

"You just wait," Amos replied.

When the large metal top of the warmer was removed, the rich fragrance of a golden brown crust covering moist, succulent steak filled the room. Along with the meat was a side of creamy mashed potatoes with thickened white gravy.

John Allen took in a long breath and smiled. He had a kindred spirit in the man who had prepared this food.

"Tell me about this guy."

"All we know is that his name is Jack."

"Where did he come from?" J. A. asked.

"No idea. He really doesn't seem to know himself. Like most of the guys here, he's odd. Doesn't say much. I think he has some kinda mental problem. I don't think it's alcohol."

"Do you think he's crazy?"

"No, not really. Just quiet and odd."

"Amos, this guy's a great cook! I could give him a job today in my restaurant. You know how much trouble I have keeping good cooks. What do you think?"

"John Allen, you know how I feel. This place is a stopping point for most of these guys. For some, like Lem, it's nothing more than a holding action before they go out into life just like before. You talk to Jack, and ask him if he wants to leave. I think I know what he'll say. He'll probably stay here. I'll warn you before you begin, you'll have to handle his money—there's something about it that scares him awful bad."

"But I can offer him a better life," John Allen said.

"I'm not so sure you can, but we'll always be here if he needs us," Amos said.

"Then you don't mind me talking to him?"

"Of course not. I want the best for Jack. Odd as he is, he's a lovable little guy. I'll go get him."

"No, let me go back there."

John Allen worked his way around the serving line and back to the stove, where Jack was busy cleaning up.

"Jack?"

"Yes, sir?" Jack replied.

"My name is John Allen St. Clair. I really enjoyed the meal."

"Yes, sir, it did taste good."

"Jack, I own the Uptown Diner across from the Peabody, and I need a good cook."

"I worked for the Crystal Palace once," Jack said. "I cut up the produce and swept up in the morning, but that was before Lem left."

"I know, Amos told me. Would you like to work for me? As a cook, I mean?"

"I don't know. All my friends are here. I'd have to make new friends. That's hard to do, you know. I guess I'd have to move. I'd have to move and make new friends. I don't know. I don't know."

"Well, you think about it. Amos knows how to get hold of me."

"I'd have to talk to Amos. He's my friend—my really good friend. He takes care of my money. I'd have to do something about that, I guess. I have to talk to Amos."

"Jack, don't worry about that," J A. said. "If you decide not to cook for me, that's okay. Let me tell you something—I know something about you that most people don't know."

"What?" Jack asked.

"You love to eat food; it's the taste and the feel and the substance of the food that are all important to you, and that's why you're such a good cook. I love to eat too, but I don't have the skill that you do. Join me, Jack."

"Let me think about it. I don't know."

"Take all the time you need; it's just life."

"I like Mr. St. Clair," Jack said to Amos. "He understands, and he's a nice man, but it scares me. What do you think?"

"Look, Jack, it's up to you," Amos said. "This is a stopping place. Almost nobody stays here permanent. We never run 'em off—they just leave. If you *do* leave, remember that you can always come back. There will always be a place for you here."

"I don't know," Jack said.

"Look, you could get your own place to live, maybe meet somebody. Buy yourself some things—new clothes and stuff. By the way, I've got your little bit of money from the Palace, and we've been putting some aside for you—with all your cooking and work, we felt we owed it to you."

Shaken, Jack said, "I don't want it—give it to somebody else."

"We can't do that, Jack. It's your money."

"But I don't want it. Do something with it."

"Why don't you want the money, Jack?" Amos asked. "What is it about the money that scares you?"

"They get louder when I have money. They say bad things to me."

"Who's 'they,' Jack?"

"I don't know who they are, but they talk to me all the time. Most of the time, it's just talk, like about war and people on the street and what's for dinner—you know, normal stuff. But when I have money in my pocket, they get louder and I can't think. They talk about somebody coming to get me, and all the bad things they're going to do to me. They come out of the bed and the sink, and sometimes out of the back of people's heads. They're real. It's only when I cook that they get quieter. Then they shut up and let me cook."

"Have you been to see a doctor about these voices?"

"No, I never thought about that. What could a doctor do?"

"Maybe they could give you some medicine that will quiet the voices."

"But they're not bad when I don't have money. It's okay, I'm used to them."

"You still probably ought to see a doctor," Amos said.

"Do you know a doctor I can go to?"

"Yeah, I got a friend over off Union—real nice guy. He stopped in here one time for a spell, just to catch his breath. He had a round with drugs and whiskey, but he's doing pretty good now. His name is Brandon—Lawrence R. Brandon."

"Will you go with me?" Jack asked.

"Sure."

"You'll call him for me?" Jack asked. "Does he charge a lot?"

Amos shook his head. "He's one of us—gives our people a discount, and says he's paying on his bill. He's a real nice guy."

Lawrence R. Brandon had a storefront office on a side street just off Union, downtown. It wasn't much—just a couple of chairs, an old wooden desk, a few medical books unopened in years, and a cot in the corner.

Amos tapped on the door. The frosted glass pane, with "Dr. Lawrence R. Brandon" and a big caduceus etched in the center, rattled loosely in its frame.

"Doc, you awake?"

"Of course I am," Brandon answered. "Who is it?"

"It's me … Amos. I got a friend that needs some help."

"Hold on, I'll be there in a second."

Behind the door, they heard shuffling as the doctor put himself in order. Presently, he opened the door.

"Doc, this is Jack."

"Morning, Jack." The fat little man extended his stubby fingers and smiled. "I'm Dr. Brandon. What can I do for you?"

"Well, Doc," Amos said, "Jack here has been hearing voices that other folks don't hear."

The doctor smiled. "I remember that part."

"But Doc, he don't drink, and as far as we know, he don't take drugs."

"Can Jack talk?" the doctor asked.

"Yes, sir," Jack said.

"Tell me, Jack, what's your full name?"

"Jack is all I know."

"Where you from?"

"I live at the mission," Jack said.

"I mean, before that."

"I don't know," Jack said.

"How did you get to the mission?"

"I don't remember, except … I remember a truck, and an old colored man feeding me."

The doctor changed course. "Tell me about the voices," he said.

"What do you want to know?"

"Are you hearing them right now?"

"Yeah, sure."

"Where are they coming from?"

"Well, right now, no place in particular—they're just there."

"What are they saying?"

"They're talking about how dirty your office is, and how fat you are, and how you must have had ribs for supper, because you smell like barbecue."

"Jack … are these voices mean?"

"Not most of the time."

"Do they threaten to hurt you Jack?"

"Sometimes, but not most of the time. They just scare me."

"How, Jack?" the doctor asked.

"They know some things that I don't know."

"Like what, Jack?"

"I'm not sure, but when I have money, they tell me to get rid of it."

"Sounds like my first wife," the doctor said.

"This seems to scare Jack real bad," Amos said. "Is there anything we can do? Any medicine or treatment?"

"Sure there is. You know us folks in medicine—there are always things we can do. There's a group of doctors here in town who've taken to giving electric shocks to patients. Thing is, Jack here don't seem to really need it." He turned back to Jack. "Tell me, Jack, do these voices ever tell you to hurt anybody?"

"No, sir, nothing like that."

"If I was you, I think I'd just learn to live with the voices the best I could. I don't think medicine really has a lot to offer you right now."

"Thanks, Doc," Amos said. "How much do we owe you?"

"Just apply it to my bill," the doctor replied.

"Doc, Jack here is thinking about leaving the mission. John Allen offered him a job at the Uptown Diner. Jack's a crackerjack cook. You ought to come have a meal with us pretty soon, just in case he leaves. Wouldn't want you to miss his cooking—when Jack leaves, that'll put *me* back to cooking."

The doctor smiled and agreed to drop by in the next day or two.

As Jack and Amos walked among the tall buildings of Main Street toward the Mission, Jack turned to Amos and said, "I think I'll go and cook for Mr. St. Clair."

"What made you change your mind?"

"I didn't. *They* told me I could. They said it would be okay."

Nothing that John Allen did ever stayed small. Within days of opening, he had put a sign out front that said, in big red letters, "Uptown Diner—Serving Central Memphis For 30 Years." By the time Jack arrived, John Allen had expanded into the storefronts on either side.

The diner sat right across the street from the biggest hotel in Memphis. The old hotel had always been known for the ducks that lived on the roof. Every day at three in the afternoon, the head bellman would bring the ducks down on a special elevator and parade them into the central fountain in the lobby. It was a big show.

John Allen put up a sign on the front marquee of his diner:

HOTEL DUCK IN ORANGE SAUCE

Needless to say, the people across the street weren't happy about this, and the hotel's lawyers were quick to serve notice on John Allen—if he didn't cease and desist, they would bury his cafe. So John Allen changed the sign to read:

BIG DUCKS IN ORANGE SAUCE

After several additional threats, John Allen took the sign down, but the whole affair was written up in the local paper, and John Allen had accomplished what he had set out to do. If the sign and the controversy attracted attention, it was the smell and taste of Jack's cooking that drew people like flies.

Soon the Uptown Diner was the new hot spot.

One evening, as they were finishing up, John Allen came into the kitchen. "Jack, I need to talk to you," he said.

"What's the matter? Did I do something wrong?"

"You didn't do anything wrong. This is good stuff. This fellow from Little Rock was in here this morning. He works for the Cotton Exchange. He comes in here every time he's in town. He wants us to come to Little Rock and look into opening a diner there. It's the big time, Jack! We could make some real money if this works."

"I don't need any money, John Allen. I got all I need right here."

"Okay, you don't have to make money," John Allen said. "What about all the new friends you could make?"

"I don't need any more friends."

"Well, Jack, I'm going to Little Rock for a day or two, and I need you to go with me."

"Okay," Jack said as he turned back to his stove.

John Allen and Jack made the trip to Little Rock, and on the sidewalk in front of the army-navy surplus store, John Allen met his maker.

And Jack's soul became consumed again by the voices.

CHAPTER 23

silver bullet

The revelation that Jack was Pauly, and that Pauly was P. J., took a while for Mary Ann to absorb. She sat in the chair beside the hospital bed and thought, *Will my friend Jack ever return? Are there other things about him that we don't know? Does it really make any difference?*

The little old man in the bed rambled on for several hours, drifting from Paul Currier to P. J. Ives to Jack. When a nurse or doctor came into the room, he became quiet and responded only with nods and grunts.

That evening, the doctor reviewed Jack's records and conducted a brief exam.

"My friend, it looks like the silver bullet whizzed right by your head. If it hadn't been for the man at the Legion Hut, you would have frozen to death. As it stands, it doesn't look like you did any permanent damage. There may have been a little damage to your heart, and you might even have had a little heart attack, but it was nothing too serious."

"Can't you tell for sure?" Mary Ann asked.

"Not really. The blood tests that we use to diagnose heart attacks are the same as the ones we use for other muscle damage, so it can be unclear which is which. That's why Jack needs to have an arteriogram on his heart before he leaves the hospital."

Jack shook his head. "I need to go home and feed my cat, Gracie. I want to go home," he said.

"We've been feeding her every day," Mary Ann said.

"But she needs a lap to sit in," Jack added.

"I'll tell you what," the doctor said, "you stay with us another night. You talk about it with your friends, and we'll discuss it again in the morning. How's that? By the way, you shouldn't be going home to a house by yourself. Have you thought about that?"

"I have," Sylvia said. "Jack and Gracie can come to live with Snuffy and me."

"Sounds good to me," said Dr. Bailey. "Is that okay with you?"

Jack nodded.

After the doctor left, Sylvia went to the cafeteria for some supper.

"I'm really tired," Mary Ann said, "and you seem to be doing okay, so I'm going to go find a quiet place and get some sleep."

"Please don't leave. I'm not safe here." Jack was visibly shaken.

"I'll be back in a few hours," she said.

"But I'm not safe here. They might come after me! You just don't understand."

"But what about the tests?" she asked.

"I'm not going to have any tests. I don't like hospitals. I want to go home tonight." As he talked, Jack looked around for his clothes. "Where's my racing cap?" he asked.

"Okay, okay," she said, "hold your horses. Give me a little while. I need to get some food in my stomach, and then I'll talk to the doctor. You're not going to run off, are you?"

"No," he said as he settled back into his bed. "But I want to go home tonight."

"What are we going to do, Sylvia?" Mary Ann asked.

"I'd vote that we not argue with him and just take him home."

"But what about the doctor and the tests?"

"Jack is dealing with a lot of things right now. Maybe when things settle down, we can talk him into coming back for the tests. But, to be honest, I doubt it."

"How did you know who he was?" Mary Ann asked.

"From the day we met, I knew there was something familiar about him. Everybody has an aura, and you never lose it, no matter how your appearance changes as you get older. In 1957, Mr. Ives did some work for Melos and me—it had to do with our wills. Melos wanted them changed after our daughter passed away. Anyway, we used Mr. Ives. Melos did most of the work with him, but I had to visit his office one day to sign the papers. When I sat down across the desk from him, I could feel that he was really troubled. I felt the same thing when Jack came and we talked about his mother. The other day, when I saw him in the back of the ambulance, it finally occurred to me—I knew it *had* to be him. Yesterday, I went by the county library and talked the librarian into letting me borrow this box from the Ives exhibit. She wasn't supposed to, but she did it anyway."

Mary Ann and Sylvia finished their supper and then went to find the doctor. Mary Ann explained to him that Jack was really getting agitated. The physician agreed that it probably would be best if he went on home and then followed up with Dr. Taylor in a couple of days. Dr Bailey wrote out a series of prescriptions, wished Mary Ann the best of luck, and went about his work.

When they entered Jack's room, he was sitting on the bed, looking out the window. The bed had been neatly made, and Jack was dressed in street clothes and his racing cap. He looked like the old Jack.

"Where do you think *you're* going?" Mary Ann asked.

"I'm going home," he said. "You said you'd take care of it."

Sylvia sat down on the bed beside him. "Which home? Saratoga Springs? East St. Louis? Memphis?"

"No," he said, "Gum Ridge. What are you talking about?"

Sylvia laid her hand on his arm. "Let's go home," she said, smiling.

"Okay," he said.

Driving back across the Le Petite River bottoms, Mary Ann looked across the cab of the truck and realized that Paul and P.J. were gone. The little old man sitting beside her was just Jack.

The late-evening sun cast a long, red shadow over the river bottoms. Off to the north of the highway, a large flock of ducks was flying in an irregular V. The flight of birds began to break up and circle a flooded rice field. Jack was completely absorbed in the birds.

"Have you heard from Moon in the last few days?" Sylvia asked.

Mary Ann shook her head. "I've only seen him a few times since Jack went to the hospital. Joy said he's breezed through the cafe two or three times. She gave me the impression that he came through, emptied the cash register, and left."

"What do you think is gonna happen Tuesday night?" Sylvia asked.

"I don't know. If he doesn't have the money and if he has any sense, he'll hightail it for Mexico or California. It's a fair bet that he won't have the money, but we all know he doesn't have any sense. I've heard people, mostly women, threaten to kill him, and I've seen him talk his way out of some pretty tight spots. But before, he always had an ace in the hole."

"Speaking of an ace in the hole—I could borrow against my house to help you keep the place going if Moon skips out. My grandson wants me to move in with him and his wife. There isn't a month goes by that Marshall doesn't offer to buy my house and the other pieces of property I own in that part of town. Now, mind you, I wouldn't want Moon to have anything to do with it, but I trust you and Jack."

Mary Ann shook her head. "Thanks, but I'd never ask you to do that. It would be the same as putting a mortgage on your life. I'd never let you do that. Besides, if the worst happens, Jack and I will hire out to the Peelers. Right, Jack?"

"What?" Jack said. He was still enthralled by the ducks flying overhead.

"Never mind. We'll cross that bridge when we come to it."

CHAPTER 24

god of chance

The Saturday-night poker game at Peeler's cabin down on High-Low Lake was Moon's last chance. Three times in the last ten days, he had raised enough money to get into a game with the high rollers in Tunica. Each time, the God of Chance had abandoned him and left him penniless. On Friday, he had won enough money at the craps table to get into the Saturday-night card game with his friends.

The weekly game was usually five-card draw, but it was a democratic process. If the dealer wanted a different game, all he had to do was convince half of the other players. There were six regulars, with a few stragglers who showed their faces from time to time.

Moon didn't drink much, so when he did, it was apparent. On this particular evening, he was in his cups when the game started. When it came his time to deal, he declared: "Doctor Pepper."

"Shit, Moon, that's a girl's game," Art said, rolling his captain's chair back from the table. "Let's play real poker."

"Let's vote," Joe said. "All in favor of Doctor Pepper, raise their hand."

Moon raised his hand, but no one else joined him.

"All opposed?"

Everyone else raised their hands.

"All right, Moon, what's your next choice?" Joe asked.

"I pass," Moon replied.

"You *pass?*" Joe said. "What do you mean, you pass? Nobody passes! The only other time anybody passed was when Art broke his hand and couldn't deal."

"I mean, I pass! This here's America, and I can pass if I want to!"

Art looked closely at Moon. "What's the matter with you? Got something in your eye? You look like you're about to cry."

"No, stupid, it's that damn cheap cigar of yours," Moon said. "I'm okay, just deal the damn cards. By the way, you got any decent liquor? I could use a drink of good whiskey."

"Look under the sink," Art said. "My old man left a half-pint of scotch. But remember the rule: if you drink the house liquor, you have to replace it."

"Sure. You guys play without me a few hands."

Moon slid his chair back, went over to the sink, opened the cabinet door, and searched around among the old bottles of detergent, ammonia, and cleansers. Under the drain trap and behind the toilet plunger was a whiskey bottle full of yellow-brown liquid. He unscrewed the top and realized that the odds were better than fifty-fifty that the contents were something other than an aged single-malt Scotch whiskey. It could just as easily have been rat poison or an insecticide. For a moment, he had a vision of himself lying on the floor of the cabin, drowning in his own saliva, the other cardplayers gathered around him, completely helpless. In his vision, Mary Ann, Jack, his mother, and all of his past girlfriends were there too. Each was recounting how good he had been to them, what a handsome man he was, how important an influence he had been on their lives, and how sad it was that he would no longer be with them. As the vision faded, it occurred to him that, in many ways that was a much better fate than ending up old and forgotten in a nursing home.

With one swift motion, he flipped the bottom of the bottle skyward and emptied its contents into his mouth with five vigorous gulps. As the last trickle flowed from the container, he noticed the wooden-cask flavor and warmth of the vapor as it filled his nasal cavity. It was scotch, all right, good scotch—smooth and easy going down. The instant he knew that he had not killed himself with rat poison, a small, clear voice from somewhere deep inside said, "Albert Lawrence Moon, you are one lucky son of a bitch. You're not going to die—at least not now. Quit feeling sorry for yourself, and find a way out of this mess."

It should be made perfectly clear that, even though Moon did not poison himself in a final, declarative way, he had stunned more than a few brain cells with the amount of beer and whiskey he had consumed over the last few days. The scotch was like the last straw, necessary only to reveal his state of complete inebriation.

"Deal me in, you unlucky shits," he said, the scotch slurring his speech. "You know, I really feel sorry for you clowns. It's not fair for you to have to go up against somebody like me."

Moon lost the first three hands, but just about the time the scotch hit its full stride, he struck a good hand. Moon slowly picked up his cards. With the first deal, he was holding three tens.

"All right boys, it's going to cost you to stay in this game," Moon said. "I'll start it out with two hundred dollars."

"Whoa, Moonshine must have a real hand," the player to his right said. "Can't stay in with these cards. I fold."

Two of the other players threw their cards on the table in disgust, but Art and Joe met his challenge.

"I'll take two cards," Moon said.

"One," said Art.

"One for the dealer," Joe added.

Joe dealt, and each man picked up his new cards. When Moon looked at his cards, it was hard for him not to break into a grin. The last card was the ten of clubs—he was holding four of a kind. Luck was with him, and he would have a stake he could parlay into some real money before Tuesday.

"Bet's to you, Joe," Art said. "What'll it be?"

"Five hundred bucks," Joe said quickly.

Art swallowed hard. "Awfully rich, but I'll stay with you. Here's my five hundred."

Moon steadied himself. "Okay, boys, it looks like we really came to play tonight. I'll see your five and raise you a thousand." He put his cards down on the table and turned to Joe with his best imitation of a poker face. "Okay, Mr. Wiseass, what do you say now?"

Joe studied his cards. Moon was either really drunk, or he had a great hand. "I got to see this hand. I'll stay with you and bump you another three hundred."

Art looked at the pot on the table. "I'm out," he said.

Moon pulled out his wallet and took out the last of his cash. "I'm short a hundred, so here's an IOU for the balance. Consider yourself called."

Joe sat there for a minute without showing his cards, and then slowly began to lay them down, one at a time—the five of diamonds, six of diamonds, seven of diamonds, eight of diamonds, and nine of diamonds—a straight flush, the only hand that could beat four of a kind.

The God of Chance had forsaken Moon again.

As Joe raked the money to his side of the table, he began to laugh, the ashes from the cigar in his mouth falling onto the table.

"Shit," he said, dropping the cigar on the red felt, "my daddy's gonna kill me if I screw up this tabletop. He just had it re-covered last week."

Moon, who was ready to get on with his winning, complained, "You know, Pitcock, even when you happen to win, you're still a slob. Get that cleaned up, and let's get on with this game."

"What do you mean, 'get on with the game,' Moon? You're busted! What are you going to play with?"

"Just because I got no cash with me don't mean I'm busted. That car outside in the yard is a classic. It's worth at least ten grand, and I got the title, free and clear."

Joe smiled. "Okay, Moon, I'll bite. I'll carry you for three thousand on the car, twenty-five percent interest for the first week. If you don't pay in a week, I get the car free and clear."

Moon's God of Chance never made it back to his side of the table. By the time Joe and Art called it quits and headed for bed, Moon was hocking his gold chains to stay in the game. His head was hurting from the scotch, and the dread of Tuesday was beginning to build.

Jack awoke to the smell of baking bread and fresh coffee. At first, he was disoriented—it wasn't his bed, but it certainly wasn't the hospital that was for sure. And then he remembered—he was at Sylvia's. More specifically, he was in the bedroom that had once belonged to Christine, Sylvia's daughter. In was impossible to tell if it was day or night, since there were no windows. A floor lamp glowed in the corner with soft, indirect light. The room was a warm, dark red color with accents of blue and green. There was a change of clothes at the foot of the bed, and his favorite cap was hanging on the bedpost. On the bedside table were his bottles of medicine and a list of instructions on how they were to be taken. He could hear Sylvia moving about the kitchen, humming.

Jack pulled back the covers and sat up on the bedside. Sitting up made him a little dizzy. *It's the medicine,* he thought. *I'll wait until later to take more of it.* When he was dressed, he walked into the living room. Sylvia was setting the table.

"You'll have to forgive me," she said. "I'm not used to having much company. Pete comes over every once in a while, but now that he and his wife have children, we usually go to their house or out to eat."

"The bread smells good," Jack said.

"I *thought* that would wake you up. It always did Melos. He would sleep forever if I let him." She put the fresh bread down on the table. "You want some coffee?"

Jack nodded. "And I'm hungry, too."

"I can believe that. You've been asleep for twenty-four hours."

"I never sleep well in the hospital. It felt good to be home—I mean, here at your house. I like the way your house feels."

Sylvia smiled. "Gracie does too. Look." Gracie was curled up on the window bench that looked out onto the porch. "I was worried that she and Snuffy might not get along, but they act like they've always been best buddies."

Jack took a sip of his coffee and began to butter a slice of the bread. "This is really good," he said.

"Have you taken your medicine? Remember, the doctor said it was important that you take it on schedule—especially the heart medicine. I woke you up and gave you a dose at midnight, and you should be due one now."

Jack nodded. "What day is it?" he asked.

"It's Sunday morning. Why?"

"I got to get to work. That is, unless Mr. Moon fired me. He didn't fire me, did he?" There was a hint of desperation in his voice.

"No, he didn't fire you."

"I could understand if he did. It's happened before, and I wouldn't blame him. He can't have his cooks running out on him like I did."

"Jack, you didn't run out on him. You got sick. You couldn't help that."

"Maybe. But still he's got to keep the cafe doors open."

"Well, you haven't been fired, but I don't think Mary Ann plans on you going back to work for a while. You've got to remember, Jack, you were really sick."

"But I'm better now, and I want to go back to work," he said.

"I'll let you and Mary Ann argue that out. She's supposed to come by and check on you before she opens up this morning."

Jack finished his first slice of bread and cut another. He put a healthy layer of butter on the second piece, and then pulled his hat out of his pocket. "When Mary Ann comes by, tell her I've gone to the cafe to get started on lunch."

"Don't you think you should wait for her?" Sylvia asked.

"I'll be okay. I need to be outside, doing some walking."

The air was clear and crisp; the colors were brighter. Jack was tired, but it was a good kind of tired. It felt as though the residue of fear had been washed away. The cool air made him think of a dream he'd had many years before. He had been flying before a storm above an orchard of giant trees, and, like an agile hawk, he flew among the treetops. He was safe from the storm, but was able to use its energy to stay afloat.

His route to work took him north on Border to the cafe. He enjoyed his walk down Border because the oak trees formed a canopy over the street. It was like walking through a tunnel. The sun filtered through the veil of leaves, creating a rainbow of yellow, green, and red. The few maples that were left along the street were the first to turn color. They were bright red in the early morning sun. From each house came the smells distinctive to that family; it was like walking down the midway of a carnival. The one smell that warmed Jack the most was the wonderful aroma that emanated from the house on the corner of Maple and Border. Jack stood on the corner by the willow tree, the colors drifting through the umbrella of changing maple, oak, and elm leaves. The aroma of fresh-baked cinnamon rolls, followed by cooked sausage, heavy on the sage, and scrambled eggs cooking gently in a heavy iron skillet filled his nose. He dreamed of flying through the treetops on a fresh new wind.

Like Jack, Mary Ann was slightly disoriented when she awoke from her sleep. A week before the blowup, she had moved in with Richard and begun the process of setting up house. Since Jack had gone to the hospital, life had been in an uproar, with several nights spent sleeping in hospital waiting rooms, and a few more in Jack's room.

Richard was always up early. This morning, he dressed, fixed a pot of coffee, and went to feed and groom the horses.

The morning sun flooded the bedroom, drawing her out of her sleep. She got up, put on her housecoat and slippers, poured a cup of coffee, and went out onto the porch. It was quiet, and the morning sun was warm. Just beyond the backyard was a large rice field. Richard's combine had reduced the field of grain to a landscape of blown golden straw. As she sat staring at the field, she noticed a streak of red moving in and out of the rice straw. Richard kept a pair of binoculars on the windowsill. She took them and focused on the moving spot of color. It was a red fox. She was so mesmerized by the animal that she didn't hear Richard walk up.

"That's Little Red," Richard said.

"You mean he's always here?"

"He, his brothers and sisters, his parents, and his grandparents."

"You mean, he's a pet?" she asked.

"I'm not sure who's the pet and who's the master. He and his family have lived on this farm for a long time. Dad told me when I was little that they were here when he was a kid."

"Are you happy, Richard?" she asked.

"Well, Ms. Random, *that's* quite a change of subject," he replied.

"Well, are you?" she asked again.

He thought for a second. "I'm happy when I'm with you. I'm happy when I'm driving. I'm happy when I'm here on the farm. Yeah, I guess I'm happy."

"No, really ... *are* you happy?"

"To be honest, I never give it much thought. Happiness is a lot like that fox out there. It's just there—it's a part of my life. But if I tried to go out and grab it, it would disappear. I enjoy it while it's there. Now, are *you* happy?" he asked.

"Being with you makes me happier than anything I can think of."

"What brought all this on?"

"Oh, I don't know," she said. "I'm worried about Jack. None of us know what's going to happen on Tuesday. Come day after tomorrow, he and I are probably out of a job. I can always find work, but what about Jack?"

"Now, hold on," said Richard. "I know you care about Jack, and I know he can be a little goofy, but he's been able to take care of himself in the past, and he'll do okay."

"I guess you're right, but I don't want to see him go."

"Do you think Moon will come up with the money?" Richard asked.

"I think Moon will skip town. That's what I think he'll do."

"Well, whatever you do, don't get between Moon and the Harris brothers. They won't put up with any of his bullshit. Have you thought about letting H. T. know what's going on?"

"If I know H. T., he already knows—or at least has a good idea. He's not going to do anything until they do something to Moon, and then it will be too late."

"Well, whatever you do, stay out of the line of fire." Richard got up and put on his hat.

"Where are you going?" Mary Ann asked.

"I told Pete that I'd help finish cutting his soybeans today. With both of us working, we should be through by about three o'clock. You going to work today?"

She nodded.

"How about Jack?"

"He probably won't be going back to work for a few days. He and Gracie are staying with Sylvia."

Sylvia was sitting on the porch with Snuffy at her feet and Gracie in her lap when Mary Ann came through the gate. "Jack left about two hours ago," she said.
"Where did he go?"
"Said to tell you that he was going to get a start on lunch."
"Did he seem upset?" Mary Ann asked.
"No," Sylvia said. "Same old Jack."

Any concern she had about Jack abated as she pulled into the back lot. He was bringing out the last of the Saturday trash. Her truck slid to a stop on the gravel.
"Morning, Jack. Didn't expect you to work today—I thought you'd probably take a few days off."
"Nothing else to do," Jack said. "I got my sleep out. Anyway, somebody's got to cook."
"Well, we shouldn't have much of a crowd today, what with the track shut down for repairs," Mary Ann said.
"Yeah, I forgot about that."
"We could probably make do with just sandwiches, if you wanted to."
"I've already started a big pot of deer stew. It should be ready by lunch."
One of the regulars had killed an eight-point buck on the first day of deer season. He had cleaned it, trimmed off all the fat, and cut up the shanks for Jack to cook. It had been in the refrigerator for a couple of days. Mary Ann had talked about freezing it on Saturday, but had forgotten to do it.
Jack's first step each morning when he arrived at the cafe was to open the refrigerator to see what he had to work with. The earthy smells, colorful leaves, and cool, crisp air from Border Street lingered as he discovered his prize for the day. *Nothing better on a fall day than a stew,* he thought as he unwrapped the packages of meat. There was something about cooking fresh, wild game—its smell, the rich red-brown color, and the texture of the flesh.
He cut the venison into two-inch chunks, dusted them in flour mixed with salt and pepper, and browned them in a small amount of oil. When the meat was seared, he added a couple of quarts of water and let it simmer. He chopped up several yellow onions, cooked them down, and added them to the mix. Later, he would add carrots, potatoes, paprika, and caraway seeds. The trick to cooking a stew was in letting the meat simmer, allowing the flavors to blend.

Like the colors of fall, Jack's stew evoked vivid memories—his mother standing at the kitchen door wiping her hands on a flour-covered apron, the soft, warm feel of a gray flannel shirt. The soupy collage of bright orange carrots, softened potatoes and onions, and the rich, wild meat with its thick brown gravy gave aroma to the blanket of vibrant red and yellow leaves that filtered the fall sunshine.

The lunch crowd was small, and the day moved along fast. Joy left early, leaving Mary Ann and Jack to clean up.

"Jack, would you mind if I asked you something personal?" Mary Ann asked.

"You can ask me anything," Jack said.

"That money you told me about … Didn't you ever wonder what happened to all the money that you left in the office?"

"What are you talking about? I don't have any money," Jack said.

"Oh, I'm sorry," she said. "I mean P. J.'s money. Didn't you ever wonder what happened to P. J.'s money?"

There was a moment's hesitation, and then the little man beside her said, "No, I ran out as fast as I could." The man speaking didn't sound like Jack. He began to sweat, and a worried look clouded his face. "I had to get away from it. It was eating me alive. It was killing me."

"Yeah, I think I understand. But it's such a shame, all that money—fifty thousand dollars—down the drain."

He looked puzzled. "What do you mean, fifty thousand?"

"I mean the fifty thousand left in the store."

"That couldn't be," he said. "There was ninety-eight thousand, eight hundred and thirty dollars in that office when I left."

"Well, I know they only found fifty thousand," she said. "They made a big deal of it being exactly fifty thousand, on the nose."

P. J. thought for a minute, then looked over at the refrigerator. Finally, he said, in a low voice, "I guess they didn't find the part buried under the floor."

"What do you mean? Are you saying there's *more* money?"

"Yeah, I guess so—about forty-nine thousand dollars."

"Is it buried here, under Moon's?" she asked.

"It should be, if they didn't dig it up."

The little man spoke about the money as though he were talking about supper.

"Let's go dig it up," Mary Ann said.

"I can't," he said. "The voices will come back. I *know* they will. The money will make them louder. You don't know what it's like."

"If you want," she said, "I'll take care of the money, and you'll never have to mess with it."

"But then *you* might start hearing the voices," he said. "I don't know, it really scares me."

"Think about this," she said. "If that money's still there, we could dig it up and pay off Moon's debt in exchange for fifty-one percent ownership of the cafe! That way, we could make sure that you and I always have a place to work, and that you would never have to worry about the money again."

"Do you really think Mr. Moon would want to sell?" Jack asked.

"I know damn well he would," she replied. "Moon will do just about anything to get out of this mess. Now, where do you think the money is?"

"It's under the refrigerator," he said, pointing behind the bar. "There are two loose boards in the very back."

Mary Ann locked the doors to the cafe to make sure that no one came in on them unannounced. Then, armed with a crowbar, clawhammer, and screwdrivers, they emptied the refrigerator and pulled it away from the wall. As he had predicted, they found two pieces of loose flooring next to the wall. Mary Ann got down on her knees and pried the loose boards up with a screwdriver. She shone a flashlight down between the floor joists. There, lying between the floor supports, as it had for four decades, was an old duffel bag, oiled against moisture. She pulled the old bag from its lodging and carried it over to the bar. She untied the drawstrings and shucked the green army bag of its contents. Inside was a flowered carpetbag that contained two narrow lockboxes—long tray affairs. She pulled the trays out, laid them on the counter, and slowly opened their lids. Each tray was filled with neat stacks of money wrapped in wax paper—forty-eight thousand, eight hundred and thirty dollars in tens, twenties, and fifties.

They both stood there, staring at the money.

Mary Ann looked up at Jack. "My friend, you have saved the day. We're going to buy ourselves a cafe."

CHAPTER 25

And where do we go from here?

It was a busy two days for Mary Ann and Jack.

Her first stop on Monday was Peeler's Cafe for a talk with Mamie—the title to Moon's and its liquor license were in her name. Mary Ann explained Moon's predicament and explained how she and Jack proposed to get him out of it. Mamie just shook her head. She understood her son, and she was overjoyed that Mary Ann and Jack would help him. When Mary Ann finished her story, Mamie reached out and put her hand on Mary Ann's arm. "Even though the place is in my name, it belongs to Moon. I'll gladly sign anything you need me to sign."

Her next stop was a lawyer's office in Batesville. He was a distant relative and a lawyer they could trust. She explained her plans and asked him to draw up the papers.

By the middle of the afternoon, they had opened a bank account in Newport with an initial deposit of three thousand dollars. The idea was to gradually make deposits in small amounts, so as not to draw attention to the money.

Later that evening, she and Sylvia re-hid the rest of the money in a place that only they knew; that way, Jack wouldn't have to worry about it.

On Tuesday, the lunch crowd came and went. Moon had still not appeared. Jack was in the back, preparing supper. Mary Ann and the lawyer were finishing work on their papers. She had decided that morning that the events about to transpire demanded a different look, so she dressed in a dark blue suit with a gray blouse. Her makeup was meticulous, with only a hint of eye coloring and neutral lipstick. In front of her was a small, black briefcase, purchased just for the occa-sion. She was studying a legal document and chewing on the arm of her glasses when Moon came in the back door. He hadn't shaved in three days, his clothes looked slept in, and he smelled of stale alcohol.

Moon walked over to the cash register and emptied it. While he was counting the money he looked around the room for unfamiliar faces. It was then that he spotted Mary Ann and the lawyer at table number three.

He walked wide around the table and stood in front of it.

"Aren't we dressed up today? Planning on a funeral?" he asked.

"Cute, Moon, cute." Mary Ann put the papers back in the case and closed it.

Moon circled the table. "Phillips, get me that bottle of scotch from my office."

"Moon, you drank that the other day, remember?" she replied.

"Oh, yeah. Get me a beer."

"How about I get you a glass of tea? We need to talk. Got a minute?"

Moon looked at his watch. "To be exact, I've got one hundred and sixteen minutes and forty-three ... no, thirty-nine seconds, and I've got to get a move on if I'm going to stay ahead of the boys across the street What do you want?"

Mary Ann went behind the bar and filled a big plastic glass with ice and fresh, unsweetened tea. She went to the end of the bar, patted the chair beside her, and said, "Here's your tea. Come sit over here. We want to talk to you about our future."

"What future? I'm gonna be dead, and you're gonna be unemployed. I'd say that about sums it up. I lost another three thousand over the weekend."

"Moon, you don't *have* three thousand. How could you lose it?"

"Oh, what the hell, how many times can they kill me?"

"I swear, Albert Lawrence Moon, you are the stupidest human I've ever known."

"No, you don't understand," he said. "I just got on a bad streak, and I ran out of time. If I only had more time. You know, I was thinkin' this morning ... I just might go down to Brownsville, Texas, for a few months. Give things some time to cool off. I've got an aunt down there. Yeah, I just might do that."

"So, you're going to run out on us and leave us holding the bag?"

"Not really," he said. "You don't owe those people nothing. They won't be looking for you."

Mary Ann got up and went to the kitchen door. "Jack, come out here, will you?"

Jack came out and stood behind the bar.

"Moon, Jack and I have an idea we'd like to run by you."

"I know, you've saved up some money and you want to help me out. That's real nice," he said. "I'm afraid you guys don't understand the magnitude of the problem. I owe these people a *lot* of money, and they're not interested in accepting partial payment. Now, anything you've got could help me get a new start down in Brownsville, but it ain't gonna solve my problem."

"First, Moon," Mary Ann continued, "before we get down to the real business, I'd like you to meet someone."

Moon turned his attention to the gentleman in the suit.

"Albert Lawrence Moon, I'd like you to meet Powhatan Jay Ives."

"You're shittin' me," Moon said.

She shook her head.

"Well, I'll be damned!" He extended his hand in the direction of the lawyer.

"No, Moon, *that's* not P. J.; that's our lawyer. *That's* P. J. Ives." She pointed at Jack.

A look of astonishment came over him, and he half laughed. "Are you telling me that Jack here is Mr. Ives himself?"

"You got it."

"Why didn't he say something?"

"He didn't know," she replied.

"Okay, now, let me get this straight. Jack nearly freezes to death, and when he wakes up, he tells you he's P. J. Ives? And you believe him? I'll be damned, Phillips, you're as crazy as he is. But okay, just for fun, I'll play along." He turned to Jack. "Mr. Ives, it certainly is nice to meet you after all these years. Where you been?"

Looking at Mary Ann, Jack said, "Here and there."

Moon smiled broadly. "At least he's consistent. I got one other question. Why the hell did you leave all that money behind?"

"What money?" Jack asked.

Moon turned back to Mary Ann. "Well, I'm convinced."

"On one level," Mary Ann said, "he knows about the money, but there's something about it that scares him real bad."

Mary Ann walked over to Jack. "Do you mind if I tell Moon some of the things you told me?" she asked.

"I don't know," Jack said. "It might get us all in trouble."

Mary Ann put her hand on his shoulder. "Moon will promise not to tell anyone, just like I did. Won't you, Moon?"

"Sure, whatever."

"Okay. If you think it's okay," Jack said to Mary Ann.

She proceeded to give Moon a brief outline of Jack's life and the places he'd been.

At the end of her tale, Moon said, "That's all well and good, but how is it going to help me now? After all these years, could he still get the money back?"

"No," Mary Ann said. "When someone disappears, like Jack did, his creditors are paid what they're owed and the state takes the rest. I think they claim it after seven years."

"And there's no way he can get it back?"

"Right, that money is gone," she said.

"Well, I guess I better start brushing up on my Spanish."

"Hold your horses. There's one more thing—something that none of us knew. The fifty grand wasn't all of the money. There was more. Hidden. Buried."

"Where?" Moon demanded.

"Here."

"You mean here in Gum Ridge?"

"No ... here in the cafe," Mary Ann said smiling.

"*Here?* Right here? Where?" Moon asked.

"Under the refrigerator."

"*That* refrigerator?" He pointed toward the bar.

Mary Ann nodded.

"You mean to tell me that the money has been right here under my feet all this time? Well, let's get it!"

"It's not there anymore," she said. "It's in a safe place, where you can't get to it."

"I'll have you know that this is my cafe, and I deserve at least half of that cash—community property, that kinda of stuff."

"Listen, Moon, this is no divorce. The fact is, you might be due most of it, but if you try to claim it, Jack and I will take you to court. That would take weeks or months. Years, even. You'd be dead and gone long before any decision was made. It might pay for a real nice headstone, or maybe a scholarship or two at the community college in Pocahontas. Your mama would probably like to have some of the money as a return on her investment."

"Okay, I give up," Moon said. "How do I get some of the money?"

"First off, the money belongs to Jack. It was his to begin with, and it's still his."

"What do I get out of it?"

"Hold your horses. Jack asked me to be the legal guardian of the money, because dealing with it makes him hear voices. It makes him sick. He and I came up with an idea. We want to buy fifty-one percent of Moon's Bar and Grill for thirty-two thousand. That will give you enough money to pay off your debts, with a little left over."

Jack walked over to Mary Ann and whispered in her ear.

She turned and asked, "Are you sure?"

Jack nodded.

"Make that thirty-*five* thousand. That way, you can pay off the rest of your debts."

"You mean you want me to give up this place I've worked so hard to build up, this place where I've slaved and worked my fingers to the bone? You want to give me a measly thirty-five thousand for it? You must be crazy," Moon said.

"Well, Mr. Albert Lawrence Moon, it's either that or you getting your skinny little ass killed at five o'clock this afternoon. Oh, and by the way, as far as anybody else knows you'll still own the place. You'll still run it, I'll still wait tables, and Jack will still cook. The big difference is that *I'll* be in charge of the cash drawer. We'll pay you an adequate salary based on how much you work. In addition, you'll get forty-nine percent of any profit after expenses."

Moon looked across the table at Jack. "Well, Mr. Moneybags, how do *you* feel about all of this?"

"If it means that I get to keep cooking and stay with my friends, I like it," Jack said.

"I guess I don't have much choice," Moon said.

Mary Ann kicked back in her chair. "Not unless you got some sweet little sugar mama who can't do without you. Well, Moon, what do you say? You want to live, have a good job, and work with people who kinda like you, even when you don't deserve it? Or do you want to die?"

"What do I have to do?" he asked.

"Just sign this contract. It says that you agree to all of the terms we've discussed. And one other thing: under no circumstances is anyone else to find out about Jack and his story until he's no longer alive. The only ones in the world who know about Jack are the three of us, Sylvia, and the lawyer. If word gets out, all of the terms of the contract are void. That means that you would immediately have to return all of the money, with interest. What's it gonna be? Yes or no?"

"Kinda hard to refuse," Moon said.

"That won't do, Moon. Yes or no?"

"What's the salary gonna be?"

"It'll be fair. Yes or no?"

"Yes. One thing, though."

"What?"

"Ain't it about time we had health insurance and a retirement plan?"

Jack began laughing. First, it was just a chuckle, but it had soon become outright laughter. It wasn't a crazy laugh, one driven by angry voices and fear—just a good, heartfelt laugh.

978-0-595-4418
0-595-44184-X